"Mr. Pei, an agent of the Internal Revenue Service."

I couldn't believe I was doing this. My name was not Tonya Weisberg and I didn't work for the Internal Revenue Service. My name was Whitney Pearl—and I was trying to clear my name of embezzlement charges.

"I'm under orders to seize the books and records of Sasha Valikov, whose business is under subpoena for suspected fraud and nonpayment of taxes. Under federal law, code section 304, you're required to allow me access to the taxpayer's place of business." I hoped Mr. Pei knew as little about the Internal Revenue Code as I did. Although I am a CPA, I don't do taxes. I'm an auditor turned forensic accountant, and I'd rather be shot than do taxes. I randomly wondered what section 304 covered.

The door buzzed and clicked and I reached to open it. Granted, this could get me ten to twenty in the slammer. But I already faced becoming a lifer, so what the hell?

Dear Reader,

In the fall of 2000, Mom and I traveled to China to visit my aunt and uncle, Glenda and Andrew Martin. I fell in love with China, the warm, friendly people, the food, the architecture and the history. Nevertheless, China does have its share of social troubles, and one that intrigues me is the shortage of women. Under the law of only one child per family, every couple covets a son who will take care of them in their old age. Baby girls are frequently given for adoption or abandoned. Because of this shortage, many men are without a wife. I had a couple of marriage proposals while in China, and when I said I was already married, they offered for my oldest daughter. I jokingly told Mom that an enterprising person could make a lot of money importing wives for these men. Thus was born the idea for this story. I hope you enjoy Pink's journey into China, and if you ever have the opportunity to go, take it!

Best wishes,

Stephanie Feagan

RUN
for the
MONEY
STEPHANIE FEAGAN

Published by Silhouette Books

America's Publisher of Contemporary Romance

SILHOUETTE BOOKS

ISBN 0-373-51401-8

RUN FOR THE MONEY

Copyright © 2006 by Stephanie Feagan

www.SilhouetteBombshell.com

Printed in U.S.A.

STEPHANIE FEAGAN

planned to be a park ranger so she could live in the mountains, marry a good-looking guy who likes bears and spend her evenings by a cozy fire, writing novels. But a funny thing happened on the way to college. Instead of a forestry degree, she graduated with a BBA in Accounting and became a CPA. Instead of a mountain man, she married an oilman. And instead of living among mountains and bears, she lives in the flatlands of west Texas, amongst mesquites and jackrabbits. That's okay for Stephanie—she happens to love the mesquites and the jackrabbits. She especially loves her oilman. And she does spend her evenings writing novels, although instead of a cozy fire, she opts for an air conditioner. Stephanie would love for you to visit her Web site at www.stephaniefeagan.com.

With much love and affection, this book is dedicated to Aunt Glenda, who enthusiastically showed me the other side of the world and shared her endless curiosity.

Acknowledgments

My sincere thanks go to the following: Leslea, for not abandoning me to marry a Chinese man; Callie, for sharing her personal phobias of big fish and murky water; and Jo George, aka Mom, for taking me to China as your "paid companion." To Mike, for your love and support and for understanding your wife's wanderlust.
Uncle Andy, for giving me a glimpse of what it's like to work in China. As always, my agent, Karen Solem, who may well be the smartest woman on the planet, and Natashya Wilson, who's definitely an editor prodigy. To the Wet Noodle Posse, may the publishing gods smile on each of you that you may sell bountiful books. And many thanks to my older brother, Dan George, who turned me on to great music at a very young age. Rock on, bro!

Chapter 1

With the phone clutched in one hand and a mechanical pencil in the other, I stared at the sequence of numbers I'd just scribbled on an already crowded notepad. "This all looks to be in order, except for one thing. You say I have another checking account, at a bank in Kansas, with a balance of over two hundred thousand bucks."

The nice lady at the mortgage company was getting less nice by the second. "It's right here, on your report. Whitney Pearl, home address in Midland, Texas. You opened the account two weeks ago."

"I've been in Washington, D.C., the past two weeks. How could I open an account in Kansas?" *Why* would I open an account in Kansas? I don't even know anybody in Kansas.

"You can open an account on the Internet, or by mail."

"There must be a mistake. They got the wrong social security number."

"Could be, but I doubt it. I suggest you get this resolved. Anything not nailed down can be cause for the application to be rejected."

Wondering why I'd been stupid enough to buy a house while I was on a consulting job over two thousand miles away from home, I told her I'd let her know, then hung up and dialed the Kansas bank. I got Shirley, in new accounts. Not sure, but based on the sound of her voice, I think Shirley started smoking at age twelve. I explained the situation, then listened while she pecked at the computer.

"Got it right here. Whitney Ann Pearl. Midland, Texas." She asked for my social security number, verified it, then rattled off some other bona fides.

"How was the account opened?"

"Through the Internet." She pecked some more. "Hang on and let me pull the signature card."

I stared out my sixth-floor window of the Mills Building and watched the guards atop the White House, one block away. It had become a favorite pastime, ever since I started the engagement with CERF, the Chinese Earthquake Relief Fund. Thus far, I'd resisted buying a set of binoculars. Still, the tall one who worked the seven-to-three shift looked mighty fine, even from a block away.

"Here we are," Shirley said. "Whitney A. Pearl."

"And the balance is over two hundred thousand dollars?"

She pecked some more and I wondered what I was gonna have to do to get this straightened out.

"It's $200,396.14. There have been twelve deposits since opening, and four withdrawals."

I'm a CPA. I know how these things work. Shirley was at a computer in a Kansas bank lobby, and there was no way she could give me any more information. "Thank you for your help," I said as graciously as possible, in spite of being seriously annoyed. After all, it wasn't Shirley's fault. "I wonder if I could speak to someone in bookkeeping?"

"Hold, please."

I watched the guards while listening to an elevator music version of Aerosmith's "Dream On." That was painful. Eventually, a woman named Courtney picked up. I asked for copies of the deposits, along with information about the withdrawals, and was pleasantly surprised when she said she'd fax me the information. Hmm. Maybe I really would open a bank account in Kansas. My bank in Midland would laugh me off the planet before they'd send me diddly squat.

Within thirty minutes, I had the copies.

And nearly had a heart attack.

Almost five hundred thousand dollars, and every single check came from CERF, the organization that had contracted me to act as accounting watchdog to ensure nobody stuck their fingers in the enormous amount of money the good people of the world donated to help the victims of the recent earthquake in China. I stared at the deposits in shock and total confusion. How had all that money ended up in a bank account with my name on it? Me, the CPA in charge of keeping an eye on the dough.

The checks were written to China Pearl, a Chinese company that manufactures generators and fuel pumps and other large equipment. I knew China Pearl was legitimate because I'd checked it out myself. Part of my job was to verify that invoices weren't paid to phony companies.

The checks to China Pearl that were deposited into the Kansas bank account were endorsed "for deposit only" to the account number. China Pearl. Not so far from Whitney Pearl. My nickname is Pink and I occasionally get a check made out to Pink Pearl, which I deposit into my account named Whitney Pearl without any questions asked. Get that last name right and the tellers never blink.

I stared at those deposits and wanted to hurl. Somebody had opened an account in my name, then deposited the China Pearl checks into it.

Reaching for the withdrawal copies, I saw that all four of them were transfers into the account of Valikov Interiors. Bells started ringing and, honest to God, my skin crawled so bad it's a wonder I didn't become an instant skeleton. I grabbed the phone and called my mother's cell, praying she was still in the airport, that she hadn't boarded the plane yet. She had a one o'clock flight to Washington, on her way to accompany me to a birthday dinner for Steve Santorelli, a senator from California who's a good friend of mine.

She answered on the fourth ring, breathless. "It doesn't matter what else you forgot, Pink. I don't have time to get it. They're boarding the plane."

"Just answer me a question. Yesterday, when you went over to my apartment to get my wool coat, remember the package you found on the doorstep that had an antique Chinese spider cage inside?"

"If you want me to go get it—"

"No. I just wondered if you remember where it came from."

"I thought you decided it was a gift from Santorelli."

"He told me this morning that it wasn't, so I assumed it

was just a mistake. Now I'm pretty sure it's not a mistake. But I have to know who shipped it."

Mom was quiet for a moment and I could hear the airport lady on the loudspeaker, calling the remaining passengers. "The company was in San Francisco, and the name was something Russian, like Vladivostok."

"Was it Valikov?"

"Yes, that's it. What's this about, Pink?"

Her Mom radar was kicking into gear, and I didn't want to alarm her, so I said easily, "I was telling someone about it and they were curious who sells antique Chinese spider cages."

"I'm about to miss the plane for this? Seriously?"

"Okay, so I have a reason. I'll tell you all about it when you get here."

"No way. I'll call you from my layover in Dallas."

She ended the call and I slowly replaced the receiver, my gaze frozen on those withdrawals. More than three hundred grand had been transferred out of an account with my name on it to the account of Valikov Interiors. And I'd received a package from Valikov.

I'm pretty much a linear thinker. Point A goes to Point B, to Point C, and so forth. Somebody set up an account in Kansas with my name and social security number. That person somehow got their hands on the China Pearl checks and deposited them into the Kansas account. They transferred money out of the Kansas account and into Valikov Interiors' account. They sent a package to me from Valikov so it would appear I bought something from them. Whoever was behind it was very clever, except for one thing. Who the hell would believe I'd pay over three hundred Gs for a Chinese spider cage? Even an antique one.

To say I was pissed off would be like saying there's a little bit of wheat in Kansas. I was so mad, my teeth hurt.

Gathering up the copies, I left my office and went down the hall toward the executive director's. I rapped on his door frame to get his attention. He looked up from some papers on his desk and grinned at me, but as I walked in his office, his grin faded.

"Pink? What's wrong?"

Parker Davis could easily be in the movies, he's that good-looking. He'd always get the part of the backup guy for Gene Hackman, the faithful, handsome, blond, blue-eyed assistant who blindly trusts Hackman's sneaky, evil character. Maybe I think so because Parker is married to a senator, and he's totally devoted to her. Not that Madeline Davis is anything like a Gene Hackman character. But Parker's unfailing support and willingness to take a backseat to his wife's career always make me think of those trusting souls in political thrillers.

"I just found out that I'm an embezzler." I tossed the papers onto his desk and briefly explained.

Looking like a diver whose equipment just failed, Parker leaned back in his chair and read through the papers. His face paled in spite of his golfer's tan. While he fiddled with his watch, a nervous habit I'd seen a hundred times, he mumbled "Oh, my God" over and over.

"We have to get to the bottom of this, immediately," I said. "Not only because CERF is getting ripped off, but because I don't wanna spend my childbearing years locked up with hundreds of other ovaries for something I didn't do."

He picked up the phone and punched in three numbers. "Taylor, I need to see you, right away."

Oh, man. Things were about to get infinitely more complicated. And aggravating.

Within a minute, Taylor Bunch sailed into Parker's office on a wave of too-strong perfume and in a lime green suit. I noted that she'd put her pale blond hair up in a snazzy little twist. Maybe I would have liked her, if I hadn't disliked her so much. I just don't feel the love for people who are mean, nasty and sneaky. If they made a movie about Taylor, they'd make her a man and get Gene Hackman to play the part.

In my other life, which ended last summer, I was a senior manager at a Big Important worldwide CPA firm in Dallas. That career, and that life, were over after I blew the whistle on one of our largest clients. Turned out the partners at my firm were all in on the cover-up to hoodwink investors—and that was the end of Big Important.

Taylor Bunch was promoted to my job the day I got fired for blowing the whistle. Regrettably for Taylor, she only got to crow about it for a few short weeks. After that, she was beating the streets for a job, and just like me and all the other CPAs who'd been in management at Big Important, she couldn't find anyone who trusted her enough to hire her. I ended up moving back to my hometown of Midland, Texas, and taking a mercy job as a forensic accountant at my mom's CPA firm. I'd gotten my watchdog stint at CERF through a contract with Mom's firm.

As for Taylor, she eventually found a job in the Texas state welfare system, churning out financial data for bureaucrats. That was how she met Parker Davis. He was the director of a children's advocacy group and came to speak at one of those lunch things that no one would go to except for the free lunch and an extra hour off work. When Parker was tapped to head up the relief fund after the China earthquake, he called Taylor and asked her to step in as treasurer. Soon after, Parker hired me to keep an eye on things, unaware of the animosity between Taylor and me.

I can only describe the expression on Taylor's semipretty face as joyful as she looked over the copies I'd brought to Parker. She couldn't have seemed more happy if she'd won the lottery, had a proposal from Brad Pitt and earned the Nobel Prize, all in one day. Yeah, I hated her guts.

She looked at me and raised one perfectly sculpted eyebrow. "Why should we believe you didn't do this?"

I ignored her and said to Parker, "I want your authorization to investigate and find out who's behind this."

Taylor stepped into my line of vision and said smugly, "Parker didn't get where he's at by being stupid. Why would he allow you to look into it when your name's on the account?"

Looking genuinely confused and freaked out, twisting his watch round and round, Parker glanced from me to Taylor and back to me. "She's got a point. I'm sure you're not behind this, Pink, but whatever comes to light, it will look mighty weird if you're the one who finds it."

Still ignoring Taylor, I stepped away from her. "Maybe so, but if you put Taylor in charge of investigating, they'll lock me up and throw away the key. She hates the ground I walk on." It was the first time I'd openly acknowledged the bad blood between me and Taylor. If only I hadn't squealed, she figured, she'd still be in a peachy position at Big Important. She never quite got that if I hadn't blown the whistle, I wouldn't have been fired, and she wouldn't have had the position. All she could see was that she'd lost her job, and it was all my fault. Never mind that thousands of people lost their life savings and retirement funds. It was all about Taylor.

"Are you saying I'd fail in my responsibility, all because of some personal vendetta?" Taylor sounded righteously offended.

"Gimme a break." I looked straight at her. "After I got promoted, you told everyone that you saw me going into the Crescent Hotel with the managing partner, effectively making my success a sexual exclamation point. You took pictures of me at Laura's bachelorette party, while I was modeling lingerie and dancing with a male stripper, then made sure those pictures showed up at the office, where they were passed around to everyone, including the managing partner. And let's not forget how the Bellington audit files disappeared from my office and turned up at the coffeehouse down the street. That made me look like a complete moron and could have gotten me fired, except that I happened to have gone to the emergency room that day because a friend was in a car wreck."

I folded my arms across my chest and stared her down. I was on a roll. "You despise me, which isn't my problem—unless you're the only thing standing between me and prison." Looking back at Parker, I said emphatically, "I am *not* going to prison."

Clearly at a loss, he focused on Taylor. "If you dislike Pink so much, how can you look into this with any kind of objectivity?"

Taylor glared at me as she spoke. "Obviously, someone is stealing from this organization. My concern isn't for Pink, but for all those unfortunate people in China who need this money to rebuild their lives. I can be objective because of them, because it's important to stop whoever's doing this."

She said the magic words. Parker is one of those people whose goal in life is to save the world, to alleviate suffering, to make certain that truth and justice prevail. And he's incapable of believing the worst in anybody. He practically beamed at Taylor. I knew I was toast.

"Pink," he said patiently, "I believe Taylor is up to the task, and I'm certain she'll leave no stone unturned to find out who's behind this. In the meantime, let's carry on as usual and keep this between the three of us. If the media get wind of this, CERF will be a distant memory. No one will send any more contributions, and even though we've got a lot to work with, we need a lot more."

I didn't have much of a choice but to accept his decision. The only alternative was to call the cops, and that was definitely not in my best interest.

With conflicting emotions that ranged from fear to fury, I made my way back to my office and did my best to concentrate on work. Thirty minutes later, Mom called from DFW airport and demanded to know what was going on. I told her.

And she wigged out. Mom is something of a pessimist, although she claims only to be a realist. She went off on me about prison, that Taylor would sell me down the river, that whoever was behind it had clearly set it up for me to be the scapegoat. "You have to look into this yourself, Pink. I'll help."

"It's out of my hands, Mom."

"That's a load of BS. Somebody framed you. For all we know, it could be Taylor, and there's no way we're leaving this up to her. If Parker Davis wants to argue about it, we'll sic Ed on him. And speaking of Ed, have you called him?"

"Ed can't do anything, Mom. Why freak him out?"

"He's your attorney, Pink. And you like him." She was quiet for a moment, then asked, "Have you talked to Ed since you've been in Washington?"

"Once."

"You've been gone over two weeks. What's up? Is this about that stupid billboard thing?"

No use lying. It would only prolong the misery. "I was so certain it was Ed who bought the billboard. After Steve Santorelli gave me a Mercedes, Ed made it sound like a contest, like he had to one-up Steve. A few days later, I see a Midland billboard that says Marry Me, Pink. Who wouldn't think it was Ed?"

"You should have found out for sure before you went over to Ed's and said no."

"Gee, thanks, Mom."

"No need to be sarcastic."

I sighed and broke a pencil in half. "I'm sorry. Just thinking about that day makes me queasy." It didn't help that my first reaction was elation. Ed wanted me to marry him, and how awesomely romantic to ask on a billboard. I remembered feeling euphoric, my mind skipping ahead to what life as Mrs. Ed Ravenaldt would be like. We'd live in Ed's quaint fixer-upper on the east side of old Midland. We'd get a cat. We'd meet at home during lunch and make crazy, passionate love to each other.

Then, less than twenty-four hours after seeing the billboard, reality set in. Bad memories from my disastrous first marriage moved in on all those squishy, happy thoughts and ruined everything. My ex-husband was a flaming philanderer. Ask any woman who's been involved with a cheater and she'll verify, it's next to impossible to trust another man. I knew I couldn't take it, the wondering every time Ed was out of pocket. I could hang out with Ed, sleep with him, spend entire weekends with him. But I couldn't marry him. So I went over there and told him. When he said he wasn't the one who bought the billboard, it was way beyond awkward.

Ed was pretty pissed, and who could blame him? I mean, what a bummer to get turned down *before* the question is asked. He was also pretty unhappy that Steve Santorelli was wowing me with romantic billboards. I had only myself to blame for that. Before I said no to Ed, I went on and on about how the billboard was awesome, how much it meant, and how clever. Blah, blah, blah. After that, Ed said he needed some space, that maybe it would be better if we didn't see each other for a while.

It wasn't just the billboard, and I knew that. As much as Ed and I are a perfect fit, our relationship from day one, when I hired him as my attorney during the whistle-blower thing, has been one of extremes. We're either completely in tune with each other, or metaphorically facing each other over pistols at dawn.

Three days after the billboard fiasco, a catastrophic earthquake hit China, killing over two hundred thousand people, with thousands more injured or missing. Mom's sister, Frederica, had spent nine years in China and still has a lot of friends there. Within twenty-four hours of the quake, she'd talked me into going with her to China, to help the survivors. After two weeks of horrors I'd never believe if I hadn't seen them with my own eyes, I came back to the States. I'd scarcely unpacked before I got a call from Parker, asking me to come to Washington and help out at CERF.

Within the week, I was living in a small furnished loft in Washington, D.C., working for CERF, feeling like I was following my destiny. After what I saw in China, I was as passionate as Parker. Maybe more so.

"Call Ed," Mom said now. "You're in a bad spot, Pink, and he can help you. Whatever personal problems you have with Ed are irrelevant."

She had a point. "He may tell me to go to hell."

"No, he won't." She cleared her throat. "I need to go. I still don't know why I let you talk me into this. The whole thing is making me antsy."

Cripes. For at least the fortieth time, I wished I hadn't convinced Mom to accept the invitation to the birthday dinner Steve's dad was hosting. She was driving me nuts about it.

Mom grew up on a dirt farm in a family of ten kids, poor as Job's turkey. She married right out of high school, had me, and became the ultimate hausfrau. When I was in college, she got up from her doormat position and told my dad to stick his autocratic belligerence where the sun don't shine. She divorced him, went to college, and became a CPA. She's a pretty woman. She's a barracuda in business. But deep inside, she's still a poor kid from the sticks, only one step away from her white-trash roots. Or so she thinks. On top of that, she has real issues with men. Now the thought of a romantic relationship flips her out, I guess because she's afraid she'll go back into doormat position. She avoids serious romance as diligently as she avoids IRS audits for her clients.

The birthday dinner posed a double threat. There would be senators, diplomats and Washington bigwigs there, and even though Mom can be as polished as the best of them, that kind of company scares her to death.

The other threat came from Steve's dad. Despite my assurances that she was invited to the party as a courtesy, her romance antennae had gone haywire because Lou Santorelli called her to offer the invitation long before the invitations were mailed.

Okay, the truth is, Lou *did* ask Mom because he's got a thing for her. But Mom couldn't possibly know that. As far as she knew, she'd never met the man.

A few weeks earlier, Lou was in Midland, working undercover for an antiterrorist group, looking for terrorist financiers. He happened to meet Mom, who had no clue who he was, or even that he was male, because he was disguised as a very large woman. Lou's pretty wacky. He was a POW in Vietnam, and like so many of those guys, it did something to him. Rules? Who needs 'em? He got it bad for Mom and asked her to the dinner via telephone, I think so he could talk to her as himself. It's kinda cute, in a weird way. And I was dying to see how they hit it off.

"Mom, you're a kick-ass CPA, and you can hold your own with überconservative businessmen. This is no different. Just be yourself."

"Don't you get it? Being myself is the bad part. I cuss like a sailor, have a tendency to bite heads off, and I'm way too opinionated. Besides, when I get flustered, this damn hick accent comes out so strong, people think I just fell off the cotton truck."

"You just don't get it, do you, Mom? All of that is what makes you so remarkable. You're unique, interesting and funny."

"And neurotic. Don't forget neurotic."

"So? Everybody's a little neurotic. Just go to the party and relax. If nothing else, look at it like you and I will have a chance to catch up."

"That's true." She sighed into the phone. "Promise me you'll call Ed."

"Fine! I promise."

Around five o'clock, Taylor came into my office and closed the door. She looked positively radiant. Tossing a stack of invoices toward me with check copies attached, she said smugly, "I called China Pearl and they say all of their invoices have been paid. Then I called Robert Wang at the CERF office in Beijing, and he checked these invoices against the copies he keeps before he mails the originals to us. He doesn't have any of these invoices. Which means they were generated by someone outside the invoicing department at China Pearl."

I eyed the invoices. "They're identical to the ones from China Pearl. Somebody went to a lot of trouble to get these printed. I wonder if they have fingerprints on them?"

Taylor looked like she wanted to cheer. "Yours, Pink. Your fingerprints are all over them. You're the one who approves all invoices for payment. Remember?" She glanced at my printer. "Did you know every printer has a unique imprint, that printer companies make them that way, so they can trace which printer was used to generate documents?" Her green gaze went to my computer. "And did you know computers have a unique identity, that the cops can trace any Internet transaction?"

My violent tendencies were coming to the fore. I guess we're not so far from our caveman ancestors. If I'd had a club, I'd have conked her on the head. "Did you know I leave this office every day a little after five and the printer and computer are alone until nine o'clock the next morning?" I leaned toward her and crossed my arms on my desk. "Give this some thought, Taylor. As much as you resent me, would you really feel good about me going to prison if I'm not guilty?"

She glared at me with open hostility. "I'd throw a party, and invite some of the staff from the old firm. You don't have a clue how many of us hated you, Pink. Always ordering everyone around, demanding we work unholy hours, giving us bad performance reviews for stupid things like wearing the wrong clothes and cussing in front of clients."

"So I deserve to rot in prison because I insisted the staff present a professional image? Because I took my job seriously and expected others to do the same?"

"You were such a bitch about it all."

"It was always all about the job, and making sure I did the best I could for the firm. That's called loyalty."

"You wouldn't know loyalty if it bit you in the ass!"

I leaned back, realization dawning on me. "This isn't about how I did my job at the firm. This is about that night you called and asked me to lie to your husband about where you were. You wanted me to say you'd been at my house, and I refused."

"We were friends! I needed help, and you blew me off."

"That was a million years ago, when we were still staff slaves. You've been divorced almost six years. And you're still blaming me?" I shook my head, more disgusted than I would have thought possible. "Face it, Taylor, I wasn't the one boinking the client's mailroom guy. That was you, and to hold such a grudge because I didn't go along with your lie is seriously chickenshit of you."

"It's not that you didn't go along with the lie. You ratted me out to the big dogs at the firm. Because of that one indiscretion, I was way behind everyone else in promotions."

"You're wrong, Taylor. I never said a word to anyone."

"Liar!" She grabbed up the invoices and waved them around. "You're gonna get what's coming to you!"

It took a superhuman effort not to lose my temper, but I managed. "If you finger me as the rat, you'll regret it, Taylor. I'm not behind this, but someone is. I suggest you find that person and lay off this immature grudge-fest."

So far, so good. I hadn't lost any ounce of professionalism, or sunk to Taylor's level.

Then she went over the line. With a smirk on her wide mouth, she said with dripping venom, "I figured out a long time ago, your problem is that you're a coldhearted, frigid bitch. George told me he had to get it somewhere else because you quit putting out." She stepped back toward the door and reached behind herself for the doorknob, just before she lobbed a nuclear bomb into my lap. "You divorced him because he slept with whores, but didn't you ever wonder if he got some he didn't have to pay for? You were the office joke, Pink, because half the women up there had a little bit of George. We all felt sorry for him, did you know that? I remember a Christmas party when George was doing Beth in the ladies' room. You went in there, and had no clue they were in the stall right next to you." She laughed. And laughed.

Unable to stop myself, I stood and shouted, *"Get out!"*

When she kept standing there, laughing, I reached for my coffee cup and hurled it at her, just as she opened the door. The damn thing flew right through the opening and crashed across Samantha Booker's desk, knocking over a pencil cup and splashing coffee all over Samantha's pretty white blouse.

I have never been so ashamed of myself. I looked at Taylor and said in as calm a voice as I could muster, which probably wasn't very, "Just know this, Taylor. If you don't do the job Parker entrusted you with, and do it fairly and without bias, you'll have a lot more to worry about than a tired grudge that's solely based on your own pathetic paranoia. Do we understand each other?"

"Are you threatening me?"

"I'm warning you. Don't screw with me, Taylor."

With one last glare, she turned and walked out.

From across the hall, in the open area of desks in the bullpen, the handful of staffers at CERF all stared at me with wide eyes and slack jaws. I didn't blame them. How often does a good catfight come along?

Chapter 2

By the time Mom and I got to the dinner party, I was ready to put myself up for adoption. All the way to Steve's Georgetown town house, she twisted one emerald earring and muttered about how she shouldn't have left Midland, that she had a million things to do, that her clients would suffer because she was gadding about the nation's capital, going to some idiotic dinner party with people she didn't know and probably didn't want to know. That led into a diatribe about politics in the United States, and it was at that point that I tuned her out.

Regrettably, the cabbie didn't tune her out, and by the time we arrived, they were in a hot debate about the state of the union. I guess Lou was awaiting our arrival because he opened the door of the cab. Mom didn't notice until after she'd summarily told the cabbie he was a socialist radical and if he hated America so much, why didn't he get the hell out?

Then Lou leaned in and handed the cabbie his fare and I honestly thought Mom would keel over in a dead faint. Her face was the color of a ripe strawberry. She took his hand and he helped her out of the cab, and while we stood there on the sidewalk, I introduced my mother to Lou Santorelli. It hit me that the two of them looked alike, with dark hair and eyes, and skin that leaned toward olive.

Lou didn't smile, didn't attempt to be gracious and welcoming, which I naturally expected because he was our host. Instead, he said in a curious voice, "If a man has a problem with how things are, does it make him a treasonous bastard who has no right to live here?"

It took her exactly twenty-three seconds to recover. I know because I counted, while I was praying she wouldn't turn around and walk off.

"If all he can do is blame the government for every stinkin' problem in his life, and insist how much better it is everywhere else in the world, then no, he doesn't deserve to live here. He should take his pissy, whiny attitude across the ocean. Any ocean."

Grasping her arm, he turned and walked her into the house. "It can be difficult to get a leg up, so maybe his pissy attitude is a result of struggling to make ends meet."

Mom appeared to have forgotten her neurosis. "It is not difficult to get ahead, if a person is willing to work hard. Especially if that person is a thirty-year-old white male, with no disability of any kind except pure laziness."

"Are you a feminist, Jane?"

Mom pulled her arm away from him. "I'm a hardworking professional woman who's got no time for labels and bullshit."

I'm still not sure why, but that struck Lou as funny. He laughed out loud, grabbed Mom's arm again and walked her into a wide living room with soaring ceilings and quite a few expensive-looking antiques. Steve's town house is beautiful, if a person is into the museum look.

The birthday boy was in the far corner, talking to a man with snowy-white hair whose back was toward the room. Looking at Steve, dressed in one of his beautiful suits, his short black hair a bit messy and his large, slightly hairy hand curled around a highball glass, I got that strange jumpy feeling in the pit of my stomach that I always get when I'm around him. It's not unpleasant at all—just unnerving. I'm afraid to put a name to the feeling because I'm fairly sure it would be something like intense, unquenched sexual desire. And as much as I like Steve, as much as I admire him and like being with him, I know it would spell disaster if I ever slept with him.

For one thing, any chance of ever making things work out with Ed would be over forever. And I wasn't ready to give that up. Not yet. For another, Steve is the antithesis of the kind of men I always assumed moved around Washington. He's a widower who lost his beloved wife, Lauren, to cancer almost three years ago, and since then, he hasn't gone out with anyone. Until me. I can't figure it out, but Steve seems to think I need to be the next Mrs. Santorelli. And that's without ever sleeping with me. If I did sleep with him, I just know he'd manage to get me to marry him. Imagine my trust issues with a senator. Yeah, it would never work.

After I figured out he was the one who bought the billboard, I told him thank you for the offer, but no. He wasn't surprised, he said, but he also wasn't giving up.

When he caught sight of me he waved me over, and I left Mom with Lou, which she failed to notice because they were really getting into it about women in America while the bartender mixed her a whiskey sour.

I was almost to Steve when I realized the old man was Richard Harcourt, a retired Speaker of the House. Steve took my hand and folded it into his, then kissed my cheek and introduced me. "Richard, this is Whitney Pearl, but she goes by Pink. We met when she testified before the senate finance committee during the Marvel Energy investigation."

Richard shook my hand and smiled warmly. "I watched it all on C-SPAN. You're a true hero." He dropped my hand, but continued smiling. "Interesting nickname you have. Lotta redheads get dubbed Red, but I'm not seeing why they call you Pink, especially with all that blond hair."

"I'm a CPA, sir. Because my last name is Pearl, people started calling me Pink Pearl, like the erasers."

"Ah, I see. Very clever, what? Mind if I call you Pink?"

I returned his smile. "Be my guest."

"Good, and you should call me Richard." He winked. "Or Very Handsome and Wonderful Old Man, if you prefer."

I couldn't help laughing, and decided I liked Richard Harcourt.

"Steve tells me you were in China for a couple of weeks just after the earthquake."

Of late, it was my favorite subject and I admit, I got kinda wound up about it. When I was done, and after I'd made the case for people to donate money to CERF, Richard chuckled and said in a pseudowhisper, "You're preaching to the choir, Pink. I wrote a check with a lot of zeroes on it just last week."

"I beg your pardon, sir, and thank you."

He lost a bit of his joviality and said, "Pretty damn good speech you've got there. I suggest you spin it to a few well-heeled people who've convinced themselves your boss should be the First Gentleman. Tell them their money's better spent on the Chinese relief effort than a lost cause."

"Sir?"

He harrumphed loudly. "Didn't you know Madeline Davis is planning to run for president?"

"I hadn't heard, no." Why hadn't Parker mentioned it? I glanced at Steve. "So a woman's going to run for president, and she's got some big money behind her. Imagine that."

"Will you vote for her?"

"Well, she is a smart woman." I turned again to Richard. "Who's supporting her?"

"Top of the list is Bill Mulholland." At my puzzled expression, he added, "Old New York family. Got money dating back to the *Mayflower,* no doubt. Sits on lots of corporate boards and hobnobs with royalty."

"And you think I should call and ask him for a donation because you're convinced any campaign money he gives to Madeline is wasted?" Maybe I didn't like Richard so much. I drew myself up a bit. "You'll pardon me, sir, if I decline to follow your suggestion. Insinuating that Madeline hasn't a prayer of winning without knowing who else might run can only indicate a gender bias I obviously don't support."

Instead of taking up the gauntlet, Richard laughed as though I'd just told a great joke. He leaned close to Steve and said, "She'll do, son. She'll do just fine."

Then he was gone, and miraculously, Steve and I were alone in the corner. But not for long. An entire flock of guests were descending on us from across the room. I quickly asked Steve, "What did he mean, I'll do?"

He grinned at me. "Richard is convinced I should throw my hat in the ring for president. He says the first thing I need is a wife, and he thinks you're just the ticket."

I was speechless. Seriously. Maybe it was the whisper of the thought of becoming First Lady of the United States of America, or maybe it was the thought of sleeping with the leader of the free world on a nightly basis, or maybe it was thinking about living at the most primo address in the country.

"What's wrong, Pink? Don't you think you're up to being First Lady?"

My mom's neurosis can sometimes be mine, as well. "Steve, I'm a CPA from a dusty oil town in West Texas. I went to a public university. I don't even have china. Come to think of it, after my apartment was broken into and ransacked last month, I don't have any dishes at all."

"The guy living at 1600 Pennsylvania Avenue right now is from your hometown. In fact, so is the First Lady. If you ask me, it's sort of cosmic. And by the way, they have plenty of dishes at the White House."

I didn't have a chance to respond, because the gaggle of guests were upon us. The rest of the cocktail hour, Steve guided me around the room, introducing me to senators and representatives, high-ranking military personnel, the IRS commissioner and the Mexican ambassador. After that we went for dinner in a dining room large enough to land a plane, where I was seated next to Steve at the head of the table and Mom was seated next to Lou about half a mile down at the far end. I was excited when the Chinese ambassador, Mr. Wu, was seated just across the table from me.

Steve noticed my enthusiasm. He leaned close and said quietly, "Most men give flowers and jewelry. You get the Chinese ambassador."

Startled, I looked into his dark Italian eyes. "You invited him just for me?"

He nodded and gave me a funny little crooked smile. "Now's your chance to ask him about Mrs. Han and the China brides."

That bizarre jumpy thing in my stomach morphed into a warm, intense feeling that was as foreign as Mr. Wu. I swallowed hard. "Thank you."

His smile kicked up a notch. "You're welcome." He turned to greet Mr. Wu, then introduced him to me.

Wu's English was perfect and we talked a great deal about the relief effort. After a while, I felt comfortable enough to ask him about something that had bothered me while I was in China. "I helped a survivor there, a pregnant woman named Mrs. Han, whose husband was killed. She was naturally very distraught, but it struck me as odd that the main cause of her distress was that she wanted to go home. The woman looked Asian, but not Chinese, and she spoke very little Chinese. It turned out her primary language was Russian. She told a story about being taken out of Siberia and brought to China as a bride. She said there are others like her, living in China, brought there to be wives to Chinese men because there's such a shortage of females. I wondered if this is something the government sponsors."

Mr. Wu looked shocked. His soup spoon clattered against his plate. "This woman, where can I find her?"

China clattered from behind the ambassador. I glanced back to see one of the waitstaff, a striking blond woman whose name tag read "Olga." When she noticed me watching her, she quickly turned and headed for the kitchen.

I redirected my attention to Mr. Wu. "Unfortunately, while I was looking for a policeman to help us, she disappeared, and I was unable to locate her again."

"This is most disturbing. Did she give you any indication who brought her into China?"

I shook my head. "As I said, she didn't speak Chinese, and the woman who translated knew only rudimentary Russian. After Mrs. Han disappeared, the CERF contact in Beijing, Robert Wang, said it's not uncommon for people to be disoriented after something like an earthquake." Remembering the poor woman, her tear-streaked face, swollen belly and woeful dark eyes, I felt a knot form in my throat. Where was she now? And what of the others? Mrs. Han said she'd been brought into China with five other young women from her village in Siberia.

Watching Mr. Wu process the idea, I said, "During my visits to China I've been proposed to several times by men in search of a bride. There's obviously a need for women."

He relaxed a bit, darted a glance at Steve, then leveled his gaze at mine. "It is true that the female-to-male ratio in China is shrinking, which leaves many of our young men without the opportunity to marry. It's an unfortunate result of our law allowing only one child in a family. Because of our custom that parents live with their son in their later years, a couple who has a son is assured of a home. Those with a daughter do not have that option."

"Because a daughter goes to live with her husband's family?"

He nodded. "Many women abandon their baby girls at birth, then try again until they have a son. Despite this, the one-child law is good, because without it, there would not be enough natural resources to support the population. The side effect is the shortage of females. I suspect that an enterprising person has been recruiting women from outside of China to fill the gap."

Olga returned and collected our soup bowls. When she asked Mr. Wu if he was done, I noticed her heavy accent. I thought she sounded Russian. Of course, to my West Texas ears, anyone from an Eastern bloc country would probably sound Russian. And I did have Russia on the brain.

"Thank you for alerting me to this problem, Miss Pearl," Mr. Wu said. "First thing tomorrow, I will contact someone who can look into this unfortunate business."

"If you hear any word on Mrs. Han, I would very much appreciate the information."

Olga hurried off with the tray of dirty soup bowls, then reappeared with the salad course. She set a plate in front of Steve, then looked a little flustered and snatched it away. He shot her a confused look, to which she smiled and mumbled an apology. "I have forgotten the garnish. Please excuse me." Before he could protest, she turned, still clutching the salad tray. She stumbled as she rounded the table and one of the salads slid off the tray and into my lap.

It took a bit to clean up the mess—this in the midst of Mr. Wu tut-tutting and Steve glowering at Olga, who looked ready to run away. Or burst into tears. Feeling for her, I hastened to assure her there was no harm done.

"But, miss, you've spots on your pretty pink dress. Please, come to the kitchen and I will clean?"

I didn't see much point. The dress was destined for the dry cleaner. But Olga was beside herself, and Steve looked uncharacteristically annoyed, so I followed her to the kitchen. Just as I suspected, club soda didn't faze raspberry vinaigrette. I thanked her anyway, assured her it was quite all right and escaped back to the table.

As I took my seat, I noticed Mr. Wu's forehead was wrinkled in concentration, his gaze fixed on a spot somewhere behind my shoulder. "Sir," I said, "my apologies if what I said has upset you."

He looked at me and shook his head. "Nothing of the kind, Miss Pearl. I am glad to have the information."

When Olga returned with a fresh set of salads and set his before him, he picked up his fork and started eating. He seemed upset, and even though I was relieved to know he would do something to investigate the China brides, I felt guilty for bringing it up.

He ran a finger along the inside of his collar as though it was too tight, then gave me a weak smile. "This earthquake is a bad, bad thing. So many homeless, and so many without families. It will take many years to recover fully. Thank you for helping my country."

"You're welcome, Ambassador Wu. I'm glad to be of any help, especially because I'm very fond of China and her people."

After all the salads had been served, the conversation turned to other topics.

The ambassador's attention was on the guest to his left, and Steve said under his breath, "You're fantastic."

"Not hardly. Just nosy."

He smiled at someone down the table, then his gaze moved to my cleavage, then to my eyes. "Nice dress, Pink. Even with salad dressing."

"Thank you." My stomach started that weird jumpy thing again. Oh, man. My first bite of salad didn't go down well, so I set aside the fork and concentrated on the wine.

"Now that the finance committee is adjourned for a while, I'll have a lot more free time. You've been here two weeks and I've only been able to see you twice."

"I'm pretty busy myself, Steve." And I was about to be a lot busier, searching for the rotten dog who set me up. I wondered what Steve would think about it, and how he'd feel about marrying me if he knew I could potentially ruin all future political races. Even if I didn't intend to marry him, I wanted us to be friends, and I prayed all over again that the culprit would be nailed before anyone else found out about it. Even being friends with Steve would be impossible if word got out about the bank account with my name on it, and five hundred thousand of CERF's dollars deposited in it.

"Is something wrong?"

I gave him a reassuring smile. "Not at all. And you're right, it will be nice to spend some time together."

Olga appeared at my elbow and pointed at my plate. "The salad is wrong?"

"No, it's fine," I said, wishing the woman would leave off being so attentive. She looked like somebody who had just realized she'd boarded a plane to Cleveland instead of the one to Paris. "I'm just not very hungry." Blame it on Steve, making my stomach do that squiggly thing.

Olga nodded and picked up my plate, then moved to the next guest.

As happens at all dinner parties, the ebb and flow of conversation created a dull roar, with no voice particularly audible. Until I heard Mom.

"You arrogant son of a bitch! You invited me and the IRS commissioner so you could get your own agenda front and center."

"The only reason you're so angry is that you know I'm right. Without people like you, CPAs on the front lines, standing up and demanding a simplified tax law, nothing will ever change. It's your duty to do so, and your life is wasted if you shrug off the responsibility."

"My life is a lot of things, buster, but it sure as hell isn't wasted! I'm calling a cab because there's no way I'm listening to any more of your bullshit. You're crazy, Mr. Santorelli."

I leaned forward a little bit and saw that she was no longer in her chair. Neither was Lou. Yet, I could hear her distinctive West Texas twang, along with Lou's deep, clipped voice. Where were they?

Steve touched my shoulder and I turned to look at him. "This is a very old house and the ventilation system's pretty rudimentary. I think they must have gone into the study, at the front of the house." He glanced up at a register close to the ceiling of the dining room. "It's like a P.A. system."

Lou said, loud and clear, completely audible now because everyone in the room had fallen silent, "I'm probably crazy, but you should know I didn't invite you because of the damn tax law. That was strictly shooting from the hip. We'll discuss it later."

"No, we won't. I'm calling a cab. Where the hell's the phone?"

"You're not leaving, Jane."

"Oh, no? Hide and watch me. Now get out of my way."

There was a moment of silence, followed by the distinct

sound of a slap. "Who said you could kiss me? Oh, my God! I have got to get out of here. If you don't step aside I'm gonna scream, and won't that be embarrassing for you!"

"I'm never embarrassed."

"Yes, I can see how that might be. You're too arrogant to be embarrassed."

Ignoring the chuckles around the room, I rose from the table, intent on saving Mom from what would surely be the most embarrassing moment of her life, but before I could step away from my chair, Mr. Wu made a strange noise. I looked across the table and saw that his face was bright red and he was sweating profusely.

"Sir, are you okay?" I asked, moving around the table toward him.

Steve stood, calling for a towel from one of the waiters, while I loosened the ambassador's tie.

"I...can't...breathe," he croaked, clawing at his throat.

"He's choking!" someone yelled.

Hauling the man to his feet, Steve moved behind him and performed the Heimlich, but when Mr. Wu vomited it became apparent he wasn't choking.

"Is he having a heart attack?" someone asked.

An attractive woman hurried toward us, shooing people out of her way. "I'm a nurse. Let me see." She took one look at him and said, "Get him to the couch, and somebody call an ambulance."

Steve and one of the generals carried the heavyset man into the living room and laid him on the couch, where he promptly threw up again. Dinner forgotten, the entire party crowded around the couch, anxiously watching. I noticed that Mom and Lou were there, but with everyone's attention on the ambassador, they didn't realize how public their private conversation had been.

I felt a tap on my shoulder, and when I turned, Olga was gesturing me toward the kitchen. Evidently I had a phone call. As if I cared right now! But recalling her persistence in cleaning the salad dressing, I followed her to the kitchen. As I reached for the wall phone, I wondered who would call me at Steve's. I said hello over the noise of the waitstaff, the cooks, water running and dishes clinking together.

"What do you want?" I heard Taylor Bunch say on the other end of the line.

"Shouldn't I be asking that question? You called *me*."

"Pink, what are you up to? I didn't call. You did. So what's this about? If you're calling to apologize for this afternoon, save your breath. You're going down, sister, and soon. When I got home from the office, I found a package on my doorstep that's gonna put you away for the rest of your natural life."

Thoroughly confused, I stared at a stack of plates. "Taylor, I'm at a dinner party, and I didn't call you."

"Well, somebody did. Told me to hang on, and here you are."

I glanced over my shoulder but didn't see Olga, or anyone else who looked out of the ordinary. The kitchen was a hive of activity and frantic chatter about the ambassador, and no one appeared to notice me. Turning back to the stack of plates, I asked, "What was in the package?"

"Everything I need to prove you ripped off CERF. I'm about to call Parker. Then I'm calling the police. Maybe the FBI."

"I don't know what you've got, or where it came from, but if it points to me, it's fake. I didn't do it, Taylor."

"Yeah, well, tell the judge." She hung up.

I returned the phone to its cradle, my mind leaping ahead, wondering what on earth Taylor could have that would hang me. And who had left it on her doorstep. Things were quickly spiraling out of control and I suddenly panicked. I felt an overwhelming need to see Taylor, to find out what she had, to talk her out of calling Parker, or the police.

Turning to leave the kitchen, I noticed Olga as she slipped out the back door. She wore a light jacket over her uniform and had a backpack slung over her shoulder, and an alarm went off inside me. I asked the waiter closest to me, "Why is Olga leaving?"

He looked confused. "Who's Olga?"

"One of the waitstaff."

"She's not with us. Must be a regular of the senator's household help."

She *wasn't* with the household staff. Steve had a house-keeper named Carla and a driver named Bill and that was it.

One of the catering staff rushed into the kitchen to announce that Mr. Wu was dead, probably from poisoning. I gasped.

My gaze went to the door where Olga had disappeared. Could she have had something to do with his death? Was that what the whole salad thing was about—she'd given Steve the wrong salad?

The thought made me breathless with terror.

I glanced at the telephone. Olga had to be the one who called Taylor, then brought me to the phone. Why? What did that have to do with Ambassador Wu?

My mind raced with possibilities, and it occurred to me that the quickest way to get answers was to ask Olga.

Not stopping to explain, or even to grab my handbag from the dining room, I took off after her, through the back door, through the garden gate and into the alleyway behind the row of houses along Steve's street.

Running has never been my strong suit and my strappy high heels took my pathetic athletic ability to new lows. Taking them off on the rough ground would slow me even more, so I hauled it as best I could out into a side street, looking both ways. I caught a glimpse of a dove gray jacket turning the corner. I ran after Olga, my mind churning through what had happened, and no matter how I sliced it, I kept coming back to wondering if I was supposed to be Olga's hit. Had my discovery that morning marked me as a dead woman?

I thought of the salad, of how disappointed Olga was when I failed to eat it. Had my salad also been poisoned? If so, it was no wonder that Olga had been upset. Someone had sent her to off me, and I had to go and be goofy over Steve, killing any desire to eat. I sent a quick thank-you to God for making me crush on Steve Santorelli.

Two blocks later, I had to admit defeat. Olga had vanished. Probably just as well, I decided, if the woman was out to kill me. Nobody but a fool chases death.

I kept walking until I came to a major thoroughfare, where I hailed a cab and gave him Taylor's address. I knew she lived in a condo complex a block over from my loft, because I'd seen her leaving a couple of times when I passed the building on my way to work. When we arrived I realized I had no money, which naturally annoyed the cabbie to no end.

"Look," I said, trying to mollify him, "if you'll just wait here, I'll be right back with some money."

"Do I look stupid, lady?"

Taking in his hairy face and hard eyes, I shook my head. "You'll just have to trust me."

"Hurry up about it, will ya? The meter's gonna keep running."

In the lobby, I signed the guest book, but when I explained that I had no purse and no ID, the security guard waved me on, barely looking at me as he read a magazine.

At Taylor's door, I sucked in a breath of courage, raised my fist and knocked.

"Come in!"

I reached for the knob, opened the door and was instantly hit with a sense of seriously bad karma. I'm not psychic or anything like that. I just get this bizarre feeling of impending doom sometimes, and it never fails to pan out.

Inside, it was gloomy, with only one lamp lit in the far corner of the living area. The wooden blinds were closed, blocking any light from the city outside. "Taylor? Where are you?" It felt strange walking into someone's home without that person there to greet me. Strange, hell. My hair was standing on end.

She didn't answer, so I went toward the only other light, streaming through the doorway to the kitchen.

I found Taylor. On the kitchen floor. With a telephone cord around her neck. Her wide green eyes stared up at me without blinking. Maybe I wasn't a fan of Taylor's, but Jesus, I didn't want her to die. I felt sick to my stomach seeing her there, so twisted and dead, a look of startled fear frozen on her face.

It hit me then. If Taylor was dead, who had called out for me to come in? The voice had been muffled and indistinguishable.

I turned quickly, just in time to see the front door closing.

I booked to the door, jerked it open and saw the sleeve of a dove gray jacket just before the fire-exit door slammed shut. I nearly fell several times rushing down the concrete steps in my heels, but I didn't want to stop long enough to take them off. Maybe I should have. By the time I reached the ground floor, the outside exit door was closed. I ran outside, into the alley, but it was pitch dark and I knew it was way past stupid to continue any farther.

Unfortunately, the damned exit door locked behind me and I couldn't get back in. I had no choice but to walk down the alley, in the dark, and hope I made it to the street alive.

For approximately one nanosecond, I considered jumping in the still-waiting cab and gettin' the hell outta Dodge. But I knew it would bite me in the ass later. I'd signed in at the front desk. I'd probably left something in Taylor's apartment, like a hair, or carpet fibers from Steve's house. Hey, I watch *CSI*. I know about those things.

There also was that pesky problem with the Kansas bank account, and all those people who saw the catfight between Taylor and me that afternoon.

Running from the problem would not make it go away. It would only make me look more guilty. Deciding to face it head-on and be completely honest, I made my way around to the street side of Taylor's building, winded and pissed off because I hadn't caught Olga. At the security guard's desk, breathing heavily, I said, "You need to call the police. I went up to see Taylor Bunch and she's dead. Whoever killed her ran out the fire exit in back."

Naturally, Mr. Macho didn't believe me. He had to go up and see her dead body for himself. As soon as the elevator door closed, I looked at his guest book to see who'd signed in within the past three hours. There were only two names. Mine, and somebody named J. Smith. Yeah, right. No doubt it was "J. Smith" I'd just chased down the stairs. I used the security guard's phone and called the cops.

They arrived quickly and we all went upstairs to Taylor's apartment, where we found the security guard wandering around, looking in closets and under the bed. Clearly, he hadn't gotten it when I said the killer ran out the fire exit.

The two uniformed officers told him to go downstairs, said that they would question him later, then asked me to have a seat in the kitchen, which seemed odd to me since Taylor was there. It unnerved me, her body lying so close, her eyes staring up at me.

"Tell me what happened," the taller of the two said as he took the chair opposite mine and the shorter one went off somewhere else in the apartment.

I'd already given some thought to what I would say, and it seemed to me that being honest was the best way to go. Start lying and I was bound to trip myself up. As briefly as possible, I told him.

He wrote it all down, then had me read it over and sign it. Several minutes later, a middle-aged, ordinary-looking man in a dull brown suit came in and walked around Taylor's body, checking her out before he sat across from me.

"I'm Detective Schumski. I know you've already given your statement, but I'd like to hear it from you."

He stared at me as I spoke, without asking any questions. When I was done, he got up and left the room, then came back and said, "Did you leave a cab driver downstairs without paying him?"

"I told you, I was chasing Olga and didn't take the time to get my purse before I left." I glanced at the entry to the kitchen. "Is he still there?"

"I paid him. You owe the city thirty-two bucks."

"Thank you."

He gave me another hard stare. "I'm taking you in, Miss Pearl. There are way too many questions I need answered, and there's a dead foreign dignitary across town. Until I have a better handle on what went on tonight, you'll be a guest of the city."

So I went downstairs and rode to the police station in the back of a squad car. Once there, I sat around and waited aeons before Schumski and another detective came in and asked a thousand more questions. Not only did they have the deposit and check copies from the office, the ones I'd handed over to Taylor and she'd conveniently taken home, but they also had the contents of Taylor's surprise package—multiple Valikov Interiors invoices made out to me, covering three hundred thousand dollars' worth of Chinese antiques and furniture. For ten thousand bucks, an antique fish pot with a wooden stand, and three pairs of Chinese wedding shoes, the tiny kind women wore when their feet were bound. A real bargain at twenty-two thousand dollars was a jade horse from the Yuan Dynasty. All of the invoices were for similar items, equally pricey.

I said to Schumski, "Why would a person embezzle money, then spend all of it on this kind of stuff? It seems to me a person would buy things like cars, or go on a trip, or maybe blow it on some expensive jewelry."

He glanced at his partner. "You tell me, Ms. Pearl. Maybe you have a thing for Chinese antiques."

"Detective, I am not behind this, and I didn't murder Taylor. I'm being honest and forthright because I want you to find the woman who did do it. Besides, if I bought all of this stuff, where is it?"

"My guess would be that it's in your home, either here or in Midland. That's why we're getting a search warrant for both places. We're also going to get the signature card from that bank in Kansas, and I'll bet it's a spot-on match with yours."

He was wrong about that. The signature card had to be my ace in the hole. I would have to remember signing a signature card. I'd hire the best handwriting expert in the country to prove it. I was not going to prison. Period.

Nevertheless, thinking of all the circumstantial evidence against me, including the phone call and the catfight, I felt my heart sink.

It sank further when Schumski implied I had something to do with Ambassador Wu's death. After he spoke to the detective who'd been at Steve's, he said I had the opportunity to put poison in the ambassador's salad when I went to the kitchen.

"Why would I tell the man about the China brides, then kill him? That makes absolutely no sense at all."

He didn't see it that way, but he was stretching it to charge me with Ambassador Wu's death, so he settled with suspicion of only one homicide, along with embezzlement and fraud.

A little while later, while I cooled my heels in the small interrogation room, they got statements from a couple of the CERF staff who'd seen Taylor and me shout at each other, and me warning her not to screw with me. They got a statement from Parker about what I'd found, and how I'd approached him about it and wanted to do my own investigation. Yeah, that didn't look good. But the last nail in my coffin was when they matched my fingerprints to those on the Valikov Interiors invoices. I knew for certain then that someone had gone to an extraordinary amount of trouble to set me up, to use me as their scapegoat. I had no idea how my fingerprints had gotten on those invoices, but I was hell-bent on finding out.

I got to make one phone call and used it to call my attorney, Ed. After I told him I was in deep doo-doo, he sighed, like he couldn't believe I was such a pain in his ass, and I decided I'd kill him if he said he wouldn't help me. Luckily for Ed's longevity, he said he'd be there as soon as he could get a flight out.

"Whatever happens, Pink, whatever they ask, or say to you, don't say a word. Understand?"

Kinda late for that, wasn't it? "I understand," I said anyway. "Ed, I left Mom at a party hours ago. Would you call and tell her what happened? They won't let me make any more calls."

"Does she have her cell phone?"

"Uh, no. It wouldn't fit in her purse. The party was at Santorelli's."

Dead silence. Then he said, "I'll call." And then, in a very cold voice, "Remember, say nothing."

"I remember."

But it was damn hard not to say anything at all, especially when they booked me for murder and embezzlement, took a mug shot, then locked me up in a room with a lot of extremely sorry-looking women. To be fair, I probably looked pretty lousy myself.

I sat there all night and ignored everyone. One chick tried

to pick a fight with me, but I turned away and closed my eyes and she finally laid off.

It's funny, the things we think of in times of major crisis. All that night, the only thing I could think about was Mrs. Han, and how much she wanted to go home, and how much I hoped that she'd gotten what she wanted. Maybe she was from Siberia, a very unwelcoming, cold place to live, but it was her home, and her people were there. I had people back in Midland, which was also somewhat unwelcoming—a long, dusty stretch of flatland, broken only by oil-lease roads and pumpjacks, covered with scrubby mesquite and cactus. I was determined to go back there, to be with my people. I vowed that I would, as soon as I found the bastard who framed me.

Chapter 3

By nine o'clock the next morning, I had a sketchy plan. But it was a start. One thing was sure—no way I was gonna sit around and wait for the police or the FBI to find out who set me up. Why would they, when they already had a perfectly good suspect?

The guard, a hefty woman named Clara, came and let me out. She walked me down a long hallway, to a flight of stairs and another hall to a door with a window. Inside was Ed.

I almost hyperventilated. God, he looked good. Like salvation and sex. Dressed in one of his killer navy suits, with a red silk tie that was exactly like every other tie in his closet and his usually longish dark hair freshly cut, he could almost pass for another one of the millions of suits walking around Washington. But not quite. Something about Ed is unlike any other man. Maybe because I know what he looks like naked.

Or maybe because he's got an attitude that even the most expensive Brooks Brothers suit can't disguise.

I've gotten in the habit of falling in and out of love with Ed, and at that moment I was dead dog certain he was the most supreme male on planet Earth. Overwhelmed with an emotion I never wear comfortably, I looked at Ed and wanted to marry him and have ten thousand of his babies.

It's probably a good thing he didn't ask just then.

Not caring if he hated my guts—and that's not to say he did—I walked to him, slid my arms around his waist and burst into tears. I was so bummed out, I wasn't even embarrassed about losing it.

Being the supreme male he is, Ed wrapped me up and let me bawl all over him and get salty tears on his tie.

Eventually, he set me away from him and pulled a chair out from the small metal table. He handed me a tissue from the box on the table and said, "This is some bad shit, Pink. They've got enough to nail your ass but good. They didn't find anything in your loft here in D.C., or in your apartment in Midland, but it turned out the manager in Midland had taken all the boxes delivered to your door and stored them for you. There's enough stuff to open a small Chinese antique shop."

I sniffled and watched him take the chair opposite mine, drag it around the table and sit next to me. "There were quite a few messages on your answering machine from a woman named Sasha, who was updating you about your plans to redecorate the house you're buying."

"I don't know anyone named Sasha, and besides, why would I make plans to redecorate a house I don't own yet?"

"You wouldn't. It's all part of the scam, Pink." He leaned forward a little and looked directly into my face. "I want you to tell me everything, from start to finish. Don't leave anything out. Got it?"

Nodding, I blew my nose, tossed the snotty tissue toward the wastebasket, missed, then turned back to Ed. I told him all of it, my tears drying up the longer I talked and the more pissed off I became. By the end of it, I could have put any televangelist to shame, I was so righteous.

In typical Ed fashion, he didn't get too worked up about it. He reached out and smoothed my hair away from my face. "You look like hell." His gaze dropped to the neckline of my dress, along with his hand. While his long, warm fingers dipped into my cleavage on the pretense of feeling the fabric, he said evenly, "Nice dress. I like that it's pink. I bet Santorelli liked it, too."

Turning away from him, I didn't rise to the remark. "What does how I look have to do with anything?"

"You need to look more conservative to the judge for your arraignment." He nodded toward a small bag next to the door. "I stopped at your loft after I left Santorelli's."

I shot him a startled look. "You went to Santorelli's?"

"Your mother is over there. She spent the night."

I stood and walked around the perimeter of the small room. "I hear about five stories in your voice. So let me have 'em. First, what did Mom say about this?"

"Lots, and most of it I can't repeat because my mama taught me better."

"So she's just mad? She's not crying? I can take anything so long as she doesn't cry. I hate it when she cries."

"Oh, she cried, then she went off on a shouting tangent, then she cried again." He smiled wryly. "I'd like to beat up the senator and leave him for dead, but I gotta say, his dad is one cool dude. Did you know he was a POW in Vietnam?"

"Yes, I know."

"It's pretty weird, watching him and your mom. Can't say I've ever seen Jane like that."

I stopped walking. "Like what?"

Ed cocked his head to one side, as though he had to think about how to phrase his thoughts. Finally he said, "There's some kind of strange chemistry there. On the surface, she can't stand Lou. She must have told him to shut the fuck up at least five times, and I didn't blame her because he kept coming up with wacked-out, commando ideas about how to help you. Jane said if we left it up to him, we'd all be in prison. Or dead." Ed shook his head like he couldn't believe it. "Lou is one of those guys who says exactly what he thinks, and to hell with being politically correct, or tactful, or whatever. He told Jane she couldn't possibly be any help because she's too damn emotional, that if she didn't stop crying and shouting, he'd force-feed her a sedative."

"Did the castration take long?"

Ed stared across the small room at me. "That's the strange part, Pink. She agreed with him. Then she sat down and asked me what I planned to do to help you out of this jam."

I told him what I knew about Lou and his attraction to Mom, and what we'd all overheard through the ventilation system before the ambassador became so sick. "I can't believe, considering how she insisted she wanted to leave, that she spent the night there."

"Naturally, after I called and told her you'd been arrested, she was upset. Lou wouldn't let her take a cab and insisted on taking her home, but when they got to your loft, the cops were all over it and wouldn't let her in. So Lou made her go back to Santorelli's house with him, and she stayed all night. When I got there this morning, she was crying and he was fixing breakfast. Gave her a couple of fried eggs, bacon, sausage and toast with butter. Jane says, that's a heart attack on a plate. Lou says, eat it now, dammit. And she picked up the fork and ate it."

Oh, man. Mom was sliding into doormat mode. This was bad. On the other hand, it meant she was definitely not wishy-washy about Lou. All her shouting aside, Mom liked him. She wouldn't be a doormat for a man she didn't like. The problem was, how could she be involved with him and not become a doormat? Jeez, I wished Mom would get some counseling.

I glanced at Ed. "You've very carefully not mentioned Steve."

Ed shrugged. "He's upset, but then who could blame him? You're the future Mrs. Santorelli. Possible First Lady. How's it gonna look if you've got a parole officer following you around the White House?"

I moved back to sit next to him. "That's not fair, Ed."

He frowned at me. "You think I care about being fair? The guy bought you a Mercedes. He asked you to marry him on a billboard. He wants to make you First Lady. How the hell can I compete with that?"

"It's not a competition."

"You don't know one damn thing about guys, Pink. It's always about competition. Always."

"So buy me a Mercedes and ask me to marry you on a billboard. You can afford it. Granted, you can't get to that First Lady thing very easily, but you could run for mayor and I could be First Lady of Midland."

"You're not even kinda funny."

"I'm not trying to be funny, Ed. I'm pointing out that what works for one guy won't work for another." I looked up at him. "As well as you know me, do you think I really give a hang about a car, or a romantic billboard, or living at the White House? I mean, seriously?"

He blinked a couple of times. "Hell, I don't know. You're a girl, and girls always go for that kinda stuff."

"I said no. About the billboard, I mean."

His laugh didn't hold a lot of humor. "I know how that feels." He leaned back in the chair until it rested on the rear legs. "Maybe you should say yes. I'm thinking being the fiancée of a Big Dog senator would get you a little more leeway. They might actually give it a shot to find who really did swipe five hundred Gs from CERF and who offed Taylor."

Shocked and amazed, I gave him a scrutinizing look. "You're serious, aren't you?"

"Damn straight."

"So I should get engaged to Steve, then break it off after I'm exonerated?"

Ed shrugged. "I guess that would be up to you."

"You really do hate his guts, don't you?"

"Not true. I actually think he's an okay guy. And it's clear he's got it bad for you, Pink. Crazy in love, even."

"It would be incredibly selfish and cruel to say yes, then break it off. I'd be using him, and there's no way I'll do it."

"Maybe you should suggest it. Be up-front about it."

"Suppose I did, and he said yes. How would you feel about that?"

He dropped all four chair legs back to the linoleum floor.

"For now, I'm willing to step aside, if it means keeping you out of prison."

I jumped to my feet and started around the room again. "Why do you do that?"

"What?"

"Be all selfless and wonderful."

"Yeah, I'll show you wonderful. Take your clothes off."

I stopped. "You can't be serious!"

He stared at my cleavage. "As a heart attack."

I began to pace again and he watched me for a while before he said, "All of our issues aside, I gotta say we're unparalleled in the sack."

"Gimme a break, Ed. It's never been just about sex."

He cleared his throat and stood. "Yeah, well, all of it's moot if I don't get you cleaned up for the arraignment. Come here and take off that dress."

I went to him and took off the dress. He rose from grabbing the bag and froze, his gaze fixed on my breasts, which were sort of way out there on account of I had on a push-up bra.

"I guess it'd be really bad form to make love to you right now."

"Really bad. For one thing, I'm not into being watched, and Clara might have a stroke out there by the window. For another, it would only be fun for you. I'm freaking out way too bad to enjoy it, Ed."

He pulled a black dress out of the bag. "Another difference between men and women."

"We wear dresses and you don't?"

As he slid it over my head, his hands brushed my breasts, and it was definitely not accidental. "We can enjoy sex anywhere, anytime."

"Yeah, you've got it made, Ed, you and the rest of humans with penises. You can pee anywhere, as well." I shimmied until the dress fell around my thighs. "Speaking of which, I haven't since before they locked me up. I refused to do it in front of all those women and the guards. It's inhumane the way they have a toilet in there, just open, for anyone to watch."

"I'll get you to a bathroom, don't worry." He pulled a toothbrush and a tube of toothpaste out of the bag. "I thought this would feel good."

"Lord, yes! You wouldn't happen to have some lipstick in there, would you?"

He produced a tube of passion pink.

"Ed, you're the man."

He pulled a black jacket out of the bag. "Put this on."

I did, and he handed me a pair of black-framed glasses and a hair clip. "Now put these on, and pull back your hair."

"But I don't wear glasses."

"They're just glass. I want you to look like a serious CPA. But not dowdy or poor. I want you to look classy."

When I was done, he inspected me. "After you brush your teeth and put on some lipstick, you'll do. Now, all you have to do in there is stand up when I tell you to, look directly at the judge and don't say anything. Got it?"

I nodded and he knocked on the door for Clara to let us out.

Twenty minutes later I was in a crowded courtroom, with a lot of other souls awaiting arraignment. When it was our turn, the room went curiously silent, which increased my tension a million times over.

To hear the prosecuting attorney tell it, I was a danger-ous, murderous, conniving thief, a real menace to society.

Lucky for me, the judge remembered my testimony to the finance committee and thought I was not so dangerous. When Ed requested that I be released on my own recognizance, the judge said he couldn't do that, based on my charges, but he thought a million bucks bail would do nicely.

I hadn't actually considered that I couldn't make bail. I might be locked up until my trial. While I was standing there, freaking out, Ed nudged me and whispered, "Let's get the hell outta here, Pink."

"But what about bail?"

He looked down at me and said with just a trace of bitterness, "Mister Billboard is gonna cover it."

Within the hour, we were riding through the streets of Washington in Mister Billboard's Mercedes and words could never describe how awkward it was. Before we even got in the car, it was awkward. Steve was pretty emotional and hugged me a lot and asked if I was okay and did I need anything, at least fifteen times. I thanked him for bailing me out, and Ed said nothing. In the car, while Steve asked a hundred questions, Ed didn't say anything. Steve insisted I go back to his place because Mom was there, and because the media was bound to descend on my building as soon as they figured out where I lived. The loft was leased to CERF, so it would take them a bit to find me, thank God.

I wanted some other clothes, so we went by my loft, and while I wandered around looking over the mess the cops had left after their search, Ed didn't say a word. I grabbed some clothes and my boots, then shoved all of it, along with some makeup, into a leather backpack.

In the elevator, Steve said to Ed, "This is gonna be a lot worse on her if you don't lighten up."

Ed scowled at him. "She's not made out of glass."

Steve glanced at me, then looked at Ed. "You got a problem with me, say the word."

"Just how long do you think it'd take them to throw me in jail after I beat the shit out of a United States senator?"

"I don't think you have much to worry about."

"Do I look worried?"

"You look like a real pissed-off guy."

"You're pretty fucking smart." He paused. "For a senator."

The door opened, but neither of them made a move to get off. I did.

And they stayed.

The door closed and I flinched when I heard a loud *thud*. I stood there and watched the numbers on the lighted panel. *Two. Three. Four. Five.*

Four. Three. Two. One, and the door opened. They both stood at the back of the elevator, looking like two guys about to kick the living daylights out of each other. A small woman and her little dog were in front, and when the door slid open, she stepped out, evidently oblivious to what she'd interrupted. Without looking at me standing there in front of the elevator, Steve reached over, pushed the button, and the door closed again.

I went to the small bench in the lobby of the building and sat down to wait.

They rode the damn elevator up to the fifth floor two more times before they got all the testosterone out of their systems. After the second trip, they staggered out and made their way to the front door of the building. Almost as an afterthought, they looked toward me and waved for me to follow. I'd say it was a toss-up as to who won. They both looked pretty ragged, but no one looked like they needed to stop by the ER.

The car ride to Steve's house was silent, but the tension was gone. When we got there, Lou took one look at them and died laughing. Mom rushed me, almost knocking me down, and before I could make any protest, she dragged me upstairs, down the hall and into the bedroom at the end. I barely had a chance to notice the furniture and the decor, which had sort of a George Washington Extreme Makeover look to it, before Mom propelled me to one of the chairs set in front of a fireplace.

"I swear to God I've lost ten years off my life," she said as she sank into the opposite, matching chair.

I noticed she had on a ratty pair of jeans and a white linen blouse, her dark hair up in a chip clip—and she was barefoot.

I was wondering about her interesting, relaxed look when she asked, "Are you okay? I mean, they didn't do anything weird to you, did they?"

"Not if you don't count making me hang out with some very smelly women. In fact, I'd really like to take a shower before I tell you all the gory details."

Looking horrified, Mom bounced up and ran to the bathroom, where she started the shower. "I'm so sorry, baby. What was I thinking? Of course you must feel icky. Oh, God, I can't believe this is happening." She came out of the bathroom and stopped by the bed to stare at me, her lip trembling. "What are we gonna do?"

I stood and slipped out of my new jacket and dress before I went to her. "I've got a plan, Mom, but I can't tell you what it is. If I did, if you knew where I was going and what I was doing, you'd have to lie if the police came looking for me."

I walked around her and headed for the bathroom, shucking my bra and panties as I went. "Just let me get cleaned up and have something to eat, and we'll talk."

Mom being Mom, she wasn't gonna let it go for another second, much less the time it would take me to shower and eat. She followed me into the bathroom and sat on the sink while I took a shower, yelling over the running water, "From what you said, I assume you're planning to do something illegal, and I won't let you do it. You can't afford to get into worse trouble. You're already in so deep, I don't see how you're going to get out."

"I told you, I have a plan."

"What is it?"

"All I'll say is that when I'm done, I'll know who set me up." I peeked around the shower curtain. "When you get back to Midland, call Aunt Fred's friend, that Chinese history guy, and ask him to take a look at the stuff sent to me by Valikov Interiors. I bet they're all fakes. One of the invoices the detective found at Taylor's was for a twenty-two-thousand-dollar Yuan Dynasty jade horse."

Mom's eyes were wide. "You could be on to something—because most Chinese antiques are fakes. Mao Zedong demolished almost everything during the Cultural Revolution." She frowned. "Did they have jade horses in the Yuan Dynasty?"

"Aunt Fred's history guy will know."

"True, but the Midland police probably have all of the stuff from Valikov locked up as evidence. They won't let him examine the pieces."

"I'll get Ed to call his brother, Hank. He's a Midland cop, and he'll work it out."

"Do you have to stay in Washington?"

"I don't know, but it doesn't matter, because I'm not."

"If you break bail it'll cost Steve a million dollars."

"The preliminary hearing is in two weeks, and by then, I intend to have everything I need to get the judge to throw the case out. I won't break bail." Looking around the curtain again, I saw that she had a huge worry wrinkle across her forehead. "Mom, I have to do this. If I don't, I'm history. You need to go home, to Midland, and not ask any questions. No matter what happens, if you don't know where I am, or what I'm doing, no one can make you tell them. It's better this way, so you need to set aside that Mom thing you do and chill out."

"It's not like I have an on–off switch, Pink."

"Okay, so worry about it, and cry a lot, and lose sleep. But the result will be the same. I'll either find the bastard who did this to me, or I won't."

"Do you have any idea who it could be?"

I let the water run down my back while I stared at the pretty mosaic tile in Steve's guest-room shower. "I wish I did." Leaning my head back, I closed my eyes. Valikov Interiors. It was a Russian name. And Olga, she of the killer salad, was Russian. Mrs. Han, the lost Chinese wife, was Russian. It didn't make any sense that the Chinese bride scheme was connected to the CERF embezzlement, but that Russian thing was way weird. And there was the phone call. I was still mulling over the significance of why Olga would call Taylor, then pretend she'd called me, in order to get me on the phone. Did Olga know Taylor had those invoices? Was she the one who put them on her doorstep?

"What have you heard about Ambassador Wu and the mysterious Olga?"

Mom didn't answer.

"Mom?"

Hearing the shower curtain open slowly, I opened my eyes. *Ed.* His bottom lip was a little swollen and his left cheek was turning an intriguing shade of blue. "If you came for sympathy, you came to the wrong place. Getting in an elevator brawl with a U.S. senator isn't in the lawyer's code of ethics, I'm thinking." I looked behind him. "What did you do with Mom?"

"She went downstairs to see the state-department guy who came by to ask questions about Mr. Wu."

I turned off the water and reached for a towel. "Will he want to talk to me, since I'm supposedly the one who killed the poor man?"

"He may want to talk to you, but not because he thinks you're the murderer. For that matter, I'm not convinced Schumski thinks you did it. I believe he was just trying to scare you into confessing to Taylor's murder."

"Have they found Olga?"

"Not yet. She left town last night, on a flight to Albuquerque, but they lost her trail after that. She's suspected of being connected to the Russian mob, which means she's got lots of connections to help her move around undetected." He leaned against the sink and crossed his arms over his chest while he watched me dry off. "I overheard what you said to Jane."

"And you're going to give me your standard lawyer lecture about letting the authorities do their job." I bent and twisted my hair in the towel, then straightened. "Save your breath, Counselor."

"Actually, I was going to tell you to let me do some investigating and see what I turn up."

After sliding into the terry robe I found hanging on the back of the door, I walked into the bedroom and curled up in one of the chairs by the fireplace. He followed and leaned against the bedpost, his hands in his pockets.

"You have permission to go to Midland. Anywhere else is not gonna happen, Pink."

"Okay," I lied.

He peered at me through narrowed eyes. "If you don't stick to the deal, they really will lock you up until your case goes to trial, and that may be months from now."

"Suppose we have enough by the prelim to prove I didn't do it?"

"Then you're off the hook, but there's no guarantee we can find what we need by then." He walked closer and stared down at my face. "You have to trust me."

Considering most of our problems were rooted in major trust issues—mostly on my part—I could see that this was going to be more than just a lawyer asking his client to hang loose and let him do his job. This was gonna be about me trusting Ed to get me out of hot water.

Well, hell.

Why did everything always have to be so complicated? Why did *Ed* have to be so complicated? The problem was, even though I did trust him, I didn't trust him enough. This was my life. Screw this up and I'd be spending the rest of it behind bars.

Looking up at him, I chose my words carefully. "I have a plan, and some of it involves doing things that aren't exactly legal. I don't think we can find this person any other way. I can't ask you to do something illegal for me, Ed."

Backing up, he sat down on the opposite chair and

stretched his long legs out in front of him, until his shoes were touching the legs of my chair. "What did you have in mind?"

"First of all, I'll call Owl Nunez to do some hacking for me, to find out who owns the Valikov Interiors checking account."

"I already did that."

In spite of what I know about Ed and his tendency to bend the rules a bit, I was surprised. "Hacking is a crime. A big one."

"I didn't do any hacking. Owl did."

"But you paid him to do it. Same difference."

"No money was exchanged, so no one could prove it."

He was blowing my mind. "What did he find?"

"Nothing yet. I should hear something in the next few hours."

"What do you plan to do with the information?"

"Pay a visit to whoever Owl tells me owns the account and find out what they did with the money, and whether they're the one who set up the Whitney Pearl account in Kansas."

"See, that's where I'd do it differently. I don't think that person will tell you, and why would they? Somebody went to a lot of trouble to set this up, to make it look like I bought expensive things from Valikov. I think it was done so that if anything went wrong, if anybody caught on at CERF, I'd be the one who did the embezzling, and whoever's behind Valikov would look like nothing more than the person I chose to buy stuff from. If a bank robber uses his stolen money to buy a new car, the dealership can't be held accountable."

"That's why I asked Owl to get Valikov's bank records. If the only deposits are from Whitney Pearl, it'll be obvious the company is a sham."

"And if there are other deposits? What then?"

He shrugged. "I'll go to the company's offices and find somebody who'll answer my questions."

"Suppose it's a legitimate company, and there's someone in the ranks who's working in collusion with the real culprit?"

Ed dropped his gaze to my chest. "I'll find out who placed the orders."

Looking down, I realized my robe was wide open. "You coulda said something." I pulled it together and tied the belt.

"That's why I didn't."

"You're a perv."

"Hmm, probably. Or maybe you just have extremely great breasts." He got to his feet and went to the door. "I'll be in the kitchen."

"Are you going to cook?"

"I'm going to eat. Lou's working on some kinda chicken thing. With mushrooms."

Turning in the chair, I said, "You hate mushrooms."

Ed stared at me. "I also hate Mister Billboard, but I'm gonna go down there and make nice with him, just like I'm gonna make like I want to eat the stinkin' 'shrooms."

"Why?"

"For you, babydoll. All for you."

I must have drifted off to sleep, and when I woke up, I was in the bed. Steve sat just next to me, reading some official-looking report. His little Chihuahua, Natasha, was curled up at the end of the bed, on my feet. Steve isn't really a Chihuahua kinda guy. He's more the sort who'd have a greyhound, or maybe a King Charles spaniel. But his mother loved Chihuahuas, and Natasha was the daughter of Mrs. Santorelli's favorite. Lou had Natasha's brother, Boris. I thought it was sweet how two extremely macho men cared for wee, tiny dogs because they'd meant so much to Mrs. Santorelli.

Gauging the light in the window, I judged it to be late afternoon, almost evening. I'd been asleep since before lunch, at least seven or eight hours.

I noticed Steve had on a pair of running shorts and a faded Stanford T-shirt. He could be any guy, anywhere. But he wasn't. He was a senator. A very rich one, who probably really could make it to the White House because he was all about integrity and hard work and he had charisma in spades.

"Where is Ed?"

"During lunch, he got a phone call from a friend in Midland and said he had to leave."

I was gonna kill him. Ed hadn't woken me up to tell me what Owl had found out. No doubt on purpose, so I wouldn't insist on going with him.

Laying the report on his thighs, Steve looked down at me. "Are you hungry?"

"Yes. And thirsty, and still sleepy, and wondering what I've missed this afternoon."

He reached for the phone by the bed and punched in some numbers. "Carla, would you bring Pink something to eat? Thanks." After he hung up, he laid the report on the table, then turned and slid farther down on the bed, propping his head in one hand while he stroked my hair with the other.

"Your face looks a little better than Ed's."

He grinned. "What can I say? I'm much better looking. It's the Italian thing."

"You know what I meant."

"True, but I'd prefer to interpret it my own way."

I stared at him and couldn't help smiling. "When's the last time you got in a fistfight?"

"Ninth grade. This kid from Australia was a foreign-exchange student, a cocky little bastard, and he told everybody he'd seen my mom in an Italian porn flick. So I beat him up—and got suspended. But it was worth it."

"What did your mom have to say about it?"

"She gave me a lecture about being a gentleman, but I overheard her tell Dad she wished she coulda been there to see it. He said he wished he coulda seen the Italian porn flick."

"Your mom must have been a pistol."

"She was." He sighed, dropped his hand and lay down on the pillow to stare up at the ceiling. "Sometimes, when I'm in a hurry and things get crazy, I forget that she's dead and pick up the phone to call her. Strange, but I never do that with Lauren. I never forget that she's gone. Maybe because I wasn't there when Mom died, so it's harder to get it fixed in my head."

"How long has she been gone?"

"Just over a year." He turned and looked at me. "I think Dad's very interested in your mother."

"I noticed. Does that bug you, so soon after your mom died?"

"Not in the least. He deserves to be happy, and if he can be with your mother, I'm glad."

It was my turn to stare up at the ceiling. "It's debatable, Steve. I've told you before, Mom has a thing with men."

"I'm thinking Dad can get around whatever thing she throws at him."

"He can be pretty persuasive, can't he?"

"Especially when it's for something he wants. And I've been told I'm a chip off the old block." He flipped to his stomach, which brought him closer. "I either have to leave, or kiss you. My mother managed to raise a gentleman, but hell if I can lie here another two seconds knowing you're half naked under those covers."

Maybe if he hadn't been less than three inches from my face, and if I hadn't had the scent of him and his subtle cologne wrapped around me, and maybe, if I'd given it ten seconds of thought, I'd have shoved him off, gotten out of bed and run like hell to get away from him. Did I mention that I'm insanely attracted to Steve? That it scares the crap out of me? And makes me wonder if I'm some kind of a ho, lusting after two different men?

Too bad for me, he *was* three inches from my face, and his cologne was seductive, and I didn't give it more than a nanosecond of thought before I whispered, "Will you think I'm a tease if it's just a kiss?"

"Yes."

I stared up at his handsome, if slightly bruised face and tried to remember why it was a very bad idea to kiss him. Then he was kissing me and I remembered, but it was way too late by then. Kissing Steve Santorelli was a bad idea because it's always next to impossible to stop. I have no idea why. He's a great kisser, extremely passionate, and I've dated several good kissers over the years, but I never had a problem stopping with any of them. With Steve, it's like breaking the laws of physics, floating in an antigravity field.

Maybe that wouldn't be so bad, except that we're not eager teenagers, dying of curiosity about what comes next. We *know* what comes next, and while Steve has no problem with that, would, in fact, be pretty damn fired up about it, I have a big, gi-normous problem with what comes next. And the problem's name is Ed. If I gave in and followed the natural progression of the crazy, insanity-causing kiss with Steve, I'd blow everything with Ed. Even if Ed never knew. *I* would know, and nothing would ever be the same again.

Still, I could *not* pull away, not even when Steve's hand slid beneath the covers to caress my breasts. He tasted like butterscotch and felt like six feet of hard, hot male. In my mind, even while I was carried away by Senator Santorelli's very talented lips and hands, I wondered how I was going to stop. I've got a lot of discipline, except when it comes to beluga caviar, Kate Spade bags…and Steve Santorelli.

Musta been my lucky day, because the decision was taken away from me when Carla knocked and said she had a tray of food. Natasha jumped from the bed and yipped at the door. I almost hated myself for the enormous sense of loss I felt when Steve pulled away and got off the bed. He looked down at the extremely noticeable bulge in his shorts.

"You'll have to get the door." He went into the bathroom. Natasha followed and scratched at the door until he opened it a few inches and allowed her in.

I greeted Carla, who entered and left the tray on the bed. "Do you need anything else?" she asked nicely.

Wondering what she'd say if I asked for somebody else's conscience, I returned her smile and said, "No, thank you. This looks delicious." I had no idea what it was.

She left, and I turned to watch Steve come out of the bathroom. I couldn't help it, but I glanced at his shorts. He was still very turned on.

What happened next still makes me cry when I think about it. It's like he knew where I was at, that the temptation was way off the page and I was completely torn up between loyalty to Ed and the powerful sexual attraction I felt for Steve. After he stood there at the doorway of the bathroom and stared at me for several tense moments, he crossed to the window and looked out at the street.

"Eat your dinner, Pink."

I couldn't move.

"Sit down and eat. Now."

Backing up, I slowly lowered myself to the bed, but I didn't eat.

"My assistant went by your loft a few hours ago and the media is camped out on the street outside. If you go there, you won't have a moment's peace. I'm also concerned for your safety. If Olga came last night to kill you, she may try again."

"Ed says she left town."

"I don't believe she's working alone, Pink. According to Dad, she's involved with the Russian Mafia. Maybe *she* wasn't able to kill you, but they may send someone else."

"No, they won't, because I'm almost certain Olga never intended to kill me. I think she came here to set me up, to frame me for Taylor's murder. If I was murdered, it would follow that I couldn't be responsible for the embezzlement, or at a minimum, I had one or more accomplices. This way, it looks like I'm the bad guy all the way around. In fact, I think she spilled that salad on purpose, so I'd have to go to the kitchen, raising the possibility that it was me who poisoned the ambassador."

"If she only came to frame you, why did she have poison with her?"

"She's an assassin. Maybe she had it in her backpack. I saw her leave with one."

He drew in a deep breath and let it out, still with his back to me. "Whether she intended to kill you or not, I think the safest thing is for you to stay here, with me, at least until the preliminary hearing. By then, we should have enough evidence to get the charges dropped, which means we'll have the evidence to point the FBI in the right direction."

"But, Steve, I—"

"Just let me finish, Pink. You know I don't give a damn about the media, or political bullshit—whatever gets said out there that isn't directly related to my performance as a senator who represents California, I ignore. But it's a double-edged sword, because when I want to use the media, or my position, for my own personal benefit, I can't. It goes against everything I believe in."

I wasn't quite following him, but he was a politician, after all. He'd get to the point, eventually.

"It would be easy to call people I know at the FBI, explain that I believe in your innocence, maybe even stretch the truth and say we're engaged, that they need to ignore the evidence they have and look for someone else. They'd do it, and eventually find whoever did this to you. If it comes down to it, Pink, that's exactly what I'll do. But for the time being, I don't want to abuse my position. I think, between me and Dad and Ed, and to some extent your mother, we can find who we're looking for."

His voice got quieter and I strained to hear him.

"I don't want you to think I don't care, or that this job means more to me than you. Nothing could be further from the truth. But until I'm in a corner, until it's a last resort, I don't want to pull rank. Do you understand?"

I mumbled an affirmative, my throat way too choked up to speak.

"As for staying here, you'll have your own room, and you can come and go as you please. I just ask that you take Bill, the driver. He's a nice guy, and he won't get in your way. Since your mom's lost the contract with CERF and you're technically unemployed for a while, I know you'll want to take part in hunting down the embezzler. If the opportunity presents itself, great, but as an attorney, I'll tell you that the worst thing you can do is go out there and dig on your own. All it will do is make you look more guilty."

Finally, he looked over his shoulder at me, his dark eyes filled with worry and an odd sadness. "You're a woman who wants to do it all by yourself, but this time, you can't. You're going to have to trust me and Ed to do it for you."

I sat there in that beautifully decorated room and wondered what amazing thing I'd done in my life to deserve a man like Steve.

"I don't want you involved in this. Not in any way beyond me staying here, and it seems to me I can maybe do that without anyone knowing. I can come and go as a maid, or in the backseat of a limo."

"I don't care if anyone knows you're staying here."

"You should."

"So you'll stay?"

"If you'll carry on as usual and not get involved with looking for the bastard who set me up."

He turned then and looked at me, and I know he lied when he said, "It's a deal."

I nodded as though I believed him, and immediately began planning to leave, to get as far away from him as possible.

Because I knew if I didn't, he'd hang himself in the political world, and no matter my feelings for him, I kinda thought I owed it to my country. Steve Santorelli needed to be the next president. It was my patriotic duty to get out of his life.

On that note, with an awkward, uncomfortable, sexually charged tension still hanging in the air, Steve left the room without another word, Natasha at his heels.

I got dressed and picked at the food. Mom came in and we watched TV, which made me all weepy because she wanted to watch *The American President*, and I was reminded of Steve's wife, Lauren, and how much he loved her, and how amazing she'd been. Lauren made a difference in the world. She was beautiful and polished, the perfect politician's wife. I'd bet everything I owned that she never would have been involved with two men at the same time. She was a nice girl.

And I wondered all over again, what did Steve see in me? Because I was the polar opposite of beautiful, perfect Lauren Santorelli. I wasn't a very nice girl.

Later, after Mom went off to her own room and I drifted back to sleep, I was awoken by a strange noise. I sat up in bed and realized someone was in the room with me. "Steve?"

"No, it's Lou," came a husky whisper. "Pink, don't go off on me—I need you to be very quiet."

I glanced at the lighted alarm clock. It was just past three o'clock in the morning. "What is it?"

He sat on the bed, his weight throwing me off balance so that I had to draw my knees up.

"I'm a farmer, you know. Our family owns and operates the largest privately owned farming operation in California. I spend a lot of time looking after things, but I also spend some of my time doing…other things."

"Like disguising yourself as Big Mama, operating a covert vigilante group and hunting down terrorist sympathizers?"

"That needs to remain our little secret."

"Because someone might kill you?"

He snorted softly. "Yeah, that, too, but I meant I don't particularly want anybody knowing I dress up like a woman. Especially your mother. She might get the wrong idea."

"Got it."

"Right now, I'm on hiatus for a while to pursue, uh, other interests. But I still have people who contact me with anything they believe might be important to know."

Somewhere, deep inside, I started shivering. Bad karma hit me so hard I was a little breathless. I scrambled off the bed and paced back and forth in front of him, barely illuminated by the streetlight outside. "Tell me, Lou. Right out. Just tell me."

He looked up at me in the half light and whispered, "I got a call about ten minutes ago, from a contact in San Francisco who's keeping an eye on the activities of the Russian mob, because we think they may be supplying terrorists with illegal explosives. He's been paying special attention to a woman named Olga, who disappeared a few days ago, then reappeared just this afternoon."

"Poisonous Olga?"

"Undoubtedly. About an hour ago, he followed her to an abandoned warehouse, where she met a man. They appeared to argue, then Olga pulled out a gun and shot the man."

I stopped pacing, my mind already screaming in denial and pain.

Lou stood and stared down at me. "It was Ed."

Chapter 4

I had a Tiny Tears doll when I was little. All I had to do to make her cry was push a button on her belly and voilà! Tiny Tears was an instant waterworks. That night, Tiny Tears and I were soul sisters. I sank to the bed, to stare at Lou.

"Is he dead?"

"No, but probably only because of my contact. As soon as he saw Ed go down, he opened fire on Olga before she could shoot again and she ran off. He checked on Ed, then called an ambulance to take him to the hospital."

"How is he?"

"Right now, I don't know his status. No doubt because he's still in the emergency room, or surgery. My contact tailed the ambulance but didn't go in after arrival. He's the kind of guy who keeps a low profile."

"Do you know why Ed was there, with Olga?" I said through my tears.

"My contact thought he might be involved with the explosives sales, so he questioned him while they waited for the ambulance. Ed wasn't forthcoming with much, other than to say it was a private matter, that he was supposed to meet a woman named Sasha Valikov about some Chinese antiques."

"So now we know for sure, Olga is involved with the embezzlement. Sasha must be the one who owns the Valikov Interiors account, and she sent Olga to get rid of Ed because he was able to find her."

"My contact, of course, had no idea I know Ed, and told me all of this so I could check his credentials and make sure he wasn't lying. We're certain there's some activity with explosives sales, and Olga is definitely involved."

"I have to go to San Francisco." I thought about the logistics. "Are you gonna tell Steve? Because no way will he let me leave."

"I won't tell him until you're airborne, which you should be in about two hours. I called my pilot and told him to get the plane ready. It'll take a little over nine hours to get to San Francisco since the plane will have to stop to refuel, so you'll be there by lunchtime tomorrow. Right now, I need to get you some alternative ID in case you need it after you get there. Give me your driver's license."

Still bawling, I went to my purse and got the license. Was the gunshot just a flesh wound? Or had it hit some major part of his body, incapacitating him for life? Was he knocking on death's door?

I stopped and closed my eyes, took a deep breath and mentally kicked myself in the ass. I had to be calm. I had to be focused. I had to get to San Francisco as soon as possible. Losing my shit wasn't going to help Ed. Opening my eyes, I wiped them on the sleeve of the T-shirt I'd been sleeping in, then turned and handed the license to Lou. "Thank you."

He was already headed for the door. "Get yourself together, and write a note for Steve. You owe him that."

True to his word, Lou had me on his plane within two hours. He went aboard with me to make sure all was well, and gave me some last-minute instructions.

"There's a car at the airport you can use. The pilot has the keys and he'll show you where to go. I'll be in California day after tomorrow, as soon as I take your mother back to Midland, and I'll help you find Olga."

"Why would I look for Olga?"

No fooling Lou. He raised one dark eyebrow. "Because she shot Ed. But take my advice—don't get yourself into more trouble. Kicking her butt all the way to Alaska might seem like a good idea, but trust me—it's not. Just go take care of Ed and wait for me before you try to find her."

It sounded reasonable. Not that I'd follow his instructions. "I left a note for Steve on the desk. It would be helpful if you'd explain things."

"I'll explain. He'll be mad, but he'll get over it." Lou looked down at his hands folded together between his knees. "You're not going to marry him, are you?"

Wow. That came out of nowhere, and I wasn't sure how to respond, so I turned the tables on him. "Do you want me to marry him?"

Meeting my gaze, he gave me a half smile. "Steve's never been one to rush into anything. He's like his mother, always careful, always considering all the angles. Me, I jump first, then find out I don't have a parachute."

"Do you think Steve's looked at all the angles? Because it seems to me like he kinda jumped without a chute on this one."

"I realize that, and it's what's got me bumfuzzled."

"Maybe he's just hot to get married because it looks better for a presidential candidate to have a wife."

Lou shook his head. "No, Steve is one of those 'what you see is what you get' guys. And if all he wanted was a wife to be First Lady, I don't think he'd choose you. Don't take offense, Pink, but you're not exactly the embodiment of a First Lady. I can think of at least ten women friends of Steve's whose lives are so impeccable, the media would have nothing to chew on. The news people would have a field day with you."

"Because I'm under arrest for murder and embezzlement?"

He shook his head. "We're gonna find whoever did this, and the charges will be dropped."

"Am I bad First Lady material because of the whistle-blower thing?"

"No. They'd probably put a romantic spin on that, seeing as how that's when you and Steve got to be friends." He gave me a wry smile. "You'd be a controversial First Lady from the get-go because you're independent, opinionated, outspoken and just too damn sexy. Americans want their First Ladies to be elegant, poised, polished and perfect. They don't want to look at the First Lady and imagine what she'd look like without her clothes on."

Maybe if I hadn't been through some pretty odd stuff with Lou when he was running around Midland dressed up as Big Mama, I would have been embarrassed. As it was, I felt sort of connected to him, like we were on the same wavelength. "Well, it's all a moot point anyway, because the chances of me marrying Steve are slim to zero."

"Then tell Steve you're never going to marry him. Don't string him along." He stood, reached in his pocket and withdrew a wad of cash. "Here's some money." He saw my expression and said, "Consider it a loan. You can't use a credit card or leave a trail of any kind. And remember, your name is Tonya Weisberg."

"Huh. I've never been Jewish before."

He shrugged. "It was all I had on such short notice." Turning away, he headed for the door and said over his shoulder, "Be careful, Pink, and call me when you get there and find out about Ed's condition."

I stood and followed him. "Um, Lou, we haven't talked about Mom."

He turned quickly and frowned at me. "What's to talk about? She's a grown woman, and your mother. If she wants to discuss it with you, fine. But as far as I'm concerned, what's between me and her is none of your damn business."

I really wanted to laugh, because he was so flustered, and being who he is, Lou isn't the type to be flustered. I also thought it was funny how he jumped to a conclusion that was way off base. Not to mention that he sure hadn't minded getting in the middle of my personal business with his son. "I don't want her to know where I've gone, but I also don't want her to worry. I was hoping you'd make it square for me, and tell her I'll call her tomorrow."

"Oh." He became even more flustered, awkwardly patted my shoulder and said gruffly, "Yeah, no problem." Then he turned and disappeared down the hall.

* * *

As soon as we took off, I used the plane's telephone and called the hospital, but they'd never heard of Edward Ravenaldt. I asked if perhaps he was in surgery, and the woman gave me the number for the surgical desk. The man who answered said there were no gunshot wounds in surgery. Since I was already three steps from irrational, I assumed that meant he was dead, which sent me off into a crying jag that nearly made me throw up.

We stopped to refuel, but I didn't get off the plane. I spent the entire flight fretting about Ed, and wondering what he'd found out, and why Olga had shot him. Every time I allowed myself to wonder if he was going to die, if he was already dead, I lost it. I used half a box of tissues on that flight.

By the time we landed in San Francisco, I'm sure I looked like a refugee with an eye condition. The pilot walked me to the parking lot where the Santorellis keep a car, and after he gave me instructions to get to the biggest hospital, he waved goodbye.

Turned out, the reason the surgical desk had no gunshot-wound patients was that Ed had been transferred to another hospital, one that specializes in trauma surgeries. My relief was so enormous I was giddy.

By the time I got to the right hospital, it was lunchtime. I found Ed in a room on the post-op floor.

It's odd the things that stand out in our memory. You'd think my recollection of that moment would be poignant and beautiful, a slow-mo move toward a prostrate Ed, my arms wide open. Instead, all I distinctly remember is opening the door and catching Ed sucking cherry Jell-O through his teeth. He caught sight of me and dropped his spoon.

"Pink! What the hell are you doing here?"

Yeah. So much for poignant. I moved close to the bed. "I came to make sure you're okay."

"How did you know?"

"The guy who saved you from Olga is a contact of Lou's."

"Olga?"

"The bitch that shot you. It was Olga. 'Heavy accent involved with the Russian Mafia' Olga. Killer-salad Olga."

He looked shocked. "Why was Lou's contact there?"

"He's been following her because the Russian mob may be selling illegal explosives to terrorists. She disappeared for a few days, then turned up again. He followed her to the warehouse where she met you."

"I wondered. After I hit the ground, this strange guy appeared. He had a gun and I thought he was going to finish me off, but instead, he asked who I was and why I was there." He looked up at me with a quizzical expression. "So he called Lou to report on Olga, and that's how you found out what happened?"

I nodded. "But Lou didn't know how bad it was, whether you were alive, or…" I turned toward the window. "Jesus, Ed, I've never been this freaked out."

I felt his hand on my arm, gently tugging me back to face him again. "I was going to call and let you know what happened, and what I found out. I'm sorry you had to go through that, Pink." He let his hand slide down to mine and gripped it tightly. "It's okay. I'm okay."

I glanced at the covers over his legs. "She hit you in the leg?"

"The thigh. They tell me I was damn lucky. A couple of inches higher and I'd be changing my name to Edwina."

That made me flinch. It also made me want to find Olga

and set her hair on fire. I reached with my other hand and caressed his cheek, rough with a day's growth of beard, still bruised from his senatorial brawl. "I'm sorry, Ed. And I'm all torn up between feeling guilty, because you wouldn't be here if you weren't trying to find out who framed me, and being really pissed off that you left yesterday without waking me up and telling me what you found out from Owl."

"Stick with the guilty thing, okay? I'm a wounded man, and being pissed off at me would be really bad manners."

"Okay, but I reserve the right to be pissed later, when you can run."

He tugged my hand, forcing me to come closer, and then my arms were around him and his were around me, and I had my poignant moment.

"Don't know that anyone's ever cried for me before," he whispered against my hair.

I held him tighter and my hand slid inside the back of his hospital gown. His skin was smooth, solid, warm. Very warm. Alive. I cried again and he murmured a lot of wonderful things to me.

That's about when a nurse came in and said, "Time for your meds, Mr. Ravenaldt. You must be feeling better, now your wife's here."

I let go of him, stepped back and wiped the tears off my face. "Oh, I'm not his wife."

The nurse, a middle-aged woman with a name tag that said she was Sally, gave me a look. "Is your name Pink?"

I nodded, then remembered my identity thing. Pink Pearl was supposed to be in D.C., or Midland, and nowhere else. I quickly said, "It's just a nickname. My real name is Tonya Weisberg."

That earned me a funny look from Ed. I smiled at him. "Rabbi Goldman wishes you a speedy recovery, sweetheart."

I watched Sally hand Ed his little paper cup of water. "How'd you know my name?"

She glanced at me. "Mr. Ravenaldt was flying high when they brought him in from recovery. He thought I was you, I guess, because he kept calling me Pink and insisting I belonged with him, and not a billboard. He got pretty excited about it all and made me promise to be married to him, and not the bill-board." She shrugged. "People say the funniest things when they come out of anesthesia." She tucked Ed in and turned toward the door. "Give me a buzz if you need anything, Mr. Ravenaldt."

When she was gone, Ed became overly fascinated with the weave of the cotton blanket on his bed. He traced the pattern with one long finger. "How did you talk him into letting you come to California?"

"I didn't tell him I was coming. I left a note."

His gaze met mine. "A note? That's kinda harsh, Pink."

"Why do you care? You hate the guy."

"I know, but I realize he's got it bad for you."

"I had no choice. If he'd known my plans, he wouldn't have let me leave. Lou promised to fill in the blanks. At least, as much as he can safely tell a senator."

"Did you fly out on Lou's plane?"

"Yes. He gave me a fake ID and some money so I won't have to use a credit card."

"And you came all the way across the country just because you thought I was mortally wounded?"

"Well, yeah."

He smiled then, and looked so happy that I found myself

wishing it *had* been Ed who bought the billboard. Maybe he wished it, too, if what he had told Nurse Sally was any indication. After all, didn't anesthesia make a person lose all his inhibitions?

Or was it only a lotta martinis that did that? Come to think of it, anesthesia usually makes people hallucinate and say crazy things they *don't* mean. Damn.

"You just went from ecstatic to depressed in a millisecond."

I looked down into his dark brown eyes and decided I was only feeling over the top about Ed because I'd been so afraid he was gone out of my life forever. I didn't really want him to want me to marry him. It was just a side effect of my hysteria. I chose to ignore what he said, and asked, "How'd you wind up meeting Olga?"

He didn't answer for a while. Instead, he stared up at me, studied my face so carefully, I began to wonder if I had a rash or something. Finally, he said, "I was supposed to meet Sasha Valikov, but when I got to the meeting place, the woman who showed up said Sasha couldn't come."

"Sasha Valikov? Is she the one who owns the bank account I supposedly transferred money into for Chinese antiques?"

"According to Owl, yes. I figure she's the same Sasha who's been leaving messages on your answering machine about decorating your house."

"How'd you find her?"

"The bank account has only a post-office box address, but Owl was able to get a phone number. I called, and she agreed to meet me when I told her I was interested in Chinese antiques."

"Didn't it give you a clue when she asked you to meet at an abandoned warehouse?"

"I didn't know it was abandoned until I got there. When she said a warehouse, I assumed it would be full of Chinese furniture and art and doodads. I'd been there maybe two minutes when the blonde you say was Olga showed up and told me Sasha couldn't make it. She asked who I was and how I knew about Sasha, and I told her it was nothing to do with her, that my business was with Sasha. That irritated her and she told me that meeting Sasha was impossible because she's too busy to take on any new customers. When I said I'd find Sasha and get what I needed from her, Olga told me all I needed to do was back off. I disagreed, and she shot me."

"Wonder if she shoots everyone who disagrees with her."

"That would be a lot of people, because she's very disagreeable."

I went to the guest chair, an uncomfortable-looking thing with harsh wooden angles and army green vinyl, and pulled it close to Ed's bed. "What did you tell the police?"

"Enough of the truth that I won't get tripped up later. I figured if I told them everything, they'd go on the hunt for Olga and Sasha, who would get wise and maybe lose any evidence of the embezzlement. So I said I was told at an antique shop that I could find some imported things at one of the warehouses at that pier, and I went to check it out. While I was looking around, somebody fired a shot at me from inside the dark warehouse. One of the cops said there've been several incidents down there since the previous lease expired and the tenants moved out, so they bought the whole story."

"They didn't find it odd you were hanging around in the warehouse district in the middle of the night?"

"It wasn't that late. I got to California at about seven-thirty, local time. I called Sasha from the airport and caught a cab to meet her."

I debated how best to broach the subject of me continuing the hunt for Sasha, and decided a full-on attack was best. "Do you have the post-office box number Owl gave you?"

"Yes, but you can't have it."

"All I have to do is call Owl. He'll give it to me."

"Pink, you can't go look for this Sasha woman. For one thing, her good buddy Olga is liable to show up and shoot you. For another, if anything goes wrong and the police get involved, you'll be caught breaking the terms of your bail and sent back to D.C. to await trial in lockup. It's not worth the risk." He turned on the television suspended in the corner of the small room and pointed. "Besides, you're all over the news, you and CERF and Taylor Bunch and Santorelli. The only reason Nurse Sally hasn't recognized you yet is that she's working a double shift and hasn't been able to watch the news."

"Why does it matter? No one knows I'm not supposed to be here."

"People are inherently nosy. Somebody might call the news people, and before you know it, you've got a couple of cameras and some microphones following you around."

After a quick glance at some old footage of me in front of the senate finance committee during the whistle-blower thing, I focused on Ed and ignored the TV. "When are they letting you out of here?"

"Tomorrow at the earliest."

"That's too late, Ed. It's obvious Valikov Interiors is a front, and now Sasha and Olga know that we know, so they're probably in the middle of packing up to leave as we speak. If they leave, we're screwed."

He gave that some thought, his dark eyes directed at the television, his long fingers worrying the blanket. "I can't in good conscience tell you to try to find her. Even if you did, what good would it do? It's not as though she's gonna confess to embezzling."

"I thought I'd follow her, see where she goes, if there's an office or an apartment or something where she keeps the paperwork for her fake company."

"What if there is?" He looked straight at me then, his expression dark and angry. "Are you gonna break in? Or just knock and ask nicely?"

I stood and shoved the chair back to its place by the wall. "You're not going to be reasonable about this, I see."

"If encouraging you to put yourself at risk is unreasonable, then yeah, you're damn right. You said you spent the past eleven hours freaking out because you thought I might be dead. How the hell do you think it'll be for me, stuck in this bed while you go out there and risk getting arrested, or killed?"

I moved close to him. "I'm sorry for that, Ed, but it'll be a lot worse if I get sentenced to life in prison. You said yourself, they've got enough to hang me without half trying."

He became more agitated, moving the bed up and down, finally throwing the covers off, then turning his body, exposing his long legs and a wide bandage, stark white against his tanned, muscular thigh.

"What are you doing? You can't get up!"

"The hell I can't," he said through gritted teeth.

"Ed, you're going to hurt yourself!"

"I'm freakin' going with you, Pink." He turned a ghastly shade of pale when he got to his feet. "What the hell did they do with my clothes?" He darted a look around the room and spied the cupboard.

Before he could head in that direction, I stepped in front of him and gently pushed him back to the bed. "If you don't calm down, and lie down, I swear to God I'll walk out and never come back. I'll hire another attorney. I'll never speak to you again as long as I live."

He would never admit it, but he was enormously relieved to be off his feet. His color began to return. Lying back against the pillows, he let out a string of cuss words that actually made foul-mouthed me blush.

"How about if I call you every so often and check in? Would that make it better?"

"How about if you just stay here and watch television with me?"

"Not gonna happen."

He stared up at me, his eyes filled with fury and an odd, helpless fear. "You are, without a doubt, the biggest pain in the ass I've ever known. You're stubborn, and foolish, and about half crazy."

I refused to get into it with him. He was blustering because his machismo couldn't stand the thought of me out there without him to look after me. Never mind that I'd spent the majority of my life looking after myself. Because he was so dead serious, I opted for funny, trying to lighten the tension.

"Aw, c'mon, Ed. It's the crazy in me you love so much."

Funny was not the way to go. His expression became so dark, I stepped back.

"If I was stupid enough to love you, it would only be in spite of the crazy."

That hurt. A lot. And the tone of his voice, as much as

his words, reminded me of my father, who we call Lurch, because he is a mean, nasty person. I swear I heard a door slam inside my head. Turning, I picked up my purse and moved away from him.

"I'll ask the nurse to let me know when they release you, and I'll be here to help you get to the airport." I pulled the door open and walked out.

At the nurses' station, I stopped and wrote my cell phone number on a chewing gum wrapper out of my bag. I handed it to Sally. "I'd appreciate it if you'd call when he's released, so I can come and get him."

"You're leaving?" Nurse Sally looked confused. "But you just got here, and Mr. Ravenaldt seemed very glad to see you."

"I have some business to take care of, and it's unavoidable. He understands."

"Oh. Well. All right then, Miss Weisberg. I'll call." She glanced over my shoulder and her eyes widened. "Good God!"

She darted around me, and I turned to see what had freaked her out so much.

Ed. He was clinging to the wall, inching his way toward the nurses' station, staring straight at me. "Don't...leave." His voice was strained and jerky. His face showed signs of the enormous effort it took to stand, to put weight on his injured leg, to move.

Our eyes met and I knew he wasn't asking me to stay, to not go after Sasha. He was asking me to not be mad at him, to not leave like this, angry and hurt.

In that moment, which is still frozen in my mind with perfect clarity, I knew just how much I really mattered to Ed. He'd never said it, might never say it, maybe wouldn't ever acknowledge it, but what he felt for me went way beyond sex and friendship. Oh, it was heroic of him to get out of bed and come after me, despite the agony he must have felt. But it wasn't that. It was the way he looked at me, almost childlike, as if his whole world depended on what I did next—leave or stay.

I stayed.

Hurrying toward him, I helped Nurse Sally get him back into the room and in bed. Sally tucked him in, then gave him a lecture.

"The bullet did a lot of damage, Mr. Ravenaldt, and you've got to give it time to knit, without any added pressure. If the wound reopens, we'll have to stitch it up again, and that will most likely mean going back to an IV, and no food for another day."

He grimaced.

"I mean it," she said sternly, hands on hips. Then she swung her hard gaze at me. "I don't know what's up between you two, but now is not the time for quarrels. Be nice to him. A patient's recovery time can be prolonged if he's emotionally upset."

"Yes, ma'am."

She turned and marched out, leaving us in silence. Not an uncomfortable or awkward silence. More like a communal "we're connected and words are so inadequate right now" silence. I moved to the bed, bent low and wrapped him up in my arms. His arms slid around me and we stayed like that for a long time, not talking, not kissing. Just holding each other. After a while, I let go and sat in the ugly green chair until he drifted off to sleep.

When his breathing was even and deep, I got up and slipped from the room.

Chapter 5

Owl Nunez has been a computer geek since he was a kid, but he always had a certain something about him that overrode his geekiness. He's Native American, and he wears his long black hair in two braids, but the coolness of that is canceled out by his round glasses with lenses as thick as soda bottles, which make his eyes look abnormally large. That's how he got his nickname.

If Owl wanted, he could probably shut down half the computer networks in the world, he's that smart. But he's not into creating mayhem. His big thing is computer games, and he's made a boatload of money developing some. Still, I guess every once in a while he likes to dabble in forbidden territory, because for the right price, he'll find out things he's got no legal right to find out.

Like who owned the Valikov Interiors checking account.

Downstairs in the hospital lobby, I called Owl from a bank of pay phones because I was worried my cell phone could be tracked. Okay, so I was paranoid. I absolutely did not want to go to jail until my trial. Owl answered on the third ring.

"Peace and harmony."

"Owl?"

"Pink?"

"What's with peace and harmony?"

"It's the name of my new company, Peace and Harmony. I want people to understand the philosophical and sacred basis of how I do business, now that I've begun my journey into the spiritual realm of my ancestors."

Remembering his tepee in his backyard, and what Ed had told me about Owl's recent fascination with his heritage, I tried to head him in another direction. It's not that I didn't appreciate Owl getting in touch with his roots. It's just that I was in a tremendous hurry. "Owl, I'm at a pay phone in San Francisco and it's kind of imperative that I get the information you gave Ed."

"No problem," he said easily, "but I'll expect the same concession I received from Ed."

Ed had said he didn't pay Owl, so I was immediately suspicious. "Concession? How much?"

"Oh, I'd say eight hours should do it."

"Excuse me?"

"Eight hours is how much time Ed agreed to spend with me in my tepee, to cleanse him of negative thoughts and achieve purity, peace and harmony."

If I hadn't already surmised that Ed felt a lot more for me than sexual attraction and growing friendship, I would have known it then. That he had agreed to do a tepee sit with Owl in order to get the account information said more about how he felt than a love note on a billboard ever could. Ed's not exactly politically incorrect, he's just more of a meat-and-potatoes kinda guy, and anything smacking of the metaphysical threatens his machismo. And yet, he had agreed to Owl's concession. How could I do any less?

"Okay, Owl, you got it."

"You won't be sorry, Pink. You'll find that the purification process is a life-altering experience, a passage into another cosmos of self-awareness and truth."

"I'm looking forward to it already, but if I don't find the chick who framed me, I'll miss out because I'll be in the pen for the rest of my life."

"Oh. Well, if you were in a hurry, why didn't you say so? This is just what I'm talking about, Pink. Once you're in touch with your spiritual self, you won't be compelled to hide the truth. You can say what you feel, without fear of rejection or retribution."

I kinda thought I already had that down pretty well, but I didn't say so to Owl. Instead, I mumbled an agreement and tapped my foot while I waited for him to get the information.

I wrote down the post-office box number on another chewing gum wrapper, along with Sasha's phone number. "Could you do me one more favor?"

"Glad to."

"Would you find out the post office where this box is located?"

I heard the tapping of a keyboard, then he said, "Pine Street Station. Pine and Larkin."

Awesome. That was only a block away from the hospital. "Thanks, Owl."

"Glad to be of service, Pink. Call when you get back to Midland and we'll set up a time for your session."

Oh, man. "Yes, I will." Eight hours? I don't even want to do stuff I like for eight hours. But I'd do it. A promise is a promise.

I hung up and headed for the hospital gift shop, where I bought a stack of postcards with the Golden Gate Bridge, Coit Tower, Lombard Street, Haight-Ashbury, Fisherman's Wharf and several other familiar scenes in and around San Francisco. I also bought a pair of sunglasses with huge frames and extra-dark lenses, the kind I'd need if I ever decided to fly to the sun. With part of my purchase in hand and the other part on my face, I left the building and walked toward the post office. The sun was high in a clear blue sky and I could vaguely smell the ocean, briny and fishy, mingled with the scents of cooking food and car exhaust. A cable car *ding-dinged* from California street, one block over, and I remembered the last time I was in San Francisco. I'd been very happy then, just married and looking forward to a perfect life with George.

I'm not really one to hold a grudge against anything but people, so my memories of a happy honeymoon that didn't foretell a happy marriage didn't make me hate San Francisco. Even with my intense agenda, I wanted to ride a cable car down to Fisherman's Wharf and eat clam chowder out of a sourdough bread bowl, just like every other tourist. But I couldn't, because timing was everything. I had to find Sasha, and it needed to be sooner than later.

Pine Street Station was a small post office, which made it harder to be unobtrusive, but as I stood at the wall counter and penned the postcards to various and sundry people, and addressed all of them to Ed's office, I was able to keep an eye on the box rented by Sasha Valikov. The light was on, indicating the mail was all up for the day, and I hoped she hadn't already stopped by. Or that she was one of those intermittent mail checkers. This I cannot relate to. I'm a mail-aholic. Even though the mail usually brings a ton of junk and bills that take all my money, there's sometimes a gem in the stacks, and it's those that I live for. Yes, I love mail. I just hoped Sasha Valikov loved mail, as well.

After I'd been there about an hour, I was almost through my stack of postcards. How could I keep hanging around without calling attention to myself? I stood in line to buy stamps, keeping my gi-normous shades on and my face angled down a bit, to avoid looking at anyone directly. When I had several sheets in hand, I went back to the wall counter and took an inordinate amount of time to stick the stamps on the postcards. After the last stamp, I went to the mail slot and dropped them in, then loitered by the racks of boxes and envelopes sold by the postal service. A dirty man with bad teeth ambled close and asked for money, which I'm certain he regretted because I talked to him for at least fifteen minutes before I finally relented and handed him ten bucks.

I'd been at the post office over two hours, and despite the constant flow of people in and out, I felt like I was more obvious than if I'd had three heads, green skin and carried a light-saber. My paranoia increased exponentially, until I was certain the counter help was eyeing me with deep suspicion. In reality, they probably never noticed me, but I was tired, and stressed, and severely pissed at Sasha for failing to show up, so my people meter was wonky.

Then, while I was trying to come up with an alternative

plan, like maybe applying for a job at the post office because then I could spend some time filling out an application, a tall woman went to the Valikov Interiors box and retrieved a few pieces of mail. Sasha Valikov? Had to be.

Her hair was short and black as midnight, her legs long and lean, her feet encased in black stilettos and her body covered by a black suit with a short, tight skirt. She had blue eyes and Angelina Jolie lips and those high cheekbones God gives only to a select few. Sasha was hot. I already despised the woman, but now I hated her even more. How dare she be a scheming, cold-blooded bitch, and be a knockout on top of it? My sensibilities were deeply offended.

Sasha went to stand in line, gaining some appreciative looks from the male customers. And a few females. Great. She picked today to buy stamps. I waited next to the parcel scale, and noticed when she got to the counter that she didn't buy stamps. Instead, she filled out some paperwork, then asked how soon her mail would begin at the new box. Oh-ho, so I was right. She and Olga were already making changes.

I trailed after her when she left the post office, and watched her go inside an apartment building a block over, on California. The Cable Carpartments. No, I'm not kidding.

The building wasn't very big, just three stories, and I suspected there couldn't be more than nine or ten units inside. There was a buzzer and intercom panel outside the entrance, which meant I had no access unless someone buzzed me in. My mind went through several scenarios, discarding each one in turn, until I hit on one that was guaranteed to get me not only inside the building, but inside Sasha's apartment.

Granted it could get me ten to twenty in the slammer if I

got caught, but I was already faced with becoming a lifer, so what the hell?

I stood at the cable car stop and looked to the east, as though I was waiting for it. Unfortunately, it did come before Sasha left, so I had to walk away and hang out inside somebody's little entrance niche, occasionally peeking to see what was going on at the Cable Carpartments. Finally, an hour later, Sasha reappeared, stood at the curb and caught the cable car headed toward the Embarcadero.

I didn't waste any time. Hurrying across the street, I looked at the directory and saw M. Pei, Manager. I hit the button a few times, and eventually a man answered, "Yes?"

"Mr. Pei, I am Tonya Weisberg, an agent of the Internal Revenue Service. I'm under orders to seize the books and records of Sasha Valikov, whose business is under subpoena for suspected fraud and nonpayment of taxes."

"Did you buzz her?"

"She doesn't answer. Under federal law, code section… three-o-four, you're required to allow me access to the taxpayer's place of business." Lord, I hoped Mr. Pei knew as little about the Internal Revenue Code as I did. Although I'm a CPA, I don't do taxes. I'm an auditor turned forensic accountant, and I'd rather be shot than do taxes. That's Mom's territory. I did randomly wonder what code section 304 covered.

"This is not a place of business. This is apartments, where people live."

"Ms. Valikov lists this as her business address, sir, and therefore, this is her place of business. I expect to gain entrance without having to contact law enforcement." Man, was I full of it, or what?

The door buzzed and clicked and I reached to open it. Inside, the foyer was small and cramped, with a bank of mailboxes on one wall and a dilapidated console table against the other. A flight of stairs faced me, and a hall to the right led to the first-floor apartments. I smelled fish. Cooked fish. Old fish. Bleh. A tiny man with a hunchback shuffled toward me.

"Mr. Pei?"

"Yes, that's me." He shook his head. "This is very upsetting. We have rules against business enterprise in the building. What sort of business is this of Miss Valikov?"

"She's a decorator who specializes in Chinese antiques."

His old eyes widened. "Where does she get these antiques?"

"From China, I presume."

"Pah! She is not truthful. There are not many antiques from China. Most all that were left after the Cultural Revolution are in museum at Beijing and Shanghai and Taiwan." He shook his head again. "And she is not paying her taxes?"

"No, which is why the IRS needs her records, to prove she has earned much more than she declares on her tax returns." I almost felt guilty for bamboozling Mr. Pei, he was such a nice man. He was clearly Chinese, an immigrant from the old days, when the borders were closed and Big Brother was all around, every day, every minute. I'd spoken to some of the old-timers while I was in China, and every story was more depressing than the last. One thing always stood out, and that was the strong belief that the government, the Party, was all-seeing, far too big and powerful to be resisted in any way.

Mr. Pei undoubtedly bought my story, hook, line and sinker, because I said I was with the government. Yeah, I felt guilty. But not guilty enough to beg off and leave. I was in it now, and I was going to stay the course. But it would be helpful if I could get to her apartment before she came home, so I tried to hurry Mr. Pei along. I knew from the directory that she was on the second floor, number 202.

"Will you accompany me, sir?"

"Is it required?"

"No. You can give me a key, if you like, and I'll return it when I leave."

"I am ached with bad knees. The stairs I avoid when not necessary." He reached into a pocket of his baggy black pants and produced a key. "Here you are, Miss Weisberg. I will be right here, in my home, should you need me."

Luck was with me. I couldn't believe he'd just handed me the key without asking for any kind of identification or paperwork verifying I had the right to take records. I guess I look honest. And as I said, Mr. Pei was conditioned to believe me. I could go into her apartment and snoop all I wanted, without prying eyes.

Which is precisely what I did. Her apartment was an efficiency, all in one room, except for a small bathroom. There was a tiny counter and sink, a two-burner stove, toaster, microwave and a small refrigerator. A double bed took up one corner and a computer desk another. On the floor in front of the desk were two boxes, each filled with files and papers. Was Sasha packing to leave, or did she just leave everything in boxes as a matter of course?

I put on the plastic gloves I'd swiped from a supply closet at the hospital and made a beeline for the boxes. Within a few minutes, I found the Valikov Interiors bank statements and hurriedly checked them out, noting that there were several cleared checks to Wang Imports. Big checks, totaling some-where in the neighborhood of two hundred thousand. Who was Wang? I looked on the back of one check and jotted down the account number endorsement. I figured on another eight-hour tepee sit to get the information from Owl about who owned that account. I was gonna be so pure of spirit I could qualify for a tax break.

Unless Sasha had written another check that hadn't yet cleared, there was still over a hundred thousand bucks in the Valikov Interiors account.

When I found a box of checks, I had the pleasing thought that vengeance would be mine. I took the book at the bottom of the box, then took one of the cleared checks from the last bank statement. Sasha's signature looked easy enough to copy.

I moved on to the next box, which was filled with random stuff, like an ad for Macy's summer clearance sale and paid electric bills. Toward the middle of the pile in the box, I ran across a couple of pages of yellow legal pad. I stared at them for several moments, my heartbeat gaining momentum as I read, the realization of what I was looking at making me a little breathless.

The top page was all in Russian, of which I couldn't decipher even one word. But the second page was neatly printed in English—perhaps for someone who didn't read Russian? There were names, dates, cities, villages and notes. One name stood out from all the rest—*Chiang Han, Beijing*. Next to his name was another name—*Anna Yakovlevna, Ko-lymskaya, Siberia. 5 June. $25,000 U.S.* It had to be the China brides.

Looking at all those names, sixty at least, and Mrs. Han's

in particular, I felt bile rise in my throat, and it took a lot of effort not to hurl. Those poor women, abducted from their homes, taken to a foreign country and sold to a man who didn't speak their language, who saw them as a commodity. It was barbaric, and terrifying, and so incredibly cold-blooded. I actually sent a prayer to God, a request that Sasha and Olga and whoever else was behind this would get a one-way ticket to hell. A vision of Mrs. Han floated through my memory and I promised myself—even if I couldn't get out of the charges against me—these women would be found and returned to their homes and families.

I folded the list and stuffed it in my purse with the checks. Then I took Sasha's door key, pressed it into the bar of soap in her shower, and wrapped the soap in a tissue. I put it right next to the list in my purse, then washed the key and beat a hasty retreat back down the stairs to Mr. Pei's door. He answered my knock and I handed him the key, which I held sideways, so that there would be only partial prints. Yes, I was paranoid. It was becoming a part of me.

Schooling my face into what I hoped was a concerned look, I said to Mr. Pei, "It appears she has moved some of her records, and I'll have to find out where. In the meantime, I wonder if I might ask you to not mention my visit? I need the element of surprise on my side, you see, and if she knows ahead of time that I am coming for her records, she might destroy them."

He nodded as he took the key. "Yes, I understand. If you need any assistance in the future, you have only to ask."

His formality was engaging, and once again, I felt like a heel for faking him out.

I stepped back and said goodbye, then headed out the

front door. Nick of time, too, because as I came out into the afternoon sunshine, Sasha was just returning to the Cable Carpartments, a Macy's shopping bag in her hand. I wondered what she had bought with her stolen money. CERF money, given by generous people to help the earthquake victims. God, I despised her. It took every ounce of self-discipline to keep myself from rushing her and tossing her in front of the oncoming cable car.

Instead, I hurried back to the hospital and used a pay phone to call Lou's cell number. He and Mom were on Steve's plane, en route to Midland, and before I could catch Lou up and ask another favor, Mom must have grabbed the phone away from him.

She said in her very best "I'm the mom and you're a rebellious daughter who's making me old before my time" voice, "You have lost your mind. That's what it is. All these years, I thought you were a sensible person, but now I find out you're crazy as a loon."

"I'd get help, Mom, but I can't afford it right now. I'm still saving up for the down payment on my house."

"You're not even kind of funny! Pink, I insist that you go to the airport and catch the next flight to Midland. Stop this nonsense and get your ass home, where you belong."

Cripes, I was so not in the mood. Sometimes Mom can be overbearing to the point of bitchy. I glanced around to make sure no one could overhear me, and all I saw were a couple of men holding hands on a couch at least thirty feet away. Turning back to face the phone, I lowered my voice a notch. "I'm going to find whoever did this to me, get the proof and get myself out of a murder and embezzlement rap. Ed can't do it. Steve could do it, but shouldn't. Lou is preoccupied with you. And as for you, Mom, how's the view from the cheap seats?"

She didn't reply for a while, and I stared at the number pad on the pay phone, wishing that just once she wouldn't pull this overprotective bullshit, that she'd treat me like I was a thirty-one-year-old professional, instead of a thirteen-year-old brat.

In the background, I heard music. Lou was playing vintage Crosby, Stills, Nash & Young. Mom used to listen to music like that. Then she did the CPA gig and started listening to jazz because she said it was more dignified. I always kinda thought it was because her favorite music made her think about the past, and the proverbial road not taken. She took the Lurch road, and it came to a dead end in a barren field. With no music at all.

When she finally replied, I seriously wondered if I needed to force her into therapy. "Why do you think he's preoccupied?"

Un-freaking-believable. "Because he's been a widower for a year and he's lonely! Because he hasn't had sex in a while! Maybe he wants you to do his taxes! How the hell should I know? For God's sake, Mother, I don't have time to dish girl talk about your new crush. Now put Lou on the phone."

His deep, even voice came through the receiver. "Pink, you shouldn't yell at your mother. She's having a hard enough time without you shouting at her. And incidentally, the answer is A and B. I already have someone to do my taxes."

"Jesus." Just when I thought it couldn't get worse.

"Now, tell me what you've learned about Ed."

Determined to pretend I hadn't just inserted my size seven

in my mouth, I told him about Ed, and Sasha and the Cable Carpartments, and what I'd found. "I may need to go back, and I don't have the heart to lie to Mr. Pei again, so I made an impression of the key in a bar of soap. I was hoping you could tell me where to get a key made. I also need to know where I can get a fake ID with Sasha's name and my picture."

"Why?"

"I can't tell you."

"Is it illegal?"

"Very."

"Got it. Okay, go to North Beach, to Carmine's Deli, and order a Bolshevik sandwich."

"I am pretty hungry, Lou, but to tell the truth, I'm kinda pressed for time. I need the ID before the close of business. I'll check out Carmine's later."

"Just order the sandwich and you'll get all the help you need. You'll also get a great sandwich. And say hello to Carmine. He's an old buddy from my days with the Mafia."

"Very funny."

"Who's kidding? Here, say something nice to your mother. She's crying again. Never seen a woman who could cry and swear like a sailor at the same time."

"Pink, I'm sorry," she said in a subdued, watery voice. "Surely you know how worried I am. Can I help it if I'm a mother who worries about her only child?"

Ah, there was the bus I'd been waiting for, stopping to pick me up for my guilt trip. I hopped on board and said to Mom, "I'm sorry I yelled at you. It's been a little stressful."

"Lou says Ed was shot. How is he?"

More emotional than I'd ever seen him. Foul-tempered and snappy, like a wounded animal. Incredibly endearing and attractive in his vulnerability. I didn't tell Mom. I was pretty sure she wouldn't really get it. "He's good. He should be released from the hospital tomorrow or the next day."

"Will you come back to Midland with him?"

"It depends, Mom. I'll let you know. Until then, please don't worry. Everything is going to be okay."

"You need help. I think I should come out there and help you find these people."

"Out where? You don't know where I am."

"I do now. Lou said North Beach, which can only be San Francisco. I'm coming out there."

I heard Lou in the background. "Like hell you are."

"I will if I damn well want to! In fact, go tell the pilot to change course. I want to go to California."

"What? You just got through telling me all the reasons you couldn't come to California with me, and now, out of the blue, everything's changed?"

"You know good and damn well why I said no. But things are different now. Pink's there. And Ed. I need to be in California."

In spite of it all, I caught myself smiling.

Lou came on the line again. "Call me after you go to Carmine's and I'll let you know where we are—in Midland, or over the Grand Canyon."

"Try to keep her in Midland, will ya?"

"Sure, Pink. Piece of cake."

We both fell silent, and I gutted it up to ask The Question. Lou read my mind and said before I had to ask, "He's a senator, and he's logical, and on that level he understood why you left without telling him. But he's also a man who thinks he's in love with you, and on that level he's pretty ripped up about it."

"Should I call him?"

"I advise against it. Just do what you have to do and leave im out of the loop. I don't know if you've had a chance to atch the news, but they're crucifying him."

I closed my eyes. Things were turning out even worse than 'd expected.

"You were having dinner at his house when you suppos-dly left to go murder the Bunch woman. He posted your bail, vhich someone leaked to CNN, and one of his neighbors was n the local news, saying he's seen you coming in and out of teve's house many times over the past few weeks."

My eyes flew open. "That's a bald-faced lie!"

"They don't care. It makes great fodder for the news, since ou're now the most notorious woman in the United States. hey're even hinting that you offed the ambassador, in spite of he state department's official statement that you're not a suspect. t's bad, Pink, and Steve's there in Washington, ignoring all of t because he refuses to get in a war of words with the press. On op of all that, you left, and he has no idea where you are, or how ou are, or what's happening to you. There are certain kinds of nisery that Steve's intimately familiar with, and I'm sad to say, e's discovering another one as we speak."

I stared at the graffiti scratched into the metal surround-ng the pay phone. *Linda hearts Oscar*. I wondered if Linda ver unintentionally made Oscar miserable. "Hell, Lou, if guilt was a commodity, you could corner the market."

"What guilt? I'm telling you what you wanted to know. 'm no good at candy-coating, so don't expect it."

"When you talk to him, would you at least tell him I'm okay?"

"No, because you're not okay. You're breaking the terms

of your bail, you're out there looking for whoever frame
you, who happens to be associated with the Russian mob, an
you're about to do something so illegal you won't even te
me what it is. Why would I lie to my own son?"

"I'm sorry," I whispered, feeling about as low as I coul
ever remember. Why had I led Steve on? What was it in m
nature that wouldn't let go? If I'd told him from the start, wa
back during the whistle-blower thing, that I wasn't inter
ested, none of this would be happening. Steve wouldn't b
involved. Maybe he'd already be going out with one of thos
ten other women Lou thought would be perfect First Ladie:
Why hadn't I told him no?

In my mind, I heard him laughing. I really loved the wa
Steve laughed. I remembered his kisses, and felt a stir of hea
in my lower body. Was that all there was? Physical attraction
Had I ruined a man's life because I was hot for him?

Then I remembered how he still wore his wedding ring
only now on his right hand instead of his left. I thought of al
the things he'd said about Lauren, the still obvious love h
had for her and how much he missed her. More than I wa
attracted to him because he was drop-dead gorgeous, I wa
incredibly drawn to him because of his depth and sincerity

"It's not all your fault, you know," Lou said, rather gentl
especially compared to his previous tone. "Steve's ver
smart, and he knew when he got involved with you that h
was setting himself up for criticism. I'm sure he had no ide:
it would be like this, but no matter what, I don't think h
regrets it, and neither should you. I do think that when thi:
is all over, you need to end it if there's no hope for him."

Was there no hope? I was always thinking Mom needed
therapy, but maybe I needed some myself. What was wrong

vith me? "Lou, you're way harsh, and I'm not exactly sure
how I feel about you and Mom, but can I just say, you're a
ighteous dude?"

"Sure, Pink. And don't worry about your mother. My in-
entions are honorable."

"For what it's worth, most women don't mind a little bit
of dishonorable intention."

"Duly noted."

"Take it easy, Lou." I hung up and headed back outside. I
vanted to go up and check on Ed, but I didn't have time. I
had to get to the bank before five o'clock.

Chapter 6

It didn't take long to find Carmine's. His deli was half a block off Washington Square, in an area chock-full of Italian restaurants and markets, with salamis and pepperonis and big wheels of cheese displayed in their windows.

Picture the sort of place you imagine mob guys would hang out and you already know what Carmine's looked like. Old, with mismatched tables, ancient linoleum on the floor and a wide array of artwork hanging on the faded, discolored walls—from a print of *The Last Supper*, to a St. Pauli Girl beer sign. The smell of stale smoke mixed with the scent of basil and oregano, yeasty bread and a smorgasbord of strong meats to create a not unpleasant odor.

But maybe that was just because I was so damn hungry.

I got some looks from the patrons, which consisted of a couple of balding guys nursing beers, some younger guys

vith a large pizza and a hatchet-faced old lady who was at-
acking a giant plate of antipasto. They all stopped what they
vere doing and stared at me as I made my way to the counter
o order. I ignored them and stayed focused. The man behind
he counter looked a little like Woody Allen. He even had the
ame nerdy glasses.

"What's for ya?" he asked.

"I'd like a Bolshevik sandwich."

"Are you sure?"

"Yeah. Real sure."

He nodded toward the tables. "Have a seat and I'll get it
ight out to you."

I took the seat closest to the counter, purposefully sitting
o my back was to the old men and the hatchet lady. In less
ime than it took me to check out the oddball artwork in my
ine of vision, a swarthy man with black eyes and black hair
nd black jeans appeared at the table, a round beer tray in one
and, a brimming beer mug in the other. He set the tray in front
f me and I saw it was a sandwich. A very, very *big* sandwich,
with all sorts of things on it that would definitely require
emergency Tums in an hour. He set the beer next to the tray,
hen took the chair next to mine so that he was close. Too close.

I guess my confusion and increasing fear showed in my face.

"You need help and I'm the one who can give it to you."
He nodded toward the sandwich. "Eat, and tell me what I can
lo for you."

He had an accent, but I couldn't pinpoint what it was. Not
talian. But then, he didn't really look Italian. He wasn't
Hispanic, either. I reached in my purse and retrieved the
soap. "Can you make a key out of this?"

"No, but I know a man who can." He looked disappointed.
"Is that it?"

"I need a fake ID, with someone else's name and my
face, but not my face. My face needs to look more like
someone else's."

"We can do that. What's the name?"

I wrote it on a napkin and he stared at it for a long time.
"How do you know this woman?"

"Actually, I don't. I just need to be her for a little while.
Do you know her?"

"Perhaps." He stood and held the soap in his hand. "Eat
your sandwich and I'll be back with a key in a little while."

"Wait!" I called before he could get out the door. He
turned and came back to the table. "Who are you? I mean,
how do I know you're not going to disappear with my soap?"

"Who I am isn't important, and you can be assured, if I
were going to disappear with something of yours it wouldn't
be your soap."

His eyes made it pretty clear what he'd take and it made
me blush. "Are you Carmine?"

"No." He turned and walked away again.

I spent the time until he returned eating the sandwich,
which, as Lou had promised, was delicious. I only made it
through half, because the thing was a monster. And I skipped
the beer because no way did I need to be fuzzy. Woody
brought me a diet cola and I donated the beer to the hatchet-
faced lady. She raised the mug in salute and downed half of
it in one long swallow.

Mr. Swarthy came back and handed me a key, along with
a small metal file. "If it doesn't work on the first try, file the
edges a little." He looked at the tray. "You're not finished."

"I can't eat any more without blowing up."

"Then come with me downstairs."

The basement of Carmine's bore no resemblance to the ground floor. There was a surprising amount of square footage, all of it painted crisp white, with new flooring and modern furniture. Mr. Swarthy took me into one room that looked like a theater dressing room, with rows of wigs, racks of clothes and a lighted mirror with a barber chair. Next to the mirror were several shelves filled with cosmetics, hair dye and bottles and tubs of oddly named stuff that I suspected was used to alter a person's facial features.

"You need a wig and some face work. Have a seat."

I did, and thirty minutes later, with instructions from me, I had short, black hair, high cheekbones and full lips. That hurt, because whatever he put on them to make them swell stung like a mother. I wasn't so sure I looked like Sasha, but I looked different enough from myself that I was sure no one at the bank would recognize me. And that was what was most important. I met his gaze in the mirror.

"You *do* know Sasha."

"Maybe. Whether I do or I don't is not something I will discuss." He lowered the chair and whipped the hairdresser cape from my shoulders. "Let's go to the next room so I can take your photo."

Within another fifteen minutes I had an authentic-looking California driver's license with my picture and Sasha's name and address. I looked it over carefully. "Are you absolutely certain this will pass as real? I don't need any attention from anyone, least of all the police."

"It's as real as it gets. What do you plan to do with it?"

"Forge a check and have the bank issue a cashier's check."

"You should have further proof of identity, just in case."

He went to a filing cabinet and pulled out a stack of cards which he then ran through a small machine. He handed them to me as they came out. Visa. American Express. Neiman Marcus. Macy's. And a grocery-store preferred-shopper card. All with Sasha Valikov imprinted on them.

"Will they check the numbers?"

"No. But if they ask for another form of identification, you can pull out all these cards and tell them to pick one. It makes you look more legitimate. Do you have a sample of her signature?"

I nodded and he pointed to the desk. "Sit down and practice."

By the time I could write her signature without hesitating, it was a quarter past four. He looked at my efforts and nodded his approval, then his gaze moved across my body. "You need other clothes. A suit, with heels. People are less likely to question a well-dressed person."

Choosing to ignore his subtle insult of my current outfit, which was a pair of jeans and a very wrinkled white blouse, I said, "I don't have time to shop for something else. The bank closes in forty-five minutes."

"In the other room there are clothes. Find something."

Maybe because I felt so different, in a vaguely out-of-body way, I chose a red suit. The jacket fit well, but the ultra-short skirt was a tad on the tight side. I found some red pumps with toes and heels that were pointy enough to put somebody's eye out.

My fairy godfather took one look and said, "Make sure you go to a male teller. Unless he's gay, and perhaps even then, he will give you the cashier's check without question."

"I don't usually buy anything red. It never looks good on me."

Mr. Swarthy walked all the way around me. "It does now." He stopped and met my eyes. "Your accent is atrocious. The instant you open your mouth you will negate your persona. I suggest you say as little as possible, and when you have to speak, do so very softly and enunciate each word, slowly."

"Maybe I should try a Russian accent. Like in *Dr. Zhivago.*"

He frowned. "They all sounded British." His expression brightened. "That would be easier for you. Don't try to sound British, because everyone sucks at British accents, but think of Queen Elizabeth. There is a car and driver out back. He will take you to the bank, wait for you, then bring you back here, where I will return you to your self."

Since I'd asked if he was Carmine I hadn't ventured any more questions about him, but by then, my curiosity was killing me. "Who are you, and how can you be sure I'm legit? Couldn't anyone come in and order a Bolshevik sandwich?"

"I told you, who I am is not important. As for the sandwich, it's not on the menu."

"But people overheard me order it."

"It doesn't matter. I knew you were coming. The sandwich is merely to let me know you are here."

"Someone called ahead. Do you know who?" I was keen to know if Lou was open about this operation, or if he operated as the big lady and everyone here only knew him as Big Mama.

"We do not use names here. I don't know yours and you don't know mine, and if we were to meet on the street, we would never acknowledge that we have met."

Odd. The whole setup was odd. My inborn inclination to be nosy was riding high, but I suspected I'd get no answers from my benefactor, so I followed him to the back exit of Carmine's without asking any more questions. The driver, a wiry man with a bushy salt-and-pepper mustache, asked where I wanted to go.

"First San Francisco Bank."

"The main bank downtown, or one of the branch locations?"

"Main bank," Mr. Swarthy said before I could answer. He looked at me. "They will be busier, and the clientele more diverse. You'll fit right in."

I swallowed, the enormity of what I was about to do finally hitting me. Even if I was justified, even if the money I took was stolen to begin with, it was still illegal to forge a check. And much like there are degrees of sin, there was a degree of money here that sent me into major criminal territory. A hundred grand was a lot worse than twenty bucks.

"You can do anything if the reward is worth it," Mr. Swarthy said, evidently reading my mind. "How important is this to you?"

"It could mean the difference between freedom and prison."

"There is a trick to these kinds of operations. While you are on your way to the bank, tell yourself over and over that you are this woman. Get inside her head, be who she is, become her. When you arrive, keep that thought in your brain and don't let it go."

"I'll try." I got in the back of the black Lincoln and looked up at him. "Thank you."

"Good luck." He closed the door, and we were off.

San Francisco proper isn't really all that big of a place. If the traffic isn't too bad, you can get anywhere in the city within fifteen minutes. And that's with lights. We made it to the bank in ten.

I wanted to throw up. Real bad. I wondered if Sasha wanted to throw up when she printed out those fake invoices, or when she called my answering machine and left bogus messages, or when she sent her blond goon, Olga, to take care of Ed.

Ed. He was almost killed because Olga was a cold-blooded murderer. On orders, no doubt from Sasha. I could do this for Ed, and for Mrs. Han and all the other women on that horrible list. And for me. I'd lived my life the best way I knew how, made an effort to be kind and compassionate and do the right thing. Now, through no fault of my own, I was facing life in prison. Maybe even execution. All because Sasha the Bitch was a greedy, conniving, evil ho.

Yeah, I could do this.

I got out of the car at the curb and the nameless driver pulled away—to circle the block until I reappeared. Striding for the door, I held my head high and looked people in the eye and kept repeating in my head, *I'm an evil ho. I'm an evil ho. I'm an evil ho. A Russian evil ho. Russian evil ho. Tally-ho, a Russian evil ho.* I spied a male teller who looked more geek than gay and walked confidently to his station.

There were two people ahead of me in line, and while I waited, I felt the stares of several men from other teller lines. I met the gaze of a young guy dressed in a gray suit and white shirt—he looked like a CPA. I didn't give him a come-on look, but I didn't look away, which is what I usually do if I catch a man staring at me. The result was freaky. He kept staring and gave me a half smile and raised his eyebrows by millimeters.

I focused on the teller, now only one customer away. *Queen Elizabeth. Pip-pip, cheerio, and all that rot. Monty Python. Elizabeth Taylor. A spot of tea. I'm a Russian evil ho with a northern Sussex accent. Mummy will be delighted, right-o?* When it was my turn, I set my Kate Spade bag on the counter and retrieved the checkbook, from which I had pulled out a few checks so it wouldn't look entirely new. Then I handed him a small piece of notepaper that had the details of my transaction.

He dragged his gaze away from my cleavage and smiled quite merrily. "Global Fund for Women. Is this who you want the check made out to?"

"Precisely." I bent my head to write the check to the bank, to cover the cashier's check. Then I glanced up and caught him staring at my cleavage again. "Is there a fee?"

"No. No fee, Miss, uh…"

"Valikov." I finished the check and handed it to him. *I'm an evil Russian ho. I can't be friendly, or pleasant, or even mildly nice.* I remembered how Sasha questioned the postal clerk about when her mail would be moved to a new box. "Will this take long?"

"Not at all," he assured me. Turning around, he walked to a door in the wall behind the teller counter and disappeared.

He was gone less than five minutes, but I swear to God it felt like a year—and a half. I could feel gray hairs popping out of my head. My arteries hardening. My stomach flipping upside down, sideways, and all the way to my feet and back. Oh, God, what was taking so long? They must be on to me.

They must be calling the— *I'm an evil Russian ho. Evil. Russian. Ho.*

The teller finally came back with a cashier's check for one hundred thousand dollars. He looked at the check I'd written to the bank. "Can I see some ID, Ms. Valikov?"

Evil hos are good at looking annoyed. I worked at it, while I slid the driver's license from my wallet and handed it to him, taking care to brush my fingers against his and bend just so, my push-up bra threatening to spill all I had out of the low neckline of the suit jacket. The evil-ho red suit jacket.

He handed the license back to me, along with the cashier's check. "My wife's a big fan of the Global Fund for Women. It's really great of you to give them this much money."

Oh, man. I wanted so bad to go off about it, and how awesome I thought they were, and how much money they gave to women's organizations the world over to help abused, starving women and their children.

But I couldn't do that. I was an evil ho who sold women. Jesus, I wanted to go take a shower. I couldn't even say thank-you to the teller. I merely nodded, slid the check into my bag, turned and walked away.

Despite my instincts screaming for me to run like hell, I calmly walked through the front door and out onto the sidewalk, where I glanced to my left, looking for the car. There it was, just making the corner. I stepped to the curb and when it pulled up I opened the back door and got in. We drove away and had made it about two blocks before I yelled, "Pull over!" It was a bloody miracle that I managed to get the door open before I lost my lunch.

As he pulled back into traffic, he said conversationally, "Don't feel bad. That happens to most people who eat a Bolshevik sandwich."

In light of my notoriety at the moment, I asked the guy at Carmine's if I could keep my dress-up clothes and fake face for a while longer. He agreed, and I headed back to the hospital. On the way, I dropped the cashier's check in the mail using an envelope and stamp I bummed from Carmine's. I figured it was the only sure way to keep the money safe, to keep it out of Sasha's greedy hands.

In the hospital lobby, which now had quite a few more people, I called Owl and asked him to check into the Wang Imports account. He said he would.

"Call me in about an hour and I'll have your information."

I agreed, then hung up and debated whether to call Lou and Mom to see where they were, but decided to wait until I'd gone upstairs to see Ed. I was worried about him and wanted to put his mind at ease that I hadn't met the wrong end of Olga's gun. With a mixed bag of feelings—enthusiasm, hesitancy and something that's about as close to love as I can get—I went upstairs to the post-op floor.

I glanced behind the nurses' station as I passed and saw three women in a windowed room, talking while they updated their patient charts. Nurse Sally wasn't among them, and I assumed her shift had ended. The hall was busy with visitors, lab techs and the guy who served dinner to the patients, his hair covered by a paper shower cap.

I pushed Ed's door open and saw he was asleep. Or was he unconscious? My gaze was drawn to an IV bag, hanging beside the bed. Had he tried to get up again? Or had there been some complication?

Worried and feeling guilty for leaving him alone, I closed the door behind me and started toward the bed, but before I'd taken two steps, the bathroom door swung open and there was Sasha, in all her evil glory. Oh, God.

She moved to Ed's bedside and held a syringe close to his arm. Then she looked at me. "Give the money back or he's a dead man."

Chapter 7

With the *Oh shit, oh God, what am I gonna do?* litany running through my head, I asked, "How did you know?"

"A teller from the bank called. You forgot your receipt." She looked me up and down. "You are not like me at all. I would never wear red."

"How did you get here?"

"I saw you outside my apartment earlier and followed you to this hospital where your lawyer recuperates. When the bank called, I knew it had to be you who wrote the check. If you do not give back the money, I will kill him."

"I can't give it back. I mailed the check an hour ago."

"Damn you!" She raised her hand, intent on stabbing Ed with the needle.

I didn't consciously decide what to do—it was strictly a knee-jerk reaction to hurl my purse at her. That it hit her in the head was a lucky break. She was more startled than injured, and her moment of disorientation was long enough for me to lunge at her. You could say I was angry. Or you could say I had enough rage to tackle the defensive line of the Dallas Cowboys. Sasha didn't have a prayer.

Maybe she knew it. Maybe she could see it in my eyes when I literally leaped through the air and landed on her. We hit the floor and the syringe went flying. I anticipated the joy of beating the crap out of the conniving, hateful bitch, but before I could even raise my hand, she made some funky moves that had to be something she'd learned through martial arts, and in the space of a few seconds she was out from under me, running for the door.

I almost got up to run after her, but stopped when I realized it would be worse if I caught her. It wasn't as though I could call the cops. They'd arrest me and she'd disappear. So I watched the door close, feeling relieved and furious and scared out of my mind. I decided to take a class that would teach me how to move like that.

When I'd caught my breath and my pulse had returned to normal, I gathered up the spilled contents of my purse. I put it on the windowsill, then searched for the syringe, which I carefully picked up with a tissue and placed in my purse, inside a zippered pocket. Then I sat in the ugly green chair to stare at Ed.

For a long, long time, I watched him sleep, and faced the fact that I'd almost lost him—again. He slept on, undoubtedly under the influence of some serious happy drugs, while I weaved back and forth between the increasing inclination to suggest some kind of commitment and the paralyzing fear that he just might go for it.

An hour after Sasha left, I went downstairs and called Owl from a pay phone, my eyes never leaving the elevator doors. He answered on the first ring, and I asked him what he'd found.

"Wang Imports' checking account is at a bank in L.A., one favored by expats in China. It's a fairly new account, opened about a month ago. The man who opened the account is named Robert Wang, and his address is listed as Beijing, but the bank statements are mailed to a post-office box in San Francisco. Guess which one?"

"Valikov Interiors'."

"Hmm, yes. The plot thickens. I find myself entangled in this mystery, Pink. You'll let me know if I can help again?"

"Yes, I will, Owl. Thanks." I almost smiled at his offer of free services. But I didn't smile. I wasn't able to do that just yet. "Is there any other information about Robert Wang?" I hoped and prayed it was a different Robert Wang from the one I knew through the earthquake relief effort.

I heard the sound of Owl's computer keyboard. "His permanent address is a post-office box in Seattle. His mother was an illegal alien from China. Hmm, so he's a long-lost son of China who returned to the homeland."

"How do you know all this?"

"I'm in a government database. You'd be amazed what they know about all of us."

"I'm sure I would, so don't tell me. I just have to know if this Robert Wang is the same one I worked with in Beijing. He's the CERF contact there, who coordinates what the agency needs to supply for the survivors."

Owl was quiet for along time, the clacking of his keyboard the primary sound I could hear. The handful of visitors in the lobby were far away from the pay phones, speaking in subdued voices.

About the time my stomach had tied itself into a third knot, Owl said in a solemn voice, "His father was executed for dissidence and Robert's mother came to the States, where he was born. A couple of years ago, after his mother died, he went to visit China and never came back to the States. Musta liked it."

"Did he renounce his U.S. citizenship?"

"Uh, no. Apparently, he's leaving his options open. Does this sound like the guy you knew at CERF?"

"Well, Robert is American, but he looks Chinese. His English is perfect. He told me he grew up in Seattle, and his mother passed away, and he went to China because he wanted to find his relatives and learn about his ancestors. His mother never mentioned his father, and she wouldn't talk about China."

"If they executed her husband, can't say I blame her." Owl paused then added, "Sorry to say, Pink, but it looks like he's your man. Makes sense, doesn't it? This guy would have access to everything needed to rip off CERF."

I was suddenly so tired. I liked Robert Wang. He was a pleasant, jolly sort, always eager to be helpful, anxious to share his knowledge of China with visitors. Aunt Fred considered him a very good friend—was, in fact, the reason Robert got the job at CERF. Because of her friendships within the Party, Fred was initially offered the China contact job, but declined because it was too long-term. She recommended Robert, who'd done a lot of work for Uncle Alvin on one of his construction projects in Suzhou.

Now, he was responsible for ripping off the earthquake fund. Aunt Fred would be heartbroken. Then she's be pissed beyond belief. I thought about her, still over there working her ass off to help all those unfortunate people, still thinking Robert was a stand-up guy. The bastard. I wanted to slug him a good one.

"Could you check one more thing for me? Could you see where the money goes from the Wang Imports account?"

"Already did that. The answer is, nowhere. Wang might be a crook, but he's a miser crook. Every cent that's gone into that account is still there."

"Thanks, Owl. I don't know how you do it, and don't want to know, but I certainly appreciate you."

I said goodbye and hung up, then asked myself, why Robert? Was it just for the money? Did he plan to acquire a nice nest egg, then move back to the States?

Or maybe this was his way of realizing revenge against China for killing his father, a man he never laid eyes on. If so, it was pretty damn twisted. Stealing money from CERF would primarily hurt the victims of the earthquake, not the Communist Party of China. But perhaps Robert viewed every Chinese citizen as guilty of supporting the government that robbed him of a father.

It dawned on me, he had to be involved with the bride scam. There would be someone in China to find customers to buy the brides. It made me sick to think it was Robert, but it made sense.

The natural progression of my thoughts brought me to another question. Was Robert doing this on his own, or was he working for the Russian mob? Olga worked for them. Did Sasha? I knew only one way to find out.

After I fished the gum wrapper with Sasha's cell-phone number out of my bag, I sucked in a deep breath, dropped coins in the phone and punched the keypad before I could lose my nerve. I'm still not sure if I was relieved or disappointed that she answered. I said in a surprisingly even, calm voice, "We need to talk. Meet me at Fisherman's Wharf at noon tomorrow."

"Unless you're giving the money back, I have nothing to say to you."

"On the contrary. I have enough to nail your ass to the wall, and that's without calling INS." She was in cahoots with Olga, who was with the Russian mob. I took a wild guess that neither of them was in the United States legally.

She laughed. Actually laughed. "You are a pesky fly. Nothing more."

"I have the syringe."

"It's saline—harmless."

"I have your list."

She was a little slower with a comeback. "List?"

"The China brides, Sasha. All those women you abducted from Siberia and shipped off to China to be sold like animals."

"There is no such list."

"Meet me tomorrow and I'll show it to you."

I couldn't be sure, but I thought I heard the sound of papers shuffling. Was she looking through her box for the list? There was a long pause. The hamster was running double time through the wheel in her brain.

"How did you get into my apartment?"

"Does it matter? The point is, I have the list."

"What is it you wish to talk about?"

I liked that she had the tiniest bit of anxiety in her voice. "Those invoices, for one thing. I want to know how they have my fingerprints on them. And how is it that the only deposits in the Valikov account are from the Whitney Pearl account in Kansas? Am I your only customer? That's gonna look mighty odd to the FBI. Not to mention that there's no record of me calling you—ever. If I never called you, how did I order all those bogus Chinese antiques? How did I ask for your decorating services? It seems to me that you did a half-assed job, Sasha, and you *so* picked the wrong person to screw over. Meet me tomorrow. Tell me why Olga killed Taylor. Tell me about those fingerprints on the invoices. Tell me who finds buyers for the brides in China."

"I'm not telling you anything. But I will tell the bank I didn't write that check, that it was a forgery."

"Yeah, you do that, and they'll be on the phone to the FBI within thirty seconds. Those guys will want to talk to you, at length. When they come to talk to me, I'll tell them what I know, and in the bonus round, I'll tell them about your relationship with Olga. The State Department and the FBI are real hot to get hold of Olga. Offing an ambassador from China in the home of a U.S. senator was pretty stupid of her. And let's not forget, she shot Ed, who got a very good look at her."

"He will be dealt with in due time. In the meanwhile, find a way to get that money back, or your lover will be dead."

"I swear to God if you kill Ed, I'll—"

"I'm not speaking of him."

I gasped so fast, I choked. Coughing, I noticed several people looked at me. Great. I was drawing attention, and that couldn't be good. I held my hand around the mouthpiece and leaned toward the back of the wraparound pay phone. "He's a senator! Are you out of your fucking mind?"

"I want that money. And you shouldn't be so emotional."

"Jesus, woman, have you got no conscience at all?"

"Who are you to judge me? You know nothing of my life."

"I don't give a shit, Sasha. Whatever happened in your life doesn't give you the right to take innocent women away from their families and sell them like cattle. And it damn sure doesn't give you the right to screw my life all to hell."

She had no reply to that.

"Are you gonna meet me or not?"

"Are you going to give back the money?"

"If I do, will you tell me what I want to know?"

There was another long pause. "You lied about mailing the check, didn't you?"

"I never lie. I did mail the check, but perhaps I failed to mention that I didn't mail it to the Global Fund for Women. Tell me what I want to know and I'll tell you where I mailed it."

"I'll think about it."

"You've got until noon tomorrow to think about it. If you're a no-show, or you show up and kill me, the money's gone for good. You're also going to be arrested, along with Olga. If I've learned only one thing over the past six months, it's to cover my ass." I hung up the phone before she could say anything else.

Paranoid about Ed, I went upstairs to check on him again. He was still out like a light. Relieved, I left again, back downstairs to make more phone calls. It was a bitch not using the cell phone, but I couldn't take the chance of it being traced to a tower in California. I did wonder if I had any messages, so before I called Lou, I dialed my cell-phone voice mail.

There were so many messages the box was full. I paged

through them quickly, deleting as I went. Most of them were from reporters, but there were several from irate citizens, people who believed I stole all that money from CERF. I was called everything in the book, some of it pretty original. I wondered how all those people had gotten my cell number.

Interspersed among the hate calls were a couple from Parker Davis, expressing his sorrow at my present circumstances and offering to help me. I thought that was nice of him, considering he was now the executive director of a deflated charitable organization whose sudden decrease in revenues was largely due to me. Granted, it was through no fault of mine, but still, it was nice.

I also had a call from his wife, Madeline. She said it was outrageous, the charges against me, and that as a woman senator, she was behind me all the way. I wasn't sure what being a woman had to do with anything, but nevertheless, I thought that was pretty nice of her, too. Especially considering she was also being groomed to run for president. My friendship with Steve was no longer a secret, and seeing as he was her main competition, I thought it was big of her to offer her support.

When I called Lou, he said they were in Midland, at Mom's house. I breathed a sigh of relief. In the background, I could hear a deep voice, which sounded angry, and Mom's voice, which sounded even angrier. "What's up, Lou?"

"There appears to be a problem with your mother's air-conditioning serviceman."

Oh, man. Mom had recently been hanging out on the sly with Harry, the AC guy, but she assured me it was nothing, that they just got together occasionally and "enjoyed each other's company." Beyond that, it was strictly a business relationship. He fixed her air conditioner and she wrote him a check.

"What's the problem?" I asked Lou.

"Jane is upset because he was here playing poker with some friends when we came in. The friends are gone now, but I believe Harry would like her to forget this and carry on with business as usual."

I heard Mom yell, "Give me back the goddamn key, right now!"

"Doesn't sound like Harry's gonna get what he would like."

"No, I'd say your mother's made up her mind, so that's that. I've noticed that about her. Not wishy-washy at all."

I started to say *give it time,* but I didn't. The less involved I was with Mom and Lou, the better. "Lou, we have a development. Is there someone I can hire to stay with Ed?"

"What happened?"

I gave him the short version. "I ripped off a hundred grand from Sasha's account, and she threatened to kill Ed if I don't give it back."

Dead silence. Well, not exactly. I could still hear Mom yelling at Harry. But Lou was silent.

"If you're even vaguely considering giving me a lecture, tell me now so I can hang up and make alternative plans."

"Okay, so I was considering it, but you're right. What's done is done. Just promise me that when this is all over, you'll explain to me what compels you to do things like this. Do you think you're invincible? Or immortal? Or is it just that you forgot to stand in line when God was passing out survival instincts?"

"Get off it, Lou, and go look in the mirror."

"I'm a decorated officer of the United States Marines, a veteran and a former prisoner of war. I'm trained for espionage tactics and guerrilla warfare. Besides all that, I'm fifty-eight years old. I've had a life. Had a wife, had a kid, had lots of experiences and life lessons. You're just getting warmed up."

"And I'll turn stone cold if they throw me in the pen. My only choice then will be whose bitch I wanna be."

"There are other ways to do this, Pink. You're not alone."

I scratched my head, which was starting to itch miserably beneath the black wig. "I'm in a hole, Lou, and the last thing I want to do is pull people I love and care about down here with me. So say yes, or say no, but back off."

"Yes. I'll take care of it. There'll be someone there within the hour. He'll be your distant cousin, uh…Bud, who lives in Mendocino and drove down to see you."

"Thank you." Preparing myself for what would come next, I let a breath out slowly and told him about the other development. "She also threatened Steve."

Lou didn't respond for a long while. I wanted to say I was sorry, that I felt worse than horrible about all of it, but it seemed so pathetically inadequate.

Finally he said, "Don't worry about Steve. Your mother wants to say hello, so I'll be off now. I'm leaving Midland in the morning and I'll be at the hospital by noon."

Somehow it didn't seem like a very good idea to tell him I would be meeting Sasha at noon, so I skipped that part and simply said, "Okay."

Mom got on the line, and after some serious Mom-lecture time, which I allowed to go in one ear and out the other, she said she had told Harry to take a hike. Then while she was telling me she was done with men for good, I heard a Buffalo Springfield tune in the background, along with the sound of ice falling in a glass. Was Lou lighting candles, too? I stared at the elevator doors and blushed. Good God, my mother was being seduced while I was on the phone with her. Time to hang up.

"Mom, I've really gotta go. I'll call you tomorrow."

"Please be careful, Pink."

I said I would and resisted the urge to tell her Lou was about to make a liar out of her. No way was Mom done with men.

When I walked into Ed's room, he was awake but looked groggy. He stared at me curiously, as though he didn't know me. I guess he didn't.

"Hi, Ed."

Recognition dawned on his handsome, if slightly hairy and bruised, face. "You lived."

Remembering my day, how I had committed several first-degree felonies and wrestled with an evil Russian ho, I thought, *Boy, if you only knew…* "Of course I lived. Who'd have sex with you if I was dead?"

"I could think of a few—"

"Never mind, Ed."

His eyes narrowed. "Damn, you look hot. What's with all that makeup, and that hair, and the suit?" His eyes widened. "Jesus, Pink, I could toss a Toyota in your cleavage. Have you been running around town like that?"

Again, I thought, *If you only knew…* "Well, Ed, it's a long story."

He waved toward the hospital bed. "I'm not going any-where. Pull up a chair and tell me."

I glanced at the IV. "You got up again, didn't you?"

He looked away, toward the television, which was on but

muted. "Not exactly. The, uh, wound started bleeding, so they had to restitch it. I didn't like it much, so they gave me something to knock me out, and I guess Sally decided to be sadistic while I was under."

"How's the leg now?"

"I don't know. Just woke up."

"Does it hurt?"

"Like a mother."

"I can go get the nurse."

"It's okay. Just sit down and tell me what I want to know."

I did, but I left out the part about me wrestling with Sasha. He needed rest, and that would be difficult if he knew his life was still in danger.

Like he always does when I tell him a very long, complicated story, Ed didn't say a word. Not even an "uh-huh" or a "hmm."

When I was done, he asked only one question. "Where'd you mail the check?"

"To Santa."

He blinked. "You mailed a check for a hundred grand to Santa Claus?"

I waved my hand impatiently. "Not that Santa. The one CIA operatives can call as a last resort. The one whose identity is so secret he's as elusive as Santa Claus. Don't you remember him from when they were looking for terrorist financiers in Midland?"

"I remember. How did you address the envelope?"

"To Santa, care of the CIA in Washington. It'll drive them crazy, wondering why I sent it to him there. And by the time they get it, I should have enough information to exonerate myself."

He stared at me a while longer before he relaxed against his pillow and stared up at the ceiling.

Then he moved so fast, I'm still not sure how he did it. In one second he was half off the bed, his hands wrapped around my arms, his face within inches of mine. "You committed a fucking felony, Pink! Your fingerprints are all over that check, and your face, which even disguised can't hide who you are from experts, is now recorded on half the security cameras at that bank. I can't defend that!"

I was already pretty freaked out by his raging reaction, but my mind was completely blown when tears welled up in his eyes.

"Do you know what they'll do to a girl like you in prison?" He gently shook me. "Aw, God, Pink, why'd you do it? Why?"

"I wanted to shake them up, Ed. I wanted something to bargain with."

Letting go of me, he plopped back to the pillow and blinked rapidly, convulsively swallowing. I wondered how often Ed cried. I had a feeling it was rarely.

Well, hell.

Desperate to put his mind at ease, I said hurriedly, "Sasha isn't going to say anything about the check, Ed. If she does, the FBI will be all over it, and nothing of hers will bear close scrutiny."

He kept his gaze on the ceiling tiles. "One way or the other, the truth will come out about Sasha and Olga and Robert Wang. You'll be exonerated of the charges against you. I have every confidence that will happen, even if it takes Steve pulling rank to get it done." Then he turned his face toward me and his expression was bleak. "But nothing can get you out of what you did today. The feds can prosecute you for grand larceny. Maybe you can plead extenuating circumstances, and the fact that the check was made out to a reputable charity might make a difference. That you mailed it to the CIA... You've left yourself wide open for prosecution, and defending you will be next to impossible."

I heard the clicking sound of a light switch in my head. He was afraid that if it came down to it, and I was tried for my high crimes and misdemeanors, he might not win. I'd be sent to prison and he would feel responsible. By committing a felony, one in which I didn't try very hard to hide my tracks, I was at risk of going to prison, and he would have to stand by and helplessly watch.

Standing, I leaned over him until my hands were resting on his shoulders and my face was close to his. "I love that you're so positive I'll be exonerated, but, Ed, what if I'm not? You know there are innocent people in prison, and I could easily be one of them. What I did today was maybe a little impulsive, but if I'd had time to think it all the way through, I'd still do it. Sasha underestimated me, and lost a hundred grand for whoever is behind all of this. Whether it's Robert Wang, or the Russian mob, or anyone else, they're gonna be furious with her. She's running scared, and I'm confident she's going to tell me everything tomorrow. Once I know the details about how they've done all of this, I can go to the FBI and explain what I've learned. They'll look into it, verify it, and I'll be off the hook. And if it comes down to me on trial for writing that check, I have no doubt you'll win. If I'm not worried, why should you be?"

He reached up and ran his fingers across my cheek. "You

really do blow me away. How'd you have the nerve to waltz into a bank and forge a check for a hundred grand? Who does that?"

I gave him a crooked smile. "It wasn't easy. I tossed my cookies when it was over."

He closed his eyes and sighed. Not an impatient sigh. More like a "What the hell am I gonna do with you?" sigh.

Leaning closer, I kissed him, a quick peck on the lips.

He opened his eyes and said, "Gimme drugs."

"Are you in pain, or is this just an excuse to pass out so you can avoid me?"

"Maybe a little of both. My leg's killing me, and your awesome cleavage is giving me impure thoughts, which ordinarily isn't a bad thing, but right now, it's a little awkward."

I unbent, turned and headed for the door. "I'll go get a nurse."

Ed got a sponge bath and a shave, courtesy of Nurse Wally. *He* made me leave the room, much to Ed's chagrin. When I came back, I questioned Nurse Wally endlessly about Ed's wound.

He said it appeared to be closing up, which was good, and if Ed was a good boy and didn't get up and screw it up again, he could get off the IV in the morning and have more Jell-O. Ed looked rather fired up about that. I guess it's the little things, isn't it?

Wally gave Ed's IV a shot of painkiller and within minutes, Ed was sound asleep. Then Nurse Wally left and I sat down to wait for Cousin Bud.

The way Ed was lying in the bed, I can't explain it, but he looked almost pretty. I'd never before noticed how long his lashes were, or how sensually his lips curved. I wondered what he'd think about being pretty, and it made me smile. I could almost hear him say, *Yeah, I'll show you pretty. Take your clothes off.* Ed is maybe the most badass, hot guy I know. Think bikers and hockey players, and Ed's somewhere in between. If there was an award for Least Lawyer-like Man in America, it'd be no contest.

Well, I guess maybe Steven Tyler from Aerosmith might beat Ed out, but it'd be close.

But he is a lawyer, and a good one. He's a bulldog, and very sly and smart. He's also from humble roots, the middle child in a family of seven kids who shared two bedrooms and an attic. I think that's why he shuns the marriage and kids thing. It was why he divorced his first wife when she fell in love with the "let's have two-point-five kids and a Suburban" idea. Ed didn't want children, and assumed by the law of averages that any woman he married was bound to wind up demanding one or two. I kinda figured that included me. And I was fine with not getting married. After George, the Prostitute King, I never wanted to walk down the aisle again. Not to mention, I'd witnessed firsthand the worst marriage ever between my own parents.

So hanging out with Ed seemed okay to me. Once I was out of boiling oil and could go back to my life in Midland, I decided it would be good for me and Ed to date, like normal people. We'd just take it nice and slow.

An hour or so later, Cousin Bud came in. I couldn't believe it, but Ed's undercover bodyguard was the counter guy from Carmine's.

"What's your real name?" I asked.

"Remember, we don't use names at Carmine's." He hrugged. "All the same, everybody calls me Woody."

"You don't say."

He smiled and shoved his glasses up his nose. "Surely you've noticed that I resemble Woody Allen?"

"Yes, I have. And don't call me Shirley." I eyed him judiciously. "Don't take this the wrong way, but you don't really look like a bodyguard."

"I'm a black belt, and a sharpshooter. And my size is a plus because no one expects me to be able to kick their ass."

"I can see how that might be the case." I glanced at Ed. "It's very important that he not know why you're here. You're my distant cousin on my father's side. Bud, from Mendocino."

"Got it. And who are you expecting to show up?"

"It could be a blond woman, or a black-haired woman who looks a lot like I do right now, both with Russian accents. But truthfully, I'm not sure who all is working with them, so it's possible someone else could come in and try to hurt him."

"What's wrong with him?"

"Gunshot in his leg. From the blonde."

Woody looked around the room, saw the extra chair and pulled it close to mine. He sat down. "Are you staying here all night?"

I hadn't actually thought about going. Even with Woody here, I didn't want to leave. "Yes, I'm staying. But I am pretty tired, so maybe I'll try to catch some sleep in this chair."

"Go right ahead," he said. "I'll be right here, awake and ready."

* * *

When I woke up, *The Price Is Right* was just ending around eleven. Ed and Woody were up watching the show. Apparently "Bud" had explained that he was there by my mom's orders to keep an eye on me, which Ed totally believed. I told him, "I'm going to Macy's to get you something to wear for when they let you out of here."

"I've got my suit."

"It's ruined with a bullet hole and blood."

"Oh. Right."

Thankful that Ed was following my cues, because I didn't want Woody to know where I was going, I looked at Woody and asked, "You wanna go with me, Bud?"

He shrugged. "If it's all the same to you, I'll just stick around here until you get back. Not much for shopping."

This immediately endeared him to Ed, I could tell. Ed hates to shop. That much is obvious by the number of identical red ties he has in his closet.

I moved close to the bed and bent over to kiss Ed goodbye.

"Good luck, and for God's sake be careful," he whispered. "Even if you get her to tell you what you want to know, she'll likely try to kill you after she realizes the money's out of reach."

"Lou will be here at noon. If I'm not back by four o'clock, send him to look for me."

His arms grabbed me before I could straighten and he squeezed all the air out of my lungs. I started to wonder if he was going to let me go.

Eventually he did, and I left without saying anything else. Things were getting complicated with Ed. Very close to can't-live-without-you. Maybe too close.

Downstairs, I went to the ladies' room and freshened up

a bit. The plasticky stuff Mr. Swarthy had used to heighten my cheekbones was miraculously still in place, and I wondered just what the hell it was. Something used in the space program? I covered it with another layer of foundation and powder, and decided that the only thing I wanted as much as being exonerated was to wash my face and take off the hot, scratchy wig. I was pretty miserable.

The suit was a little wrinkled. Not that I cared. I was going to meet Sasha, and if she disapproved of my lived-in look, I couldn't give a shit.

Outside, I walked a few blocks over to Kinko's, where I made a copy of the China brides list, then couriered the original to Ed's office, with a note to his assistant not to over-handle it, to preserve fingerprints and to lock it up in a safety deposit box as soon as she received it.

Then I caught a cable car to Fisherman's Wharf.

I was frightened, and tried to stay angry to counteract the fear. It worked. Sort of. By the time I got off the cable car and began walking past the tourist and T-shirt shops, I was as psyched as I could be. Gulls flew overhead, making their weird seagull squawks. I wondered if they were telling the other gulls about possible food sightings. Hey, guys! Fish guts at Pier 27! Me first!

There were lots of people milling up and down the street, which was why I'd picked noon to meet Sasha. I figured the more people around, the less likely she was to shoot me.

It was still a quarter of twelve, so I wandered down the street, stopping to look in the windows of the shops, thinking I should buy Mom a T-shirt that said *Road Trip: We're All Here Because We're Not All There*. It seemed to fit.

At Ripley's Believe It or Not museum, I stopped and

picked up a brochure. Standing next to a streetlight pole, I leisurely looked over the pamphlet's pictures and descriptions, not actually seeing the *Mona Lisa* painted on a grain of rice. With my head slightly bent, as if I were reading, I looked over the top of the paper through my shades, searching the milling crowd for a tall, black-haired woman with high cheekbones.

From my left, I heard a man's voice. "I dunno how a kid of mine could be stupid enough to wanna go in there. Nothing in that place is real!"

And a woman's soft, timid voice. "Ripley's is the only place she wanted to go. What's the harm?"

"The tickets are a rip-off!"

Then, a wee little voice. "It's okay, Mom. Really."

I had to look. And when I did, it was like a rush back through time, to when I was eight and Mom and Lurch took me to Disneyland. To this day, I have no idea why we went. I guess Mom insisted, and Lurch agreed because she so rarely insisted on anything. It was, bar none, one of the most miserable experiences of my life. We practically ran through the park, and I rode a total of three rides. Lurch bitched about the waste of time and money, and Christ, didn't any of those people have something better to do with their time than gad about like a bunch of idiots, squealing and laughing?

I looked at the little girl, who had blond hair and blue eyes, just like me. I looked at her mother, who was very pretty, just like Mom. And I looked at her father, who was scowling so hard his face took on an evil cast—dark and forbidding. Just like Lurch.

They moved on past the museum, and I returned to my subtle search for Sasha in the throng of people. But I'd been distracted by the encounter with my clone family. That must be why my bad-karma radar never gave me a warning and I missed seeing Olga until she was within twenty feet of me.

Chapter 8

I began backing away, and she continued toward me. I
couldn't believe she'd shoot me in the middle of all those
people, and I knew I was right when I caught the glint of
metal in her hand. A switchblade.

Sasha had sold me out. No surprises there, but I'd been so
sure she'd cooperate in order to get the money back. Instead
she sent her goon to get rid of me.

I had no weapon other than my brain and it switched into
overdrive, searching for possible ways to escape Death By
Olga. I considered running into Ripley's, but then I thought
of all those kids inside, and how traumatized they'd be if she
knifed me to death in front of them. I darted a glance across
the street, to the fish market. Worst case, I could grab a tuna
and stave her off while yelling for help.

I turned and ran, but my pointy red pumps weren't designed for fleeing from murderers, and she was right behind me by the time I got to the first booth of the smelly market. I had no time to slow down and grab a fish of any kind, much less a tuna, so I just kept running, weaving my way through the swarm of people buying cups of clam chowder and big plastic baggies of shrimp and crab legs.

To tell the truth, I had no plan. I was so scared I ran blindly, my only thought to get away from the cold death in her icy gray eyes. Every time I glanced over my shoulder, she was the exact same five feet behind me. And in the way you know there's no way to avoid a car wreck, even though you can see it coming, I knew there was no getting Olga to change her mind. She was going to kill me and there wasn't a damn thing I could do about it. I considered screaming as I ran, but I worried she'd kill anybody who got in her way. She was that scary.

The end of the market gave me no choice but to leave the illusory comfort of the milling crowd and continue along the pier, the pointy red pumps making me stumble on the rough wood. I headed down a marina arm of the pier, between rows of boats bobbing in the water, and a gaggle of gulls must have assumed I was there to offer food. They swooped down to land on the narrow planking, further inhibiting my ability to run.

When I risked a glance over my shoulder, I saw a couple of the big birds swoop down to land at Olga's feet. She attempted to kick one out of her way and it pecked her leg. I stopped and turned, morbidly amazed when she slashed downward with the switchblade and cut the poor thing, causing it to flop about, its blood spurting everywhere.

Olga started to move around the dying gull, but before she could, the gulls surrounding me caught the scent of blood and moved next to the wounded one, pecking at it and squawking excitedly, flapping their wings, covering the narrow pier. She tried kicking them away, but they attacked her legs, their very long beaks breaking the skin exposed by her midthigh skirt. Olga's eyes met mine and we locked gazes for several seconds, just before she began hacking at the gulls.

Good God she was malevolent, indiscriminately swinging the lethal blade. The birds weren't intelligent enough to fly away and save themselves, but they were in a frenzy, which served to keep the blade from finding its mark very often.

Feeling bile rise into my throat, I wished with all my heart that I had my little Beretta Bobcat with me. I'd have taken great pleasure in shooting Olga right between the eyes. Even though I'd probably miss, hell if I wouldn't enjoy trying.

But I didn't have a gun, or anything more dangerous than a paper clip in the bottom of my purse. MacGyver I'm not.

While Olga was fighting through the gulls, I turned and scanned the boats docked there, looking for any sign of someone who might help me, but there was no one. There weren't even any tourists walking around the boat slips, feeding the gulls. Just my luck. I could see throngs of people walking up and down the street in front of the wharf, but because of distance, and the obnoxious boom-box music of street dancers, no one would hear me if I yelled for help.

"It's no good," Olga called from across the melee of the gulls.

"What about the money? If I'm dead, it's gone."

"You think me a fool? The money is gone already." She managed to cut another bird, sending the rest of them into screeching madness. Some of them flapped their wings hard enough to fly up a few feet, right at Olga, who held her arms up to protect her face.

"Did Sasha tell you I have the China brides list?" I yelled. "It'll be handed to the State Department as soon as I'm dead."

Despite the birds, she answered calmly. "The brides are Siberian, the grooms, Chinese. American government has no cause to care." Trying to push through the hysterical gulls, she managed to look back up at me. "You discovered the Kansas account and sent your lawyer to find us, but all you've learned will never be told. Dead people do not speak."

People. Plural. "You can't get to Ed."

Her demeanor was pure business. Even the attacking gulls didn't seem to scare her. The woman had all the emotional reaction of dirt. "He's being dealt with."

Oh, God. Sasha hadn't come because she'd gone to the hospital. I prayed Woody was able to protect Ed. No way could I allow myself to think otherwise. I turned away and scanned the waterfront again, yelling for help at the top of my lungs.

"You are ridiculous. It is your day to die."

The boat directly in front of me was *SeeLegs*, and had a woman's legs painted next to the name, along with Cap'n Johnny Charters. I didn't see Cap'n Johnny, but I jumped on his boat anyway, planning to run toward the front, then hop from boat to boat until I was back at the main pier, where I could jump to safety and run. I had to get to Ed.

I hurried around the cabin, along the edge, then stepped out onto the front of the boat, but those damn shoes were slick on the bottom, and before I could catch myself, I slipped across the sloping surface of the hull and straight into the water. It was so cold my body immediately stiffened, and only by the grace of God did I not gasp and suck in a mouthful.

The dank, dark, oily water around the Fisherman's Wharf marina was like my worst nightmare. I've had a deadly fear of water since I was four years old and Mom thought the quickest way to teach me to swim was to throw me in the pool and shout, "Swim!" I came close to drowning that day, and I never forgot my fear of the water, even after taking swimming lessons.

With a superhuman surge of energy, I swam toward the pier. I slid my purse over my head so it would stay with me, but the shoes were goners.

When I got to the pier, I reached up to grab something, anything, to pull myself out of the horrible water. There was nothing. I wanted to scream in terror, scream for help, scream for mercy, but the water lapped over my head, and I knew if I opened my mouth I'd swallow a gallon of water, and drown for sure.

Then Olga was there, reaching down, offering me a way out. "You have no choice," she said in her heavy accent.

Like hell.

I have no idea how I got the guts to do what I did next. I looked up at Olga and certain death, glanced back toward the boat slips and a slim chance of survival, then closed my eyes and sank beneath the surface of the water.

I swam through that cold, dark, ungodly creepy water, around the boats, toward the end of the slips, ducking in and out of the water, catching glimpses of Olga as she ran along and looked for me. It would have helped if I'd had a plan, a way to get out of the water and away from her, but I didn't. All I could do in my mindlessness was swim back and forth between the boats and around the boats, dodging Olga.

My teeth chattered, my body shuddered, and I knew I was

going to die from hypothermia if I didn't get out soon. But the only way out was with Olga's help, and I couldn't give up. Not yet. I held on to hope that someone would come along, one of the boat captains, or a tourist.

Still, in my heart of hearts I knew I'd eventually have to give up. I was tiring quickly, short of breath, and my fear of the water was starting to paralyze me despite my determination to keep a steady mind, to not allow my nightmarish phobia to overtake rational thought.

But I was so afraid I would drown, and the dread of not being able to breathe, of sinking to the bottom, where I'd be lost in the murk and no one would find me, consumed my soul. I began to cry, sobbing helplessly, desperate to get out of the water.

Without warning, in spite of my will, I lost my grip on reality. Fear is an intimidating thing, and my mind played tricks on me, convincing me there were monsters in the water, that they had hold of my ankles. I struck out for the narrow arm of the marina, between two boats, my only thought to get out, to save myself from the evil things grabbing for me, trying to jerk me beneath the surface.

By then I was so far gone it didn't really register that the woman waiting to help me out was going to stab me to death. Swear to God, by that point it wouldn't have mattered if I'd been fully aware. Nothing mattered more than getting out of the water.

When I was maybe six feet from the wooden pier, a tremendous splash hit me in the face and I was powerless to avoid swallowing a great deal of the disgusting water. In my terrified alternative reality, it was one of the monsters, coming out of the water to shove me under.

I clawed at the side of the boat, screaming and kicking my legs as hard as I could, trying to find purchase and only sliding back into the ghastly, freezing water.

In the midst of my hysteria, something bumped me from behind. I screamed louder and surged away, frantic to get far from it, still grasping at the glossy side of the boat, unable to get hold of anything, least of all my sanity.

Whatever was left of it went south when Olga floated close. Her eyes stared up at the sky, seeing nothing, and her mouth was open, allowing the water to slosh in and out. While I watched in horror, her face was covered by the water, then she slowly drifted down, toward the bottom, a circle of pale, sucked into the darkness. Mother of God! I went over the edge completely and consciousness began to fade.

"Give me your hands!" a deep, heavily accented voice commanded. Miraculously, a set of arms appeared overhead, along with a stranger's face.

More afraid than I could ever remember, I responded to the authority of the voice and raised my arms out of the water, kicking to stay afloat. Giant hands grasped my wrists and I felt my body being lifted from the water. Seeking warmth and solace, I moved toward the solid wall of humanity that had saved my life, not knowing or caring who it was. For the briefest of moments, the wall was welcoming and those arms wrapped around me.

"You are good now."

The arms fell away and the giant stepped back, leaving me bereft and afraid again. I blinked in the bright sunlight. His hair was the color of wheat. He looked like a Viking.

He turned and walked away.

Sliding my purse from around my neck, I clutched it and

hurried to get off the boat, to follow the Viking. But he was too quick, and I lost him in the crowd along the wharf. Who was he? Had he killed Olga to save me? He had a heavy accent, much like Olga's and Sasha's.

I got some very odd looks. Not surprising, considering I was wet, shoeless, and my fake cheekbones had slipped down my face, no doubt making me look like a chipmunk. Even worse, I could tell by the feel of wet hair against my neck that I'd lost the wig. I felt naked and vulnerable, and my focus switched from finding the Viking to finding a way to hide my identity. With a dead woman in the vicinity, one with ties to the Russian mob, I had a healthy case of anxiety. Her body had sunk, but it would surface again, and I wanted to be very far away when that happened.

I was still shaking with lingering horror and bone-deep cold. More than anything, I wanted to see Ed. I had to get to the hospital as soon as possible. Just the thought of anyone hurting him sent a jolt of rage through me. If he wasn't alive and well, I'd find Sasha and kill her with my bare hands.

Hurrying across the street, I ducked into one of the shops, and grabbed a pair of sweatpants, a long-sleeved T-shirt and the only shoes they had, which were lime green flip-flops with orange Hawaiian flowers on the soles. I took all of it into a dressing room to change, then used the mirror to try to fix my face. The cheekbones were history, and it was a killer to peel that stuff off my skin. I covered up the red spots with powder, amazingly still dry because I'd put all of the cosmetics in a Ziploc bag.

Everything else in the purse was waterlogged, but the purse itself was still in good shape. I thought maybe I'd send one of those goofy, happy customer letters to Kate Spade. *Your product is so durable, it looked great even after I fell into San Francisco Bay while escaping a hit lady with the Russian mob!*

I tried to rub the dried mascara from beneath my eyes, and when I looked less like Rocky Raccoon, I brushed out my hair and put it into a ponytail with the rubber band that had held the flip-flops together. Then I left the dressing room, the red suit folded beneath my arm. I'd removed the tags from the clothes, and when I went to pay for them, the clerk looked at me like I was nuts.

I moved my arm, indicating the suit. "A man across the street spilled a whole bowl of clam chowder on me." I spoke carefully, trying to keep the Texas twang out of my voice. I didn't want anyone to remember me as a Texan.

He nodded and gave me a sympathetic smile. I grabbed another pair of huge shades, and as he was checking me out, I spied a cap on a rack behind him and bought it, as well.

I walked out of the shop and sauntered down the street, looking like any other badly dressed tourist. Not running like the hounds of hell were after me was difficult, but I couldn't afford to draw attention to myself.

Halfway to the end of the block, I went into another shop and bought a big pocketknife with a cable car imprinted on the yellow plastic. It wasn't much of a weapon, but it beat nothing, and I had no idea what I'd find at the hospital.

As soon as I was off the street that fronts Fisherman's Wharf, I flagged down a cab and took it to the hospital, so anxious to see Ed that I sent mental messages to the cabbie to speed.

Once there, I took the elevator up, hurried toward Ed's room and pushed the door open.

I froze in my tracks.

The room was empty.

I'm pretty sure the woman at the nurses' station thought was an escaped metal patient. Not that I blame her. I was vay past frantic, my hands twisting the plastic bag that held he wet, filthy suit and my voice close to a shriek. "What have ou done with Ed? Where is he? Oh my God, he didn't die! 'ell me he didn't die!"

"Ed who?"

"Ravenaldt!" I pointed down the hall. "He's not in the oom! It's all made up, like he was never there!"

She was an older woman, and must have had experience vith panic-stricken people. She moved around the desk, closer o me, and said in a low, calm voice, kinda like how I imagine a horse whisperer would speak, "He was released about an our ago. He had several visitors, and there was some kind of ltercation. One of his visitors, a tall man, asked that Mr. Ravenaldt be released into his care. Mr. Ravenaldt signed a elease form, and very shortly thereafter, they left the hospi- al."

"What did the tall man look like?"

She gave me a look. "Very handsome. Dark and maybe a ittle like a thinner Robert De Niro."

Lou. My relief was so great, my already rubbery legs ecame jelly. I held on to the counter and asked, "This alter- ation—was anyone hurt?"

"No, but there was a small man who chased a larger man own the hall, into the stairwell. I don't know what happened o them, and it was just after that that Mr. Ravenaldt signed he waiver and left."

A larger man. Not Sasha. Who was it? And where had ou taken Ed?

The nurse was staring at me pretty hard and I knew she was trying to place me. My shades and cap weren't disguise enough. The longer I was out in public, the more likely I was to be recognized.

Anxious to get away from her, I thanked her and headed back to the elevator. Thinking it would be best if I left the hospital altogether, I avoided my usual pay phone and left the building, debating where I could go to call Lou, trying to figure out who'd tried to hurt Ed. If not Sasha, then who?

I glanced up and saw that I'd walked to California Street. Fingering the folded knife in my pocket, I made a snap decision to go to Sasha's apartment.

When I arrived, I buzzed her, but she didn't answer, so I punched Mr. Pei's button. He did answer, and I asked, in a Russian accent, "Buzz, please? I have forgotten my key." The door clicked. I opened it and hauled ass up the stairs.

Mr. Pei called after me, "Miss Valikov, you are good?"

I slowed and said carefully, "Yes. Good." It came out *guut*, which sounded more German than Russian, but I suppose Mr. Pei was satisfied. I heard his door close.

After a soft knock didn't result in an answer, I tried the key Mr. Swarthy had made for me. As he'd warned, it didn't work at first. I filed it a bit, and finally got the door open. I went in, locked the door behind me and looked around for a phone. There wasn't one. Dammit!

My pissed-off level was so off the charts, it's a wonder I didn't stroke out. They say all women have testosterone, that it fluctuates during the month. Mine must have been at an all-time high because I was consumed with the very unfeminine desire to get my hands on Sasha and hurt her. Badly. She'd tell me what I wanted to know, by God, or I'd strangle her. I'd had

e Silhouette Reader Service™ — Here's how it works:

NO POSTAGE
NECESSARY
IF MAILED
IN THE
UNITED STATES

BUSINESS REPLY MAIL

FIRST-CLASS MAIL   PERMIT NO. 717-003   BUFFALO, NY

POSTAGE WILL BE PAID BY ADDRESSEE

SILHOUETTE READER SERVICE
3010 WALDEN AVE
PO BOX 1867
BUFFALO NY 14240-9952

Play the Lucky Hearts Game

and get...

2 FREE BOOKS
and a FREE MYSTERY GIFT...

yes! YOURS to KEEP!

I have scratched off the silver card. Please send me my *2 FREE BOOKS* and *FREE mystery GIFT*. I understand that I am under no obligation to purchase any books as explained on the back of this card.

Scratch Here!
then look below to see what your cards get you...
2 Free Books & a Free Mystery Gift!

300 SDL EFX9

FIRST NAME

200 SDL EFWX

LAST NAME

ADDRESS

APT.#

CITY

STATE/PROV.

ZIP/POSTAL CODE

(SL-B-04/06)

Twenty-one gets you
2 FREE BOOKS
and a **FREE MYSTERY GIFT!**

Twenty gets you
2 FREE BOOKS!

Nineteen gets you
1 FREE BOOK!

TRY AGAIN!

enough of getting jerked around, of being scared out of my wits, of my boyfriend being threatened.

I didn't have a great plan, but I figured I'd wait for her, and when I heard the key in the lock I'd hide in the tiny bathroom. With the element of surprise on my side, I'd hit her with a solid object, like maybe the toaster, to daze and confuse her. I could tie her up with something, then demand answers to my questions. The money wouldn't work for leverage, and the China brides list appeared to be a nonthreat. All I had was death, and at that moment in my life, I was willing and able to threaten it.

I moved around her one-room apartment looking for anything I could use to tie her up. In the top drawer of a flimsy chest, I found fishnet stockings. Those would do nicely. When I pulled them out to untangle a pair, a stack of Polaroids came with them and scattered on the floor.

Glancing down, I drew a startled breath. There were four pictures, all of the same man. The same *naked* man with a very gi-normous Johnson. I looked at her extra-tall double bed, at the cheap bedspread and old wicker headboard. Yep. Same bed as in the picture. Man, oh man, I'm serious when I say he was porn-star huge.

The *ick* factor for me was way off the page. Not that I have anything against large penises, but knowing Sasha took those pictures less than five feet away from where I stood was grossing me out. I bent and picked them up to get a closer look. Not at his anatomy—at his face. He had a neatly trimmed beard, sort of like how I imagine Robin Hood's beard would look. Almost pointy. His hair was not quite black and his eyes appeared to be light in color, but it was hard to tell since the camera had done that red-eye thing.

Something about him was familiar, but it was difficult to focus on his face.

I shoved the photos back in the drawer. I would ask Sasha about him. Was he involved with the embezzlement? The China brides? Was he the one who tried to hurt Ed at the hospital? Or was he just a guy she asked up to her apartment so she could take nekkid pictures of him with his willy at full salute?

My nosy nature was in high gear, so I continued going through her drawers. The second one revealed some cotton knit shirts and a few nighties. The third held scarves, belts, a couple of squished-up jogging bras—and more pictures of the bearded, naked man. I was dumbfounded all over again by the size of the man's equipment. And the very odd predilection of Sasha's to take its picture. In my limited experience with men, I couldn't remember ever wanting a lasting memento of their penis, erect or otherwise. I imagined Ed's reaction if I suggested taking a picture of him, naked and ready. He'd say, "Yeah, I'll show you ready. Take your clothes off."

There were several pictures of Sasha, as well, but she was fully dressed—thank God. I left the pictures in the drawer and continued to the fourth and last drawer. It had black hair. A large mass of black hair. What the hell? It was a wig. Just like the one I'd recently lost to the monsters in the ocean.

I stared at it for a moment, then saw a tube of that painful stinging crap Mr. Swarthy had put on my lips to make them swell. There was a small container of the space program plastic stuff that works so well for fake cheekbones. And in the corner of the drawer, I found a contact case, with blue contacts.

Sasha wasn't real. Who the hell was she? *Olga?* Could it be that Sasha was Olga, in disguise? If so, then Sasha wasn't coming back to the Cable Carpartments. Sasha wouldn't be answering any questions. Sasha was lying at the bottom of the ocean. I shuddered at the thought.

Who else knew of her deception? He of the Jolly Pecker? Robert Wang? Why would she take on another identity? Was she covering her ass in case she was implicated in the embezzlement scheme? Sasha could disappear, permanently, and no one would be able to find her.

On impulse, I took the wig, the painful lip goop and all the rest and stuffed it in my purse. If no one knew Olga and Sasha were one and the same, it could work in my favor. I also swiped some of the Polaroids, just in case I needed to remember what Sasha looked like. I pinched a couple of photos of Mr. Johnson, as well. Maybe I could find out who he was. At a minimum, I could play a game of *Believe it or Not*! with Ed.

Someone knocked on the door and I nearly had heart failure. What if it was Sasha's well-endowed lover? I tiptoed to the door and peered through the peephole. It was the Viking. "What do you want?" I called.

"We need to talk."

Did he think I was Sasha? "About what?"

"Boating."

Oh, man. "Did you follow me?"

"I won't hurt you. Just let me in so we can talk."

I was curious, and there was the fact that he had saved my life, for which I would be forever grateful, so I pulled the pocketknife out and opened it, then reached for the knob to let him in. The man was a giant, and I could easily see him wearing one of those pointy iron hats with horns on either side. As he closed the door behind him, his pale-blue eyes moved to the pocketknife and he chuckled.

"You are not serious with that toy?"

"Why not?" I was stupidly offended. "I could at least poke you in the eye."

He didn't look the tiniest bit nervous. "You are either very brave, or very foolish."

"Who are you? And why did you kill Olga?"

"I am Alex. And why are you questioning my reasons? I saved your life."

"Yes, and I appreciate it, but I suspect it was only a side benefit to you."

He stared at me for a while, his eyes narrowing as he studied me carefully. "You are smart, Pink."

I stepped back. "So you recognize me."

His gaze went to the hideous hat, then fell to the DayGlo flip-flops before settling on my face. "I might have, but I already know who you are because of a mutual friend, a large woman we call Big Mama." He smiled slightly. "You are very well thought of. I was told to trust you completely, that you have full clearance."

I wondered if the Viking named Alex knew Big Mama's real identity. "Have you been following Olga?"

He nodded, then moved around me to walk the perimeter of the small apartment, looking in drawers, poking through the boxes still on the floor in front of the desk. He moved to the bed and lifted the mattress, looked beneath it and found nothing. Then he dropped to his knees and bent to peer under the bed. "You may not yet know it, but the woman who lived in this apartment was not Sasha Valikov. She was Olga Petrovich, the woman who tried to kill you. She worked for a crime syndicate in Moscow."

He stood up and sat on the bed. "I've been monitoring her

movement for some time, but it wasn't until last night that I discovered Sasha. I have you to thank for that. You swiping that money shook her up enough to forget herself." As he spoke, he leaned over and opened the narrow drawer of the tacky nightstand. His expression was gratified, as if he'd finally found what he was looking for. Retrieving a cell phone, he flipped it open, pushed a button, then lifted it to his ear.

Had Lou told him about the money? Why? I thought about Ed freaking out because it would be so hard to defend me. Now here was Lou blabbing about it to a stranger. Of course, the Viking wasn't a stranger to Lou. Or was he? Maybe I was becoming cynical and jaded and mistrustful, but who could blame me? I'd have to figure out a way to verify if he really did know Big Mama. In the meantime, I decided not to acknowledge the mention of money.

When he lowered the phone and snapped it closed, I said, "I don't understand."

"Olga's apartment is in Oakland, and I've spent a lot of hours there, watching her come and go. Since she returned from Washington she hasn't been there at all, undoubtedly because the authorities are looking for her. Through our monitoring of her cell-phone calls, I found her at this address most of the time. I noticed a dark-haired woman who lives here, but it didn't occur to me until last night that she might be Olga in disguise."

"I didn't know you could put a bug in a cell phone."

"Not a bug. We have equipment that can monitor where a cell phone is, as well as eavesdrop on any number we give it. With the monitor, we discovered that later tonight Olga was supposed to close a deal for a large amount of explosives to be moved from Russia to Afghanistan."

"That'll be a one-sided meeting, won't it?"

"Actually, no. We've got someone to stand in for Olga, a woman who can gather intelligence about the purchasers."

"So the reason you killed Olga was to keep her from going to the meeting?"

Alex gazed at me patiently, as though I didn't get it. "My intention was to keep her from attending the meeting, which I planned to do without killing her. It wasn't until I got to the wharf and saw you in the water that I knew I had no choice." He stared at me for several heartbeats. "You're very afraid of the water, are you not?"

"Very." I moved to a small café table and took a chair. I set my purse on the table. "I'm still not sure how you knew Olga and Sasha were one and the same, and how I have anything to do with the discovery."

"Olga screwed up and used the wrong cell phone to make a call, I think because she was flustered over the money you took. She had two cell phones—one for Olga and one for Sasha." He tossed the phone to me. "That's Sasha's. Last night, Olga dialed a number from her cell and spoke with a man named Gromyko. I was intrigued because I'd never heard of him, because she sounded so different, and because he called her Sasha. I put Gromyko's number in the monitor, and a short time later he made a call to Sasha on the cell phone you're holding in your hand. I put Sasha's number in the monitor, and within the hour, guess who called her?"

"Me." I looked at the phone in my hand. That was how he knew about the money. "You heard our conversation, so you knew I was meeting Sasha today."

"I knew. I also knew Sasha was actually Olga."

Looking up, I tried to make sense of it. "How? For all you knew, Sasha was a friend of Olga's who picked up her phone and used it by accident."

"Yes, that's just what I thought at first, but during Sasha's second conversation with Gromyko, he suggested they get rid of Olga because she was a liability. Not only are the authorities looking for her to question about the death of Ambassador Wu, but Gromyko was worried the Russian syndicate bosses would discover Olga was helping him and Sasha with their project and demand a piece of the pie. That's when Sasha gave herself away, to me, anyway. She said dealing with Olga would have to wait because she'd been called back to Moscow, in serious trouble for bumping off Wu. Gromyko said he hoped the Mafia would take care of Olga permanently because they wouldn't have to cut her in for part of the money."

"But Olga didn't go to Moscow."

"Of course not. She was supposed to have a meeting tonight to finalize a high-dollar explosives sale to a terrorist faction. As for the Russian syndicate, the only reason they'd care that Olga killed Wu is if she was paid for it, and from what Gromyko said to Sasha, she wasn't. It was a spur-of-the-moment thing. Call it honor among thieves, but there is a code that says people in the organization don't make money outside the syndicate. If they knew about Olga smuggling Siberian women into China and making serious money doing it, they'd kill her within twenty-four hours."

"That must be why Olga dreamed up Sasha."

"I'm sure of it, and it appears she went to extreme lengths to keep the two personas separate—from everyone. Gromyko definitely believes there are two different women."

"Who is Gromyko? The name sounds Russian."

"His accent is closer to Romanian, and in fact, he spoke a bit of it during their conversation. Sasha was angry and reminded him she cannot speak his language. He did not speak Russian, so they made do with bad English."

Romanian? I wondered how they had met, and how they came up with their plan. How had Robert Wang become involved? The embezzlement hadn't begun until recently, after the formation of CERF, but the bride sales had been going on for quite some time.

Alex shot me a sideways glance. "Did you see the photos in the drawer?"

I nodded and blushed.

He grinned. "That is Gromyko. He came to see Sasha last night while I was watching the apartment, and didn't leave until early this morning."

"You stayed outside all night?"

"I left around midnight and monitored their cell phones from Carmine's. It's impossible to watch around the clock, mostly because we don't have enough manpower."

"Did you see me come here yesterday?"

"No."

Leaning back in the chair, I rested my head against the wall and stared across the room at the narrow window covered with a dingy set of sheers. "You planned to keep Olga from attending the meeting, but it isn't until tonight. Did you decide to get her at noon because of my meeting with Sasha?"

"I didn't plan to pick her up until early this evening. I showed up at the wharf because it's my job to keep tabs on her."

Looking directly at him, I raised one eyebrow.

He shrugged. "So maybe I was curious. I'd have been there sooner, but there were so many people and I couldn't spot Sasha in the crowd. It was a while before it occurred to me to look out on the pier."

"Thank God it occurred to you at all."

"After I left, I called Big Mama and told her Olga is dead. Naturally, she wanted to know why I killed her, so I told her what I'd learned, and about you." He shook his head and sighed heavily. "Other than what I've seen in the news, I didn't know anything about you, or that Big Mama knew you, so I was surprised when she became angry with me."

Poor Alex. Got ripped up by the Boss Lady.

"She was very upset that I didn't call her last night, as soon as I found out about Sasha and your meeting." He gave me a crooked smile. "I reminded her that I did, and she didn't answer or return my call."

I knew exactly why Lou hadn't answered or called him back, but of course I didn't say so. I also tried not to think too much about what Lou was doing with my mother when he missed the call.

Alex continued. "She was even more upset when I told her what happened to you. Gave me instructions to find you and help in any way possible. I had a feeling you would come here."

"What, exactly, did you tell her happened to me?"

His gaze shifted away from mine and he looked almost embarrassed. "When I came around the market and onto the pier, I saw Olga dashing about, looking in the water. Then I saw her stop in a space between two boats, as if she was waiting for something. As I got closer, I saw you." He stopped and didn't say any more.

"It musta been ugly."

His light-blue eyes met mine. "I didn't give killing Olga a second thought. All I could think about was getting her out of the way so I could pull you out of the water. I knew she'd never let me do that while she was still alive."

The memory made me shiver. I wrapped my arms around myself and focused on the spotty carpet. "It's not dying that's so frightening—it's the idea of dying like that. Thank you."

"You're welcome."

Raising my gaze, I said soberly, "You also saved Ed from Olga."

"Ed, is he important to you?"

"Yes." I was overwhelmed with the need to see him, to feel his warm body next to mine, to hear his deep, steady voice. "Very important. I'm indebted to you, Alex."

"No such thing. I was just doing my job."

"Are you Russian?"

He shook his head. "Bosnian." His expression was inscrutable. "Actually, I'm an American who started out in Bosnia."

"How did you end up working for Big Mama?"

"It is not something I care to discuss. All I will say is that she saved my life and I am indebted to her."

I liked Lou more and more. And Alex's sincerity convinced me he was on the level.

Glancing around the apartment, I asked, "Were you only looking for the cell phone when you came in?"

"No, I was also searching for any documents she might have that would help with our investigation of the explosives sale."

"If she set that up as Olga, wouldn't any documents be in her apartment?"

"I thought so, but I went there from the waterfront and found nothing."

I stood and went to the boxes, dropped to my knees and began going through the first one.

"What are you doing?"

"Collecting information that'll help exonerate me. As soon as Olga's body is discovered, Gromyko will most likely clean out this apartment."

"Why would he do that? He will think Sasha is still alive," Alex said.

"True, but what about the police? They may take it all and stick it in some dusty evidence room. I need it for my defense."

"The boxes will be right here until the end of the month, when Sasha fails to pay the rent and the landlord comes calling. The police don't know about Sasha."

"Good point, but maybe there's something in the apartment leased to Olga that would lead them here," I said.

He shook his head. "I saw nothing that could tie her to Sasha." He glanced at the boxes. "I suggest you leave everything here, in case Gromyko comes around. If anything's missing, he will be suspicious."

Rocking back on my heels, I gave that some thought. "He's going to find out eventually that Sasha is gone, when he keeps calling and she never answers, or if he comes over and she's never home."

The Viking didn't respond. Instead he stared at me curiously, as if waiting for me to get something. After a while, his gaze went to Sasha's phone. "Perhaps you should listen to her voice mail."

Flipping the phone open, I pulled up the voice-mail screen

and punched the talk button. She had one saved message—the one Alex had just listened to. A deep, foreign-sounding voice said, "I expected verification of the completion of the Pearl job, but you have not called. I trust you were successful. Unfortunately, I was unable to expedite the attorney and will have to follow up. Wang tells me you still haven't transferred the funds, as we discussed last night. I will not tolerate insubordination, Sasha. If you've already left for Vladivostok, this is not an excuse. We want the money before close of business today or you will suffer consequences."

I started to close the phone and end the call, but stopped when I heard Gromyko say something else. His voice became different—softer—and what he said embarrassed the hell out of me. Sweet Mary and double ick.

Alex was watching me and I had to look away. My memory flashed one of the pictures of Gromyko and Mr. Gigantic Johnson. Oh, man. Finally, he came to the end of this message and I gratefully closed the phone, thinking I'd like to take a shower.

"Well?" Alex asked.

"Apparently, Sasha was supposed to kill me. I have to wonder why she came as Olga."

"I theorize she tried to keep Sasha as clean as possible, without any murders to her credit. It's a mental trick used by people who frequently don disguises. Helps to keep the personas separate." He glanced at the phone. "What do you think about Sasha going to Vladivostok?"

"I assume she was going to collect more brides. Now that she's dead, there are some Siberian women who just got lucky."

"Pink, give this some thought. Sasha told Gromyko she

was on her way to Vladivostok so she'd be free to be Olga and have her meeting tonight without any intrusion from him. Because I was monitoring her, I know Olga had a flight to Moscow tomorrow, where she would hand over the money from tonight's sale. Perhaps she planned to then travel to Vladivostok as Sasha, to take the train into Siberia and collect more brides to take to China."

"It makes sense—but what's your point?"

"Think about what you need to prove you're not responsible for the CERF embezzlement."

My gaze fell to the boxes. "The bank statement might do the trick. I'm the only customer of Valikov Interiors."

"When was the company started?"

"Very recently. There's only one bank statement." The significance of that hit me. "I suppose it's not unusual that a fledgling interior design business would have only one customer." I looked up at him. "But I never called her. Phone records would show that. No way can they prove I solicited all those antiques."

He shrugged. "You could be right, but these are professionals, Pink. They've thought of everything, and I would not be surprised if they covered that, as well. You can't count on it as a defense. You've got to go on the offensive, force them to make a mistake and use it against them."

I stared at the phone in my hand, my mind racing a million miles an hour. I wished Gromyko had said something more concrete, something that would give the D.C. police someone else to look at as a suspect. "If I disguised myself as Sasha, I could wear a wire and get Gromyko to incriminate himself."

Alex shook his head. "They were lovers, Pink. If you

get close to him, he will know in an instant that you are not Sasha."

I became very excited all of a sudden, and wondered why I hadn't thought of it before. "What about the recordings you have from last night?"

His expression turned to stone. "No."

"Whaddaya mean, no? You've got Gromyko talking about offing Olga, and Sasha telling me she'll kill Santorelli if I don't give the money back."

He shifted and faced me more directly. "The monitoring system we use is strictly for use by government agencies. Everything recorded is illegally obtained and would never hold up in court. Not to mention, taking the recordings to the authorities would expose our organization, which isn't supposed to exist, leading to indictments against all of us, including you. According to Big Mama, you've participated in some of her operations. Forget the recordings, Pink."

Dammit. I continued to consider my options, trying to figure out a way to use Olga's alter ego to my advantage.

In the quiet of the apartment, I heard the soft scrape of a key in the lock. My wide-eyed gaze met Alex's. He raised a finger to his lips while his other hand slowly withdrew a pistol from the back waistband of his slacks and slid it into his jacket pocket. He waved me to hide beneath the bed.

I quickly scooted under the box spring, and bumped my head against a Polaroid camera. Oh, man. I prayed the person on the other side of the door was no one more menacing than Mr. Pei.

I saw the bottom of the door as it swung open, heard the squeak of the springs as Alex came off the bed, felt the supercharged tension in the air. If there'd been gasoline in the room, the sparks would have ignited it.

"Who are you?" a voice I instantly recognized as Gromyko's demanded.

"I am a friend to Sasha," Alex said calmly. "And you?"

"None of your affair. How did you get in?"

"Sasha gave me a key. I am waiting for her."

"You lie. Sasha is away and not expected to return for some time. I ask again, who are you?"

"I tell you again, I am her friend."

I saw a pair of very nice shoes move toward the café table. "Is this yours?"

Shit! He'd seen my purse.

Alex said with just the right amount of offended male sensibility, "Of course not. I assume it is Sasha's."

"We shall see," Gromyko said. His shoes moved closer to the table.

"Put it down." Alex's voice was cold and menacing. "And step back, toward the door."

The shoes stopped. "A gunshot will bring everyone in the building."

"True, but you will be dead and that's your choice. Leave, or die. For me there is no difference."

I watched the shoes move to the door. I held my breath as the door slowly opened. I prayed he would leave without incident.

Without warning, the door quickly closed, the shoes turned and I heard what sounded like a heavy book slamming shut. Alex crashed to the floor, his big head turned toward me, his lovely blue eyes staring without blinking.

Oh, my God! The bloody bastard had shot Alex.

His hand still held the gun, scarcely two feet from where I hid.

I was debating whether I could get to it before Gromyko shot me when he said in a deeply ominous voice, "Whoever you are, come out from under there. *Now*."

Chapter 9

Alex's gun was close, but it might as well have been across the bay in Oakland for all the good it did me. Gromyko squatted next to Alex, the business end of his silencer pointed right at my midsection. If I reached for Alex's pistol, Gromyko would shoot me in a heartbeat.

"Why should I come out? You're going to kill me, either way."

He didn't respond for a moment. Then he said in a surprised tone, "Ms. Pearl, you are alive."

"No thanks to Olga."

Again, he didn't speak right away. After a pause, he asked, "Olga?"

"Tall blonde, heavy accent, makes a killer salad." He was confused. Olga was supposedly in Russia, getting her comeuppance from the mob. "Now she sleeps with fishes."

"You killed her?" His astonishment was evident.

"Does it matter? She's dead."

"What are you doing here?"

"Looking for Sasha."

"Why? And who is this man?"

"None of your business and…none of your business. Why should I make it easy for you?"

"Come out from under there so we may talk. Perhaps I will not kill you."

Yeah, I'd believe that as soon as it snowed in hell, or Lurch bought Halloween candy, whichever came first. Nevertheless, I couldn't stay under the bed forever. I'd die for sure. If I moved, at least I'd have a slim chance of escaping.

When I began to move, my head bumped the camera again. Inspiration struck and I grabbed it, hiding it beneath my belly as I scooted from beneath the bed. Without stopping to think about it, I rolled to my back and pressed the button, sending a very fervent prayer that the flash would go off.

God gave me a break. Gromyko was confounded long enough for me to have time to jump to my feet and give him a mighty shove, sending him backward across Alex's prone body. I leaped over him and grabbed my purse on the way out the door, but not before I noticed Gromyko wore a dove gray jacket, just like the one Olga had worn the night she killed Ambassador Wu.

He followed me, just as I knew he would, and I had a helluva time running in the plastic flip-flops, but I had enough of a head start that I managed to catch a cab and lose him over on Larkin.

I had the cabbie drive me all over San Francisco while I concentrated on keeping my shit together. My overwhelmed mind wanted to blow a circuit. My heart wanted to explode, filled to capacity as it was with pain and sorrow and anxiety.

When we were on our second time around the Embarcadero, I directed the cab driver to the Mark Hopkins Hotel. I had to find Ed, and I needed to call Lou. I still had Sasha's phone but thought it best not to use it.

The looks I got at the Nob Hill hotel most likely had less to do with who I was than with my horrible clothes. I ignored them and went in search of the house phones, where sure enough, there was a pay phone.

The area was low-key and quiet, and I knew I wouldn't be able to talk freely, but I had to contact Lou. He would know where I could find Ed, and I had to give him the bad news about Alex. He answered on the first ring, and the instant I heard his voice, a safe voice, I started crying.

"Pink, where are you?"

"The Mark Hopkins," I whispered.

"Are you okay?"

"No…not exactly." I choked back a sob. "Where are you? Where's Ed?"

"We're on the way to the farm. Ed will be safe there." He said something as an aside, I suppose to Ed. "Did the Viking find you?"

I squeezed my eyes shut. "Yes," I whispered, "but, Lou, he's dead. Gromyko shot him."

"Is Gromyko a dark-haired man with a beard?"

Awed by his calm demeanor, I said that he was.

"We'll talk tonight, Pink. Right now, you've got to get out of town. You have the car, right?"

"Right." It was still parked in the hospital garage. "All I need are directions."

He told me how to get to the farm, and I wrote it all down on the small hotel memo pad.

"That's about two hours from where you are. If you like, I can send the pilot to pick you up."

"No, it's okay. I'll bring your car." A drive through the California countryside didn't sound half bad. I needed some downtime to collect my breath and reevaluate where I stood and where I needed to go. "Can I talk to Ed?"

"Hang on."

Ed's voice sounded raspy, and I knew he was in pain. "Pink, how did it go?"

"Not so good. Are you okay?"

"Good. Great. Just fine."

"You're lying."

"Nothing a couple of painkillers won't take care of."

"When are you due for more?"

"About five hours ago."

"Why didn't you take them when you were supposed to?"

He didn't answer, and it dawned on me that it was because he hadn't wanted to be out of it while I was seeing Sasha. That was particularly heroic and awesome, I thought. "You can take some now, Ed. I'm okay. I'm good. I'm leaving San Francisco."

"Be careful on the road."

Lou came back on the line. "Take your time. Pay attention to who's following you."

I said I would and replaced the receiver on its hook, then turned to go. In my peripheral vision, I thought I saw someone dart around the corner. I went to look, but all I found was an empty hallway. Maybe I was losing my mind. It wouldn't have surprised me.

Outside, I had the doorman hail a cab, and directed the driver to take me to the hospital parking garage. Once I was in Lou's car, I finally relaxed a little—enough that driving through San Francisco, with traffic and buses and cable cars and pedestrians, didn't faze me. I was alive, and that made everything possible and nothing improbable. Not even going to China to kick Robert Wang's ass.

I wasn't totally prepared for the Santorelli farm. Maybe because I knew the family was wealthy, and by that, I mean stinkin' rich, I expected some kind of amazing house, a mansion of great beauty and National Treasure–style architecture. Instead, after I drove down a narrow paved road between two rows of cottonwoods, I was stunned to find a white clapboard farmhouse, with forest green shutters on the windows. I will say, what it lacked in interesting architecture, it made up for in size. It was huge, with two stories and several stone chimneys.

I parked the car and got out, then went up a set of wooden steps to the front porch, which was a wraparound with big ferns hanging from the eves and white wicker rocking chairs. There was even a swing. The door was painted green, like the shutters, and when I rang the doorbell, it sounded just like the one at the house where I grew up.

No one answered. I rang the bell a few more times, knocked as loud as I could, but no one came to the door. Frustrated, because I was certain Lou and Ed had had plenty of time to beat me there, I went against my upbringing and walked into someone's house without an invitation. Inside, I hollered, "Hello!"

Nothing. It was eerie.

I caught the scent of roast beef, faintly tinged with the smell of apple pie, and my mouth immediately watered. Maybe someone was in the kitchen and couldn't hear the door?

I went through a formal and very lovely living room, a large dining room, a big study with lots of bookshelves and old farm pictures, into a pretty sunroom at the back of the house, and through the large, cozy den. I wound up in the cavernous kitchen. Lou's little teacup Chihuahua, Boris, yipped excitedly and launched himself at me, so that I automatically held out my hands to catch him. He licked my face and yipped some more, and when I went to put him down, he whined, so I kept him tucked under my arm.

Standing there, inhaling the scent of food that sent me back to childhood, I turned slowly, wondering what to do next. That was when I spied another swinging door.

Still holding Boris, I went through the door and found another hallway. I passed a large laundry room, a small room with a flagstone floor that had to be a mudroom, and another room that I decided must have been Mrs. Santorelli's workroom.

Farther down the hallway was a whole suite of rooms, an add-on to the house, I supposed, judging by the difference in building materials. There was a small kitchen, a breakfast nook, a petite living area and two bedrooms. I wasn't sure if it was designed for household staff, or a mother-in-law suite, but at the moment it was Ed's suite. I found him in the second bedroom, at the back of the house.

He was asleep. I entered the room and closed the door, and when I got close to the bed, Boris caught Ed's scent and barked, all excited to investigate and maybe get some more licking time in. I scratched his head and shushed him, but it was too late. Ed's eyes opened a bit and he smiled slowly.

Raising his arm, he twisted two fingers together and whispered in a groggy voice, "Me and God...we're tight."

"Did you find religion at last, you heathen man?"

His eyes just wouldn't open all the way, and he finally gave up and closed them. I thought he'd drifted off again, but then he whispered, "You're alive, aren't you?"

"Miraculously, yes."

"Like I said...me and God..."

He didn't talk any more because he was back in dream world. I sat in an easy chair on the other side of the bedside table and watched him sleep, stroking Boris's soft coat while he lay in my lap and dozed off. It was peaceful and quiet and I was more glad to see Ed than I'd ever thought possible.

"Should get a dog," Ed mumbled.

"You can get a dog. I'm getting a cat."

"Hate cats."

"You're a communist."

He was quiet again, and I thought he'd gone back to sleep, but after about ten minutes he called my name.

"I'm here, Ed."

"Lou wouldn't tell me. Said you should tell me. What happened to you?"

"Why do you think something happened to me?"

"Lou was upset, and you smell funny. Like fish and motor oil."

"I went fishing and changed the oil in the boat."

He turned his head and opened his eyes. Barely. "Nice shoes. Do they glow in the dark?"

"Watch it, buddy. I'll sic Boris on you."

He stared at me for a long time, first at the shoes, then the sweatpants, then the shirt and the hat, which was emblazoned with a big ship's wheel and the words Fisherman's Wharf in orange letters. His eyes met mine. "She pushed you in the water, didn't she?"

"Not exactly. I sort of fell in, trying to get away from her."

His expression was sad. "Aw, hell, Pink. It's a wonder you didn't drown. You can't swim for shit."

In Ed-speak that meant, *Oh, my God, you poor baby, I'm so sorry you had to go through that.* "It's okay, Ed. I didn't drown and she didn't kill me. But if boating is a big thing in your life, maybe you better find somebody else. After today, I'm all done with non-chlorinated bodies of water."

"No worries. Not into boats, or fishing, or fish for that matter. Probably because the closest my family ever got to fish was out of a box from the frozen food section."

We fell quiet again and he continued to watch Boris as he slept on my lap. Then Ed got the funniest expression on his face—like he probably looked before he sat for the bar exam. A little anxious, and seriously concentrating. "Pink, I've been meaning to talk to you about something, and now is probably—" He stopped and stared at me, his expression never changing. I heard him swallow. "Not really a good time." Turning his head on the pillow, he stared up at the ceiling until his eyes closed and his breathing became even.

He chickened out.

I wasn't sure if I was disappointed, or glad. The Talk was inevitable, and I was unpredictably ready for it, but the timing was all wrong. He was on drugs and I smelled bad. Not to mention, my emotional trailer was packed to the roof. One more feeling to deal with and I'd spin out of control.

Watching him sleep, I feel a fierce sense of protectiveness, and something I wasn't sure was a good thing—possessive-ness. One word: *mine*.

When he moved his arm, he shoved the covers farther down his torso, until the waistband of his boxers was in view. And the waistband was not at his waist. Oh, man. He was asleep, so I stared. Ed is some kind of wonderful to look at.

He startled me when, out of the blue, with his eyes still closed, he said, "I work a lot of divorce cases, and one of the main reasons people get divorced is that they wake up one day and realize they have nothing in common."

"Are you saying that if we got married, we'd end up divorced because we have nothing in common?"

He opened his eyes. "Not exactly. I just think it would be nice if we found something we both like to do, and did it."

"For instance?"

He started listing out activities like bowling, horseback riding and clay shooting.

"Ed, this is us, in our thirties. We're not going to camp."

"Then you make suggestions."

"How about square-dancing lessons?"

"How about a suicide pact?"

"We could fix up your house."

"What's wrong with my house?"

"Ed, you have a wagon-wheel light fixture in your den."

"Maybe I like the wagon wheel."

"Please, God, tell me you don't."

"Okay, I don't. But I'm not into decorating my house. I don't even notice stuff like that."

"Then we can decorate my house—when it's actually mine."

He didn't respond right away. After a while he turned to

look at me with that bar-exam face again. "Has you mortgage come through yet?"

"I don't know. I haven't had a chance to check my messages."

His gaze was stuck to mine. "Don't buy the house, Pink. Tell them you changed your mind. If decorating houses is you thing, decorate mine. When we get back to Midland, move i with me."

Wow. I hadn't expected The Talk to start out like that Before I could respond, Boris suddenly jerked awake and looked toward the door. "Somebody must be coming."

"Probably Steve, looking for his First Lady."

Steve was here? I wondered why he was in California, especially since the Senate was in session. It wasn't like Steve to ditch his responsibility. "I haven't seen Lou, or Steve since I got here."

"Steve had to go to San Francisco on some kind of business and Lou went to check on a crisis with a hired hand."

"Is no one in the house?"

"There's the housekeeper, Koi. Vietnamese woman. Real nice. A guy named Rolly who looks after the horses. But he' probably out in the stables."

Maybe Koi had been outside when I came in the house.

Boris became more agitated.

I'm not sure how I knew it wasn't Steve or Lou coming toward Ed's room. Maybe because a bad-karma feeling hi me like a ton of bricks. Or maybe because Boris started growling, which was very out of character. Boris loves everybody, even if he is a shaky, nervous little Chihuahua.

I set the dog down and stood. "Ed, I think we need to get out of here. Can you walk?"

I heard a loud crash. Breaking glass. Boris scurried beneath the bed. "Scratch that. Can you run?"

Ed threw the covers off and got to his feet. "Follow me." With a strong limp, wearing only his navy boxers, he hustled toward a set of French doors.

Surprised by how fast he was moving despite his bum leg, I hurried after him, closing the door behind me, out onto a small patio, down a couple of steps to the back lawn. To tell the truth, I had no clue where he was going, and didn't question. He appeared pretty clear about his intentions, so I trusted him to find us a hiding place.

Until I saw the pond. He was headed straight for it. I hadn't noticed the pond before because it was set far to the west side of the house, behind some kind of big gazebo thing that had a gigantic brick barbecue pit on one end. "Ed, why don't we go over to that big barn? Or the stable. That looks like a stable. We could hide with the horses. In fact, we could get a horse and ride away from here. I don't know how to ride a horse, but it can't be that hard, can it? Ed, where are you going? Oh, my God, you can't be serious! I'm not getting in that water! It's slimy!"

A gunshot sounded from the house. Ed grabbed my arm and pulled me with him to the water's edge. "I'll buy you forty cats and take square-dancing lessons if you'll get in the water."

"I just want one cat, and I hate square dancing."

He continued tugging me and I wasn't sure which was more frightening—the water, or the gunman in the house. There were water lilies on the surface, which meant there were long, slippery strings of green stuff beneath the water. Long, slippery things equaled bad. Very bad. They could wrap around my legs and get tangled and pull me under. How deep was it?

"This is the only place no one would think to look. Now get your ass in there and stop being a big baby."

"I see where you're going with this, and pissing me off isn't going to work." His fingers were digging into my arm. No way was he letting go of me. "This is stupid, Ed! Your leg's gonna get infected, and then you'll get gangrene, and then they'll have to amputate, and then... Why can't we just go to the barn?"

"There's no time! And whoever's in there with a gun will keep looking until he finds us. I didn't come this far with you to get dead now, dammit, and you're gonna get in that pond."

He was right. "I hate you. I really, really hate you." I allowed him to pull me to the water's edge, into the squishy mud that instantly sucked my ugly flip-flops from my feet. He bent to pick them up, then stuffed them inside my sweat pants. He swiped my cap and it followed the flip-flops into my pants. "Oh man, you are so never getting sex again."

"If they're not hidden, anyone within fifty miles could find us. We might as well send up a flare."

On into the water we went, and the feel of the slimy bottom of that pond against my feet was like nothing else. I took it all out on Ed. *"I hate you."*

"You said that already." We were maybe ten feet from the edge, still standing, the water to my chest. "We're going to stay over there, where the grass is high and the lilies are thick. If anyone comes close, go all the way under and hide your face beneath one of the leaves, with just your nose and lips above the surface. Got it?"

"I loathe and despise you."

He ignored me, pulling me farther through the water until it was over our heads and we had to swim. I felt something brush against my leg and bit the hell outta my lip to keep from shrieking. Maybe I wouldn't have been quite so wound up, except that I was still recovering from the horror at Fisherman's Wharf. I couldn't believe, after living through that, that I was in water again. Murky water. I was shaking so hard, I don't know how I managed to swim.

When we were in the middle of the lilies, my prediction came true. The stems wrapped around my legs as I kicked through the water, and every nightmare I've ever had about drowning, and there've been a lot, came screaming to the forefront of my brain. It always happens that way, with long, slimy things grabbing at my legs, pulling me beneath the water, down, down, to the bottom, where it's silent and dark and, oh my God, so damn scary, I always wake up screaming and gasping for breath.

From the direction of the house, a man shouted, "It's useless to hide! Come out now!"

Raising my head just a little, I saw a man standing in the backyard, holding what looked like a rifle. Gromyko!

Ed raised himself up a bit and looked, then ducked and pulled me with him deeper into the grass and lilies. I could touch bottom there, and even though it was squishy, icky mud, at least my imagination didn't have the bottom pegged at thirty or forty feet.

"What can we do, Ed? You can't stay out here much longer, or your leg will be in seriously bad shape."

"I'm okay. When he gets close, do what I told you."

"Does it hurt?"

"Don't worry about it, Pink."

We had our arms linked. I slowly drifted closer to him and kissed his cheek. "I don't hate you, Ed."

He shot a quick glance at me before returning his focus to Gromyko's progress. "I know. I'm sorry it had to be the pond."

"Me, too, but you're right. This is the only place he won't look. Not closely, anyway."

We watched him go inside the barn.

"Who is he?" Ed asked.

While we waited, I whispered to Ed what had happened at Fisherman's Wharf, and later, at Sasha's apartment.

He asked, "How would he have known we'd be here?"

"I thought I saw somebody lurking around the corner when I was on the phone at the Mark Hopkins. But I was very careful about what I said, and I'm positive I didn't say anything about a farm. I asked for directions, but I didn't say where."

"What did you write them on?"

"A memo pad by the house phones."

"If you left the memo pad, it's like leaving the original. All he'd have to do is shade over it with a pencil. Oldest trick in the book, Pink."

"Well, hell."

Gromyko pressed on to the stables, going in one end and coming out the other, occasionally yelling our names, his frustration obvious by the increasing volume of his shouts and the way he sprinkled his words with Romanian. He went from outbuilding to outbuilding, even looked in a doghouse. After we'd been in the pond over an hour, I was feeling waterlogged, pruney and pretty damn cold. I figured Ed was more miserable than he'd ever been in his life, but he continued to assure me that he was fine and I shouldn't fret. The sun had set and dusk colored the sky dark lavender.

That was about the time Gromyko finally headed toward the pond. And that was when I had to gut it up and put my face beneath a lily pad. In the water, Ed gripped my hand tightly, whether because he was in pain or to give me strength I wasn't sure. I will say, it was probably only because he kept hold of me that I was able to not get the screaming meemies with all those slithering stems around my legs while darkness continued to fall. If all of that wasn't enough, with my ears below the surface of the water I couldn't hear anything. I knew Gromyko was yelling, but I couldn't make out what he was saying. Ed held my hand even tighter.

Suddenly there was light. Then I heard another voice, a deep, rumbling voice that seemed closer than Gromyko's, but I still couldn't make out the words. I heard a gunshot and thought, Holy God, he's firing into the water. We're goners for sure. Another gunshot, and then a big disturbance in the water. Was he coming in after us? I wanted so bad to raise my head and look, to know what was going on. But I didn't dare give away where we were.

"Ed! Pink! Are you here? Come out! Show yourselves!"

I could hear the voice then. It was Steve. He had to be standing only a few feet away from where we hid in the lilies.

"He's dead, Pink! For God's sake, if you and Ed are hiding, please come out!"

Ed squeezed my hand and I felt the water ripple as he lifted his head from the water. Taking his cue, I lifted my head. Sure enough, there was Steve, standing by the bank of the pond, a rifle in one hand, backlit by the lights in the gazebo.

"Thank God! Are you okay?"

"We're okay, but I think you're going to have to help Ed."

"You first," Ed said in a low voice. "I know you're scared to death."

I saw that his face was pale. I hoped and prayed the wound hadn't opened again, that he wasn't bleeding. "No, Ed. You first. I'm okay."

Steve laid down his gun and waded in to reach for Ed's hand. He put an arm around his waist, hauled him up and out of the water, then helped him to sit. I was struggling against the horrible lily stems and the sucking mud around my feet when Steve turned and waded back to extend his hand to me. I reached to take it, but before I could, something really did wrap around my ankles and pull me back into the water.

It wasn't the lilies.

As in all my nightmares, my paralyzing phobia became a reality and I screamed and screamed, until the water closed over my head and the monster pulled me deeper, toward the dark, silent horror that was the bottom.

Chapter 10

I sat in an old-fashioned tub, with lots of bubbles and blessedly warm water. I felt confused, because the last thing I remembered was reaching for Steve's hand. I turned my head, and met a set of compassionate dark eyes.

"Lou? What's going on? Why are you sitting on the floor, watching me take a bath? This is kinda over the top, dontcha think?"

He reached for me and smoothed my hair away from my face. I'd never, my whole life, been touched like that—almost as if he was talking to me without saying a word. My eyes welled with tears. "What's happening to me? Why am I here? Why are you here? Why are we crying?" His dark eyes were suspiciously watery and I heard him swallow hard.

"You needed a little help," he said. "Since there isn't a woman here to help, I volunteered."

I blinked and looked at the bubbles. "Lou? Why did I need help to take a bubble bath?"

"Sometimes people need help, even when they don't know it."

Why the hell did I need somebody to help me take a bath? Why couldn't I remember drawing the bath? Or taking my clothes off? Or deciding to take a bath in the first place? I wasn't even sure which bathroom I was in. I looked around, and still had no clue.

Decorated in chocolate and tan and apple green, it could be masculine or feminine. There was a large shower in one corner, and a long antique cabinet, with what looked like a granite top, spanned one wall. From the bathtub, I could see there were two faucets. There was a large overstuffed chair in one corner, with a smallish tea cart next to it, a footstool in front of it and a basket of books beside it.

I met Lou's gaze. "This is your bathroom."

He nodded. "It has the best bathtub, and it's bigger. And it's easier to take care of you here, in my room. I'll wash your hair."

"'Sokay, Lou. I'm a big girl and I can wash my hair."

"Let me help you get started." He got down on his knees and reached for a coiled silver hose that was attached to the bathtub faucet.

He tilted my head back and warm water flowed over my head. I stared up at the ceiling, painted a nice shade of tan. Or was it khaki? Then Lou was washing my hair, massaging my head with his big hands. It felt good, but I didn't smile or make any sound. I just cried. And cried. He rinsed out the shampoo, then applied conditioner. When that was all rinsed out, he took a terry cloth and washed my face.

Looking back, it does seem very strange, but at that moment in time it wasn't the least bit weird.

He got to his feet and reached for a gigantic white towel, which he held up so I could get out of the tub with some modesty. When I was wrapped up in it, he guided me to a small vanity I hadn't noticed before because it was on the same wall as the bathtub. I sat on the low stool where Mrs. Santorelli must have sat every morning to put on her makeup, and while I looked in the mirror and watched, Lou combed out my hair. When he was done, he handed me a T-shirt and underwear.

The T-shirt had to be his, because it had a Marine symbol on it. The panties were mine, a pair I'd folded into my backpack.

Lou turned his back while I dressed. When I was done, he took me by the hand into the dimly lit bedroom. The king-size bed was turned down, and there was a fire in the grate and a tray of food on one of the large ottomans before the fire. My stomach growled and I realized I hadn't eaten anything but a bag of almonds since early that morning, when I'd bought myself and Woody an egg sandwich at the hospital. That seemed like a lifetime ago. In a way, I guess it was.

I sat down and ate the food—a turkey sandwich, some grapes, two chocolate chip cookies and a glass of milk. No kidding. It really was like reliving my childhood. But I didn't think so at the time. Extraordinary, I know, but everything seemed just as it should be. Lou played with Boris while I ate, tossing a small ball across the room and waiting for Boris to go get it and bring it back, then throwing it again.

"You like dogs, don't you, Pink?"

"Yes, but I've never had one. My dad wouldn't let us have any animals. I had a cat when I was very small—well actually, it was Mom's cat. Blix. He was a mix. Dad ran over him." I started crying again, but Lou didn't go all mushy on me.

Instead, he handed me a tissue and simply said, "Accidents happen."

"I guess so. Mom was so mad at him, I don't think she ever got over it. When he wouldn't let her get another cat, well…" I looked up from the cluster of grapes. "You'd let her get a cat, wouldn't you?"

"Pink, it's not my place to let her do anything. If she wants a cat, she should get one."

"Do you like cats?"

"Not overly much. We have them here at the farm because they're good mousers, but for a companion, I'll take a dog any day."

It seemed important for some reason to know that he would have a cat. That he wouldn't make a big deal out of it and fuss at Mom if she wanted a cat. "But if Mom wanted a cat, you'd be okay with that, right?"

He held the ball in his hand, driving Boris crazy because he didn't throw it right away. "Pink, you may as well know, the chances of anything serious between your mother and me are slim to none. She's not in for anything long-term, and that's all I'm in for." He threw the ball at last, to Boris's delight.

Leaning back in the big chair, I stared at the fire and wished I could talk to Mom. But something in me wouldn't make the effort to get up and call. Subconscious, I'm sure. Hearing her voice would have sent me off like nothing else, and on some level I knew that.

Why did she blow off Lou? I knew she liked him. It almost seemed like she couldn't allow herself to be happy. Naturally, that made me sad, so I cried again. "Jesus, I've never cried this much, ever. And I don't know why. How stupid is that?"

"It's been a hard day for you. Maybe you should climb in bed and get some sleep."

It did look inviting. I stood and went to the bed and got between the covers. Staring up at Lou's ceiling, I heard him humming something, and the sound of the soft rubber ball when it hit the wall, and Boris's claws, clicking on the hardwood around the edge of the big rug that covered most of the floor. I heard the *hiss* and *crackle* of the fire and watched the flicker of light above me.

"How did you meet your wife?"

"In the military."

"Mrs. Santorelli was in the military?"

"Call her Jenny. She worked in munitions procurement. I asked her out and we dated about two months before I shipped out to Vietnam. I was twenty-one and she was nineteen. She got pregnant, so we got married before I left and she came here to have Steve. That was 1968. I didn't come back until he was four years old."

"And Jenny was here, waiting on you, all that time?"

"Not the whole time. After I was captured, she went to Washington and drove everyone crazy, trying to get me out. There are some old-timers in D.C. who still remember Jenny, hauling her little boy around, pestering people. She actually got in to see Nixon, cussed him out, and the Secret Service labeled her a dangerous agitator. Jenny thought that was damn funny, and when Steve was elected to the Senate, she had a dinner party and invited all the warhorses who had blown her off. Gave each of them a button pin that said Agitators Never Shut Up, the Santorellis Are Back in Town."

It was maybe the most romantic story I'd ever heard, and—wonder of wonders—it made me cry. "You really miss her."

"Every day. All the time."

"I think I see now why you like Mom. She's like that a little bit, isn't she."

"She's like that a lot."

I wished with all my heart and soul that I'd had a dad like Lou. Then I felt guilty, because even if Lurch is a son of a bitch, he's my father, and I was a traitor to think such things. But I couldn't help comparing. Lurch would never, ever do what Lou had just done. He wouldn't be compassionate. He'd shout at me and tell me to gut it up, that my fear of water was all in my head and I was alive, wasn't I? So what the hell was there to squall about? He'd probably go as far as to take me back out to the pond and toss me in, and tell me I had to get back on the horse.

That was what it took for everything to come rushing back. Cold fingers, in a vise around my ankles, that wouldn't let go no matter how hard I kicked and clawed at them. The inky blackness of the water. The absolute certainty that I would die, that I'd be anchored to the bottom, in the mud, in the dark, in the silence. And the suffocating feeling of desperation, of needing to draw a breath, and instead of sweet air, sucking in only filthy water.

There's fear, there's fright, then there's a kind of terror that does something to a person, that scars their psyche for all time. Oh God, it came back to me and I relived it, over and over, until the reality meshed with the phobic dreams and my mind took me to a place I never imagined, a place I pray to God I never go to again, a place I know is visited only by the insane.

I don't recall much of the rest of the night. Only bits and pieces, but every memory has Lou, front and center. He never raised his voice, never flinched when I struck out or kicked away the imaginary hands, never did anything but hold me, say unbelievably beautiful, calming things, and make me tell him exactly what was going on in my head. All of it. I wonder sometimes what I said, because I do vaguely recall talking about Lurch, and Mom, and Ed and Steve and the whistle-blower thing, and Sasha and Alex and Taylor Bunch. I was confused and disoriented; I couldn't remember who was good, and who was bad.

It would be a long time before Lou and I talked about that night. And it would take me a long time to understand what happened to me. Something like post-traumatic stress. I essentially drowned in that pond, literally checked out for a short time. I guess that will mess with anyone's head. Add to it my phobic fear of water and all that had happened in my life since the beginning of the whistle-blower thing, and I was ripe to go off the deep end.

When I woke up, sunlight filtered through the sheers over the window facing east, at least a thousand birds were chirping and Lou was right there, in a chair before the fireplace, reading a book. I knew, without asking, that he'd been there all night, awake and watching over me.

He heard me stirring and looked up. "How're you feeling?"

"My eyes are swollen, and I'm hungry, but otherwise, okay."

"Steve will be up with some breakfast in a little while."

I said that sounded nice, while I gazed at the painting of Jenny Santorelli. She was very young, dressed in a flowing white dress with flowers in her long dark hair, wisps of it blowing in the breeze. Barefoot, she stood in a field of wildflowers that merged into a blue sky. It made me think of the peace movement, of hippies and free love and John Lennon. And it occurred to me that Lou woke up and saw her that way, every morning.

Still focused on the painting, I said, "Is Ed okay?"

"Ed's good. Steve took him into Sacramento to have his leg looked at and they had to restitch it, but he's back now, and resting downstairs."

"His leg was bleeding again?"

"Yes, but it's better than being dead, and that's what he'd be if he hadn't run outside. He said you knew beforehand that something was wrong."

"Boris growled. Remind me to buy Boris a T-bone steak."

The little dog heard his name and barked beside the bed. I reached out my hand and he jumped into it, then scrambled across the sheets to curl up beside me. "What happened, Lou?"

"You up for it, Pink?"

I kept my gaze on Jenny. "Yes." I heard him drop the book on the small side table.

"When Steve got home, the house was empty and he suspected something was wrong, so he got a rifle and went looking for Ed. Then he heard a shot and saw Gromyko out by the pond. He circled around through the trees and fired at him. Gromyko faked a hit and went into the water, where he must have hidden in the lilies and grass. I suspect he planned to wait until everyone was away from the pond and make his escape, but it must have occurred to him that he needed to kill you. He swam up from behind and grabbed you. Steve went in after you, and saved you from drowning. Gromyko climbed out the other side. His car was parked out of sight, and he ran for it. Ed tried to catch up, but couldn't."

He stood and went to the window, staring out as he spoke. "Gromyko arrived before you did, parked behind the stable and tied up Rolly, the guy who cares for our horses. Then he came in and tied up our housekeeper, Koi, in the basement. After we found her, I sent her home."

"Is she okay?"

"A little shook up, but otherwise fine. I gave her the rest of the week off."

"Is that why you were the one to take care of me?"

He didn't answer right away. Finally he said quietly, "I took charge because Steve and Ed didn't have the first clue what you needed. As much as they wanted to help, they'd only have made it worse." He paused, then added, "If you say thank you, it'll piss me off."

"Can I say I think you're awesome?"

"That'll work."

I stared at him for a long time and thanked God he'd been there. Without a doubt, I'd have been in a lot worse shape without Lou.

"How did Gromyko get here before me?"

"I figure he chartered a puddle jumper to Sacramento, then rented a car." He sighed. "I should have called some of the other men to stay here at the house when I left. But Koi is an excellent shot, Rolly is an ex-special-ops guy, and I took extra precautions to set things up so no one would know where to find you and Ed. It mightn't have been so bad, except that Steve had to go into San Francisco and I had a problem with one of the hands."

"Don't blame yourself, Lou. Gromyko found us because I was careless. You told me to watch for anyone following me."

"You're a CPA, Pink, and not expected to know how to avoid a tail." He glanced over his shoulder at me. "Keep getting into the middle of things, however, and I'm going to force you into espionage training."

"Did he shoot anyone? I heard several shots."

Lou looked at Boris. "From the bullet holes, I assume he was trying to kill the dog. I'm sure Boris was barking his head off."

I laid a protective hand on Boris. "The man has no soul."

Returning his gaze to the window, Lou said softly, "I would really enjoy killing the son of a bitch."

I relaxed against the pillow. "Tell me what you know about Gromyko."

"Alex was working on it, but he wasn't able to find anything. We spoke with contacts at the FBI and the CIA, and they've never heard of him. I had the Carmine crew check out his cell-phone number, and it's one of those you can buy with some built-in, prepaid minutes. He registered it under John Smith." He remained by the window, staring out at the farm. "Things are getting out of control, Pink, and time's running out. You need help and I'm going to give it to you, no arguments. Tell me exactly what you've learned."

In spite of my intentions, there were now other people involved—people I cared about. He was right. It was no longer just about me. So I told him everything, and ended by sharing my thoughts about what to do next.

"They're bound to find Olga's body within the next few days, and identify her as an affiliate of the Russian mob. Her fingerprints are all over the apartment she leased as Sasha, as well as the Valikov Interiors records, and there are no fingerprints that can belong to Sasha because she wasn't real. Seems to me, the D.C. district attorney will have to take that into account and have it investigated further."

Lou turned and came close to the bed. Looking down at me, he said solemnly, "There is no apartment. There are no records. There was a fire."

"Oh, no." I thought of Mr. Pei. "Was anyone hurt?"

"A few minor cases of smoke inhalation, but nothing serious. The west side of the apartment building, however, was gutted. The police suspect the fire was started with an incendiary device."

I sat up. "Do you think it was Gromyko?"

Lou shoved his hands into the pockets of his Levi's. "That's my conclusion. The fire began late yesterday afternoon, not long after you called me. Gromyko started the fire to get rid of any evidence tying him to Alex's murder. Clever bastard, because he moved Alex's body to the apartment next to Sasha's, and that's where he set off the bomb."

My confusion must have shown.

"Gromyko wouldn't want the cops looking for Sasha to question about a murdered man in her apartment."

That old familiar feeling inched its way through my body, and within seconds, I was flushed with righteous fury. I looked across the room, at Jenny. Her pretty dark eyes seemed to be gazing right at me. "There are still the phone calls. Or lack of. Phone records will prove that I never called Sasha."

Lou shook his head. "Maybe you didn't, but somebody

did. The D.C. police looked at the CERF phone records and there were several calls made to Sasha's number from your office. They've also determined that the fake China Pearl invoices came from your printer, and the Kansas bank account was opened from your computer's IP address."

"How? Olga wasn't in D.C. when those invoices were printed, or when the bank account was opened."

"My guess is Gromyko was the one who did all the legwork in Washington. He could have gotten access to your office by subbing for delivery people or building maintenance personnel. You spent a lot of your time in meetings, and around town, drumming up donations. Your office was unoccupied for long periods of time during the day."

"There's still the signature card. What did the handwriting expert come up with?"

"You must have been tricked to sign it, Pink. It's a spot-on match with yours."

Good God, they'd thought of everything.

I told Lou about Gromyko's jacket, the one that was just like Olga's. "Now I have to wonder if it was Gromyko I saw going through the fire-exit door at Taylor's apartment building. All I saw was a sleeve, but it was definitely dove gray." I crossed my legs and set Boris in my lap. "I'm still trying to figure out why they killed Taylor."

"They did it to frame you, Pink. Olga called you to the phone that night at Steve's, but Taylor said she didn't call you. They left the invoices at Taylor's, to set you up for the fall on the embezzlement, but also, I think, because they hoped she'd taunt you with them."

My heart sank further. "Taylor died because I took the bait. If I hadn't gone over there, she'd still be alive."

"Maybe. You can't know for sure."

I stared up at him. "Why is this happening, Lou? Is it all because I found out about the account?"

"That's my take on it. Had you not found out about the Kansas account, I suspect they'd have continued milking CERF until the organization became obsolete and dissolved. But you did find out, and they had to make certain the embezzlement charges stuck to you, that the police wouldn't look elsewhere. Taylor's murder did the trick."

"What about the China brides? They can't make me look guilty of that, no matter how clever they are."

"They don't have to. Their only exposure over that endeavor is if the Chinese or Russian authorities find out. The U.S. doesn't have a dog in the fight."

Still grasping for something, anything that would help me, I asked, "What about Robert Wang? What about all that money that went out of the Valikov Interiors account and into the Wang Imports account?"

"He's the one supplying Valikov with Chinese antiques. Where's the crime?"

"So what you're saying is, I'm screwed."

He returned to the chair and leaned back with his legs stretched out and his head against the cushion. "You're screwed if we don't think of some way to catch them at their own game, to think of the one thing they didn't consider when they set this up."

"I think our ace in the hole is that Gromyko and Wang don't know Sasha and Olga were one and the same. If I go to China as Sasha to hand off more abducted brides, I can record Robert in action with one of those tiny little video cameras. If Robert is caught selling foreign women to

Chinese men, the Chinese government will lock him up for the rest of eternity. They may decide to execute him, particularly since his father was executed for dissidence. Once I've got the goods on him, I'll threaten to turn him in if he doesn't agree to sign an affidavit, then come back to the States and exonerate me."

"It could work, particularly if we agree to help him cut a deal for providing evidence implicating Gromyko. He appears to be the brains behind all of this. But someone else should film the video and serve as a backup, in case you get into trouble. I'll go with you as Big Mama."

I shook my head. "That'd be a dead giveaway to Robert. Except for Gromyko, it appears Sasha worked alone."

"Then I'll go as Gromyko."

I looked at him for a while, gauging the laugh lines around his eyes. "Gromyko is in his thirties. Can you look like you're in your thirties?"

"He can't, but I can, because I *am* in my thirties," Steve said from the door.

Holding a tray, he walked in the bedroom and set it on the nightstand. He was dressed in faded Levi's and a plaid flannel shirt, the sleeves rolled up, exposing his forearms. He looked nothing like a senator. He looked like a very hot farmer. He looked like my hero.

"Morning, Pink. I brought you some breakfast."

I set Boris aside, got off the bed and threw my arms around him.

"Hey! What's this?"

"Thank you," I mumbled against his neck. "Oh, my God, thank you."

His arms squeezed me tightly. "It's only breakfast."

"You saved my life," I whispered against his ear.

"It's okay." He rubbed my back gently, swaying back and orth. "Everything's going to be okay."

He was warm and wonderful and I was overcome with motion. When I finally let go of him, he smiled down into ny face. "Come on now, and eat some breakfast."

I dutifully sat back on the bed and he set the tray beside ne. I looked down at a piece of grilled toast with a fried egg n the center and blinked. "It's an egg-in-a-hole. Mom used o make this for me every day before school." I glanced up t him. "Imagine you knowing how to do that."

He shot a look at Lou and I suddenly understood. Leaning over, I peered around Steve, toward the door. "Where is she?"

"Talking to Ed. She'll be up in just a minute."

I turned to Lou. "You called her, didn't you."

He shook his head. "Ed did, but we all agreed she needed o be told, Pink. And we thought you might like to see her oday, after what happened."

I'd considered asking everyone not to mention the pond hing to Mom, so as not to upset her, but now that she knew, was actually in the same house with me, nothing seemed quite so important as seeing her.

Moving the tray, I got off the bed and anxiously headed for the hall, but halfway there, I saw her come through the bedroom door. "Mom!"

"Pink!" She threw her arms around me; I threw mine around her.

"Oh, baby, I'm so sorry." Her voice was clogged with tears. "It killed me, hearing what happened. And not being able to get here until this morning. Please, please, come home with me."

I started to tell her why I couldn't, but Lou beat me to it.

"She can't go home, Jane. There've been...developments, and her only choice now is to go to China."

"China?" Mom held me away from her and stared at me with a tear-streaked face. "Over my dead body."

"Hey, here's an idea," Lou said, coming close. "How about you calm down and hear the facts before you freak out."

She frowned at him. "Last time I looked, this isn't your daughter." Jerking her head toward Steve, she said, "How would you feel if your son was framed, had a contract out on him and was almost killed?"

"I sure as hell wouldn't stick him under my wing and insist he ignore his best chance at staying out of prison."

I waited for Mom to let him have it.

Instead she looked at me and asked, "Okay, so what on earth do you hope to accomplish by going to China?"

With Lou's help, I told her.

She gave him a look of disbelief. "And you're going to go along as Gromyko?"

Steve cleared his throat. "No, Jane, I'm going with Pink to China. I'll be Gromyko."

Chapter 11

I broke away from Mom and faced Steve. "Have you lost your mind? You're a senator, and if we get caught, you'll be impeached. Or whatever it is they do to senators when they kick them out."

"I'm pretty much headed that way now, so what the hell? I'd rather help you than try to salvage what's left of my reputation."

"Is it that bad? Really?"

"Damn straight. Four years of nonstop work down the drain. They're comparing me to Richard Nixon, only most of the talking heads say Nixon was a lightweight compared to me. I've heard so many lies, so many spins, it's damn near funny if it wasn't so infuriating."

Swear to God, my heart broke right in half, and the guilt trip I packed for was permanent. Steve's political life was in shambles, and his personal life wasn't far behind—all because of me. "What are they saying?" May as well hear all of it.

"I put you up to the embezzlement because I wanted the money for my presidential campaign. You killed Taylor in a jealous rage because you thought she and I might be involved. You and I have been sleeping together since long before the Marvel Energy scandal, and you only blew the whistle so I could come in as the conquering hero, which would help my campaign for president. We're the scum of America, Pink."

I moved to the bed and sat on the edge. "Jesus, this just gets worse and worse. I hate these people."

"So I've got nothing to lose by going to China. I want retribution from Gromyko and Wang for what they've done to you, and I want to personally beat the shit out of both of them for what they've done to all those Siberian women."

Mom and Lou moved to the chairs before the fireplace and sat down. Boris hopped onto Mom's lap and she idly stroked him. I noticed she was staring up at the portrait of Jenny. I noticed Lou was staring at Mom.

I refocused on Steve. "What about you? Because of them, your whole political career is screwed."

His smile was wicked. "Did you know my great-grandfather was Sicilian?"

"Are you gonna make an offer they can't refuse?"

"As soon as Wang sings and gets you out of trouble, he's toast." He pointed at my breakfast. "Eat up, Pink, so we can get ready. I can have a visa for us by early tomorrow, and there's a flight out of San Francisco to Beijing at ten o'clock in the morning. If we're going, we'll do this right. You need accent lessons and some clothes, and you're gonna have to work with Dad to get Sasha's face right. You'll also have to help me with Gromyko's face. I wish we had a picture."

"I have a picture of him I got from Sasha's apartment. It's in my purse, in the car."

He turned and walked out. I glanced at Lou, who was still watching Mom. "Do you think he's doing the right thing, going with me?"

"Doesn't matter what I think. Steve's always done pretty much what he wanted and any advice I give goes in one ear and out the other."

"If he asked your advice right now, what would you tell him?"

Lou gazed at me with a funny little smile playing on his lips. "My grandfather came over on a boat from Sicily. He was a goatherd with no education who couldn't speak English." He waved his hand, I assumed to indicate the world that was the Santorelli farm. "His son bought this land and built the first version of this house with money from questionable sources. Our family has a long history of jumping from one side of the law to the other, but after he started this farm, my father decided we'd be one hundred percent legitimate. Since then, we've stuck to that policy, except in rare instances."

"Are you serious?" Mom asked. "Your family was involved with the Mafia?"

He raised one eyebrow. "Kind of makes your white-trash ancestors look not so bad, doesn't it?"

She suddenly became very interested in Boris's ears.

Lou looked at me again and nodded toward the door. "It's in his blood to go after someone who threatens his family, who brings shame to his family name. So it wouldn't matter what I said to him—he's going to China."

When Steve came back he handed me the purse and I caught a whiff of San Francisco Bay. "Wow, that is funky."

As I opened the purse, the smell became stronger, making me nauseated, whether from the actual smell or the memory it evoked, I'm not sure. I handed it to Steve. "Would you get the pictures?"

He pulled out the wig and the other disguise things and dropped them on the nightstand. "Souvenirs from Sasha?"

I nodded. When he reached in for the pictures, I said, "Get ready."

"For what?" he asked, followed quickly by, "That's freaking amazing!"

To my intense mortification, he handed one of the four photos to Lou, who was equally impressed, though in a far more clinical way.

"Hmm, wonder if he had an implant? Not sure that could be real." Lou looked at me and raised one eyebrow. "Young lady, I'd like to know what possessed you to steal this picture."

"Let me see," Mom said, holding out her hand.

Lou had a devilish smile as he handed it over. I thought I might die of embarrassment.

"There's more," Steve said, glancing at each of the others, then handing them to Lou.

Lou kept his gaze on me. "You stole *four* naked-man pictures? Pink, what were you thinking?"

Mom laid the first picture on the side table, glanced at me and winked, then turned her attention back to Jenny and Boris.

I worked on my very best innocent look. "I only took them because I thought we might need to know what Gromyko looks like, and as you can see, we do. So it's a good thing I swiped them."

"He looks vaguely familiar," Steve said thoughtfully. "Maybe because he resembles Robin Hood."

"God help Maid Marion."

Downstairs, Ed was on the couch in the den, watching cartoons. He was wearing a pair of faded blue sweatpants, so I couldn't see his injured leg. He wasn't wearing a shirt. I took a seat on the edge of the large square coffee table and we stared at each other for a long time.

With Tweety Bird in the background, Ed said quietly, "If your mother doesn't stick with Lou, she's an idiot."

"I'm gonna talk to her about that, as soon as I get back from China." I waited for him to argue about the trip, to tell me I was risking everything by leaving the country.

Instead, he blew me away. "It's bumming me out I can't go with you, but with this leg, all I'd do is slow you down. Steve is better suited to this sort of thing anyway. Knows how to keep his cool. Me, I'd probably murder Wang and get thrown in a Chinese prison. Then where would you be?"

"On my back, bribing somebody to let you out."

"Well, there you have it. Me not going will save you having to prostitute yourself, so it's actually noble of me to stay home."

"Surely you don't feel guilty about this, Ed? You've got that hole in your leg because of me. I couldn't, and wouldn't, expect you to put yourself at further risk. Besides, going with me would make you a criminal, maybe get your law license revoked, and I couldn't live with myself if that happened."

"But it's okay for Santorelli to get kicked out of the Senate, or have his law license jerked?"

"I didn't say it's okay. But he's got a stake in this, and that makes a difference."

Ed looked as though I'd just slapped him across the face. Stunned and hurt. "Why do you do that?"

Confused, I frowned at him. "Do what?"

"Act as though anything I do for you is some kind of favor. Or duty. I've got news for you, Pink—I don't go around getting shot for just anybody, and for you to say I have no stake in this really hurts."

I got it then. Gromyko wanted him dead. His life was at risk. "Okay, I stand corrected and I see your point."

"*No*, you don't. My stake in this isn't about me."

He sat up and put his feet on the floor, so that my knees were in between his. His brown eyes, the color of chocolate, looked straight into mine and I could sense the tension in him.

"One of the reasons I dislike cats is that you never know where you stand with them. One minute, they're rubbing your leg, purring and affectionate. Ten seconds later, they're climbing up your leg and trying to take your nuts off. They spook at nothing and attack imaginary enemies. They frequently bite the hand that feeds them, then expect that same hand to scratch behind their ears." He shrugged and shook his head at the same time, as though cats were too bizarre to figure out. "You're just like a cat."

Ouch. I wasn't hip on his analogy. At all. "You just said you dislike cats. Is this your way of telling me something, Ed?"

"Yeah, Pink." He leaned closer and grasped my thighs, his long fingers splayed across my skin. "I have absolutely no clue where I stand with you. Every possible hint I might get, you manage to deflect, to turn it around so I'm left just as clueless as before. One minute you look at me with those ooey-gooey blue eyes and I'm thinkin', whoa, man, we are so cookin'. The next minute you act like I'm just some do-gooder guy who's taken pity on you, who's doing you a favor, and you're grateful. You know what it's like?"

So shocked that we were having The Talk at that particular moment in time, I wasn't really able to string together a sentence. I shook my head.

"It's like getting invited to a party, then having to stand outside and look in the window. You keep inviting me over, but you always slam the door in my face. And I don't know if it's because you regret the invitation, or because you think I only showed up to be nice." He leaned even closer, until his nose was a few inches from mine. His hands moved farther up my thighs and under the hem of the T-shirt. "Trust me when I say, my interest in you has nothing to do with anything nice."

"I know that. You know I know that. I just can't help it, Ed. You get too close and I back off. Then you back off and I want you to come back. I'm jerking you around. I see that, and I'm sorry."

"It bugs the crap outta me the way we're on again, off again. Hell, Pink, we've spent the night together exactly once, and had sex maybe three times, all on the same weekend. I can't think of any other woman I've been involved with that we didn't have sex all the time. In fact, it says a whole helluva lot about where I am in this that I'm even still trying."

"Am I supposed to find it romantic that you're still interested in me even though you can count on one hand the number of times we've had sex?"

While his hands gently moved my thighs apart, his thumbs slid all the way up, until they were lightly stroking me through the panties. "That's my girl. Make me out to be a bastard so you can feel righteous about shoving me away. So I like sex. Sue me. As far as I'm concerned, a relationship without sex is friendship, and no way do I wanna be friends."

His thumbs slipped inside the panties and I inhaled, a little shocked that he'd be so bold, right there in plain sight of anyone who might walk in.

Just his thumbs were driving me crazy, and I squirmed this way and that, trying to get away, then trying to get closer. I suspect if we hadn't been right there in a wide-open space of the Santorelli house, things would have gone way further than Ed feeling me up with his thumbs.

Nevertheless, I managed to go over the edge, and I don't mean the edge of the coffee table. I grabbed Ed's shoulders, bit my lip to keep from making any sound and let the enormous, pleasurable shudder run through my body. Having an orgasm via thumbs, while sitting on a coffee table in a T-shirt, with no kisses, no touching other than those thumbs, was definitely a first for me, and maybe if Ed hadn't looked so pleased with himself I might have been vaguely embarrassed, or felt a little awkward.

But he had a satisfied smile while he smoothed the hem of the T-shirt across my thighs, and I was anything but embarrassed. I wanted Ed. I was in love with Ed. "Just curious, but why now?"

He brushed his lips across mine before he leaned back against the couch cushions and stretched his legs beside my right hip, resting his bare feet on the coffee table. "You're about to leave the country with my archrival. I wanted to get some things off my chest and clear the air, but mostly, I want you to remember me when you're over there."

Before I could respond or argue, he said evenly, "I know ou can't stay away from him. I see it every time you look t him. Whether it's the senator thing, or because he's Italian, r a sad and lonely widower, I have no idea. But I do know hat if I didn't exist, you just might wind up married to him."

I rested my hand on his knee. "I could never forget you, d, no matter where I go, or who I'm with."

His gaze met mine, and he sighed. "I know that, Pink. Why lse would I keep waiting for you?"

Before Lou could take me shopping in Sacramento, I had o go through my Sasha transformation. It took him longer han it had taken Mr. Swarthy, but maybe that's because all he ad to go on was a picture. On the other hand, it may have aken longer because Mom kept pestering him, insisting he ad the cheeks too big, then too small. He finally made her eave.

"Go check out the horses and pick one. We'll ride later."

"I don't ride."

"Bullshit. You grew up on a farm."

Mom looked like she was excited at the prospect but unwilling to voice it. She turned and left without another word.

When Lou was done, I put one of Jenny's scarves around my hair to hide the blond until we could get to a wig shop. I sure as hell wasn't gonna wear Olga's. The ick factor on that notion was off the page.

Mom wanted to go shopping with us, but Lou said no, we had to hurry and two women shopping in a hurry was an oxymoron. He turned out to be about as excited over shopping as Ed. Everywhere we went, he was impatient, and whatever I tried on, he loved. "Perfect," he'd say, glancing at his watch. "Buy one in both colors. And shoes to match. Got it? Okay, let's go."

He spent close to five thousand dollars on clothes in less than two hours. I kept trying to go to less expensive stores, but he said Sasha would only wear the best, and I had to be like Sasha.

In addition to the clothes and shoes I needed to be Sasha, he insisted on two new Kate Spade bags and a wallet and business-card case because he said I had to toss everything that reeked of San Francisco Bay. He also bought me a pair of shoes that cost almost one month's rent on my Midland apartment, and a pair of diamond earrings I'd swear were fakes if I hadn't seen the price tag. Those sent the day's total close to twenty grand. I am not kidding. Lou appeared to enjoy himself hugely, and to be honest, I hadn't ever had anybody do anything remotely close to spoiling me rotten, so I thought, what the hell.

In the car on the way home, watching the farmland roll by the passenger window, I said, "Thank you, Lou."

He was gruff when he replied, "You're welcome."

We both knew I wasn't thanking him for all the stuff.

When we got back to the farm, I went into the kitchen to get something to eat and looked through the doorway to the den. With only the backs of their heads visible, I saw Steve and Ed on the couch, passing a bag of Cheetos back and forth while they watched *Two Mules for Sister Sara*. It was the part where Shirley MacLaine has to climb up the Mexican train trestle and set the dynamite that will blow up the train carrying the evil French ammunition, or soldiers, or whatever. Clint Eastwood is wounded, and drunk and pretty damn impressed with the little nun's spunk. And her very nice ass. I heard Steve say, "I had the hots for a pretty nun when I was in junior high. Probably gonna roast in hell for that."

"Hey, man, if God didn't want a guy to have the hots for a nun, he oughta not make her good looking. In fact, there should be a law or something against hot nuns."

I glanced at Lou, who slowly shook his head, then turned and left the kitchen. Maybe it was tacky of me, but I stood there and listened in on Ed and Steve a while longer.

"I always wondered how they go without sex their whole life. I mean, who does that?"

"Not sure, but I'm getting freakishly close to it."

I saw Ed's head turn toward Steve's. "Are you shittin' me? Since your wife died, you haven't—"

"No." He paused. "It's the senator thing. People expect me to be a saint. One-night stands tend to be frowned on, and somebody always finds out and squeals to the news and before you know it, you're a horny son of a bitch who can't keep his pants zipped. The only alternative is a girlfriend, or a wife, and that's no picnic, either." He paused. "Mostly because of you, you selfish bastard."

I tensed up, expecting Ed to fly off the handle.

Instead, he handed the Cheetos to Steve and said, "There's a lotta women in the world. Find one."

"Why don't *you* go find one?"

"I already did." He took the Cheetos when Steve handed them back. "You should let it go. She's gonna end up with me because I'm a homeboy. Where we're from, it's like a whole other country. The place is in her blood." Ed's head turned toward Steve's. "If she married you, she'd wind up miserable because she'd want to go home."

"On the contrary. She loves politics. Loves stirring thing up. How's she going to get that in a backwater like Midland You're wrong, Ed. She'll wind up with me. You should back off and go find somebody else."

"Wish I could help you out, but that's not gonna happen."

They fell quiet while the train was blown up, and then heard Ed say, "You're about to spend a lot of time with her alone. You won't forget our agreement."

"I didn't get to where I'm at by blowing off agreements Besides, the whole point of this is to help her. What kind asshole do you think I am?"

"You're not. And that's the whole problem. This would be so much easier if you were one."

"Same goes for you. In fact, it's a pity I'm hardwired to hate your guts. Otherwise, we'd be pretty good friends."

"Yeah. Pity."

I stood in the kitchen and considered all the possibilities about an agreement. My curiosity was killing me, and that's the curse of all eavesdroppers—not hearing quite enough to fill in the blanks.

When Shirley and Clint were on their way to the French garrison, I heard Ed tell Steve, "Your dad's an amazing guy. Last night, what he did for her…it's…"

"Yeah. I know."

They fell quiet again and went back to watching the movie. I went to the refrigerator to get something to eat. But my mind wasn't on food. Not really. I wanted to know what sort of an agreement they had, and what had passed between them the night before that had changed everything. Because for all their talk about hating each other, it was obvious they had become fast friends.

Maybe I'd been to hell and back, but the upside was that the tension and awkwardness between Steve and Ed were gone. Way gone. It made me glad on the one hand, because I really do hate confrontational situations, but on the other hand it kind of bummed me out. Their distance from each other was all that allowed me to keep some semblance of sanity. If the two of them started hanging out together, I was afraid I'd spontaneously combust.

Not that I was complaining. My God, what woman in the universe wouldn't die and go to heaven to have two men like Ed and Steve fighting over her? The problem was, I was in love with both of them, each for very different reasons.

But did I want a permanent relationship with one or the other?

Standing in the kitchen with a dish of Koi's leftover pot roast in my hands, I was stunned to realize I did.

After what had happened the day before, everything was different. I wasn't going to spend the rest of my life alone, out of fear that any man I was involved with might turn out like my philandering ex-husband. I wasn't going to keep my distance because I could get hurt again. What did it matter, after all? I died last night and came back from the other side. From here on out, I reasoned, everything was gravy.

Ed wanted me to move in with him. Steve wanted me to marry him. Clearly, I couldn't have both. I'd have to decide.

And I would—just as soon as Gromyko and Wang were exposed and brought to justice. Until then, I needed to stay focused. Otherwise, the choice would be made for me. Nobody would want me if I was spending my life in the pen.

There's no doubt I had some kind of weird daddy thing going on with Lou, and it became ever more apparent as the day passed. We spent hours closed up in his study, working on my Russian accent, along with some useful phrases and a down-and-dirty Russian geography lesson. We'd already gone way beyond the usual courteous distance people keep between them. My sojourn into the land of maniacs took care of that. I mean, hell, the man had seen me naked as the day I was born, literally and figuratively. What was the point in acting as though he hadn't? He felt the same way, if his words and mannerisms were any indication.

He sat on the rug, leaning against the seat of a leather chair, watching me pace back and forth while I tried to mimic the accent. "You're extremely intelligent, Pink. Why is this so hard for you? Listen to the tape again."

I was beginning to feel like Eliza Doolittle. Listening carefully, I repeated the sounds on the tape, then parroted the phrases.

"Better, but it's got too much British in it. Too proper. Try again."

Over and over I said the words, trying to imagine myself standing in Red Square, in the snow, wearing a furry hat, anticipating eating some borscht. I have no clue what borscht is, but it sounded very Russian-like.

When I got frustrated and testy, I asked, with a trace of a whine, I admit, "How come I have to do this and Steve gets to sit on his ass and watch movies with Ed?"

"Because Steve can mimic anybody on the planet. Has a natural talent for it. And he knows some Russian. And German and Chinese and Spanish and a whole lotta Italian."

"What about his disguise?"

"He's got it figured out, and he's using his own beard,

which is growing at the speed of light. The boy always did have a thick beard."

"He's got to work on his wardrobe, doesn't he?"

"Well, since the only picture of Gromyko we have available to us right now is a naked one, it's a bit hard to figure out what he might wear."

"His trousers were charcoal gray, a nice wool, and his shoes were leather slip-ons. Black. And that dove gray jacket."

"That's good enough to go on," Lou said.

After another hour, Lou turned off the tape player and shook his head. "You'll have to practice on the plane with Steve. I don't know how you do it, but you've still got that Texas twang in some of your words and it'll be a dead giveaway."

"Well, shit!"

"See? You just did it. How the hell can you make a one-syllable word into two? *Shee-ut?*"

The phone rang and he got off the floor to answer it.

Mom came in while Lou was taking the call. "How's it going?" she asked.

"Not so good." I filled her in. She just laughed.

I left her there and went to the kitchen for a diet soda. Steve and Ed were still on the den couch, watching TV. *Jaws* was on, killing any urge to stick around. I hoofed it back to the study.

But when I got to the door of the study, I stopped in my tracks.

"Janie, you're good at that martyr routine, but I can see right through it, and this is not about me or what I want. This is all about you, and some cockamamy idea you've got about who I am."

"Oh, I know exactly who you are. That's the whole problem. You thought you could argue your way into something, and when that didn't work, you conned me into bed."

Aw, hell. I should have left. Right then. But I couldn't.

"If this is the part where you play the offended, righteous paragon, skip it, will you? Don't forget who you're talking to. I was there, remember?"

"So it was good. So what? Sex doesn't make a relationship." She paused. "Aren't you going to respond?"

"How can I? Whatever I say can only be counterproductive. Would it make you feel better if I get angry and yell a lot? Because it's not a problem. Trust me, I'm close."

"You're frustrated."

"Whaddaya expect? I'm Italian and a product of the sixties. Hell, yes, I'm frustrated."

It was quiet for a moment and I told myself I should leave, immediately. Again I didn't.

Mom said, "I really don't get you at all. How can you be so sure of yourself?"

"Because I'm not twenty-five goddamn years old anymore! Neither are you! And you can tell me all day long that you want to finish things up on your own, but you're lying, and I know it."

"You're a bulldozer."

"Maybe I am, but we both know the possibility wouldn't even be on the table if I was anything different. You'd run from any man who didn't have the balls to stand up to you."

"Look, it's not just me we're talking about. I have my daughter to consider."

"Jane, she's thirty-one years old. Besides, that card's already been discarded, so don't play it. Ask her what she thinks, but don't expect her to defect. Pink and I are simpatico, and whatever happens between you and me won't change that." All was quiet, then he said, "Your reasons get flimsier and weaker. If you just flat out don't like me, have the grace to say so and I'll leave it alone."

"You know I like you. I'm just confused, because you don't know me. Not at all."

"I married Jenny within two months of meeting her—because I knew."

"How do you know about me?"

He sighed. "Because you've pulled yourself out of nothing and made a big something. Because you're ungodly beautiful. Because I just know."

"What are you saying?"

"Jesus Christ, woman, you drive me fucking crazy! Do I have to draw a picture?" I heard his footsteps crossing the wooden floor. "I'm in love with you! I don't care where you came from, or who you know, or how much money you've got in the bank. I want you today, and I'll want you tomorrow. All five feet six inches of you, every swear word, every funny look, every incredibly bright brain cell, and every little gasp you make when you try to be quiet. What's up with that, anyway? If you wanna scream, you should go for it."

Holy shit! Over-share. I heard more footsteps moving farther away from the door. Mom running away?

"You don't play fair at all, Santorelli. You come to my house and fix things. You ply me with whiskey and Buffalo

Springfield and make me crazy. You take care of my daughter when I can't get to her. You take a lot on yourself. That's all."

"Just tell me, yes or no—do I stand a chance?"

It was so quiet, I feared they would hear me breathing.

"You know the problem, you bastard."

"You're lonely and sex-starved."

"No."

"You're afraid I'll turn into your ex-husband?"

"Not a chance."

"Ah. Well, then the only problem I see is that you're hardheaded. Will it really kill you to admit you could fall in love with me?"

"It just might."

He laughed. "So don't admit it. Let's go for a ride, Farm Girl, and you can *not* admit it while I show you around and brag about how much land I own."

"You're such a peacock. You're everything I despise in a man."

"And you're a bad liar. Worst I've ever seen."

"I know. It runs in the family."

They were coming toward the door, so I did what all good eavesdroppers do. I hauled ass.

When they were gone, I came out of my hiding place in the sunroom and returned to the study. I turned on the tape player and started another round of Russian while I stood at the window and watched them lead a couple of horses out of the stable. And I didn't look away when he kissed her. Instead, I thanked God for Lou Santorelli. He had to be a gift. For both of us.

Chapter 12

Because Steve and I were on an international flight, we had to arrive at the airport two hours before departure. To be on the safe side, we got there three hours before. I played my "I am Sasha, the evil Russian ho" head game, and Steve was a very convincing Gromyko—at least, he sounded authentically Russian. His redefined face, along with the beard, effectively disguised him.

We got through check-in with no problems at all. Scary, really, how all of our fake documents passed without so much as a blink from anyone who looked at them. Despite Gromyko's cleverness at moving Alex's body to another apartment before he blew the building, I worried I'd be detained for questioning by the police. I'd made an attempt to cover my ass by calling Mr. Pei, as Sasha, on her phone, and asking him about the explosion, telling him I was out of town and unable to be there to see about my salvaged belongings. He told me there was nothing left, that he would convey my concerns to the authorities. I hoped it would keep me from being stopped at the airport, but I was nervous until we were through security and had our boarding passes.

In the clear, we went to one of the crowded airport eateries and had coffee and watched CNN's *Headline News*. Not gonna lie—it was very strange to see myself on television and hear the awful things people said about me. Same for Steve. Knowing what kind of man he is, and how much he'd done for America just in the short time he'd been in the Senate, it turned my stomach to see how badly he was maligned. One thing's sure—from then on, I've never listened to anything on the news without a saltshaker nearby.

There was one lonely voice in the crowd who pledged support for Steve, and that was Madeline Davis. In light of the fact that she was his main competition for nomination as their party's presidential candidate, I thought it was pretty big of her to stand up and say she wasn't willing to believe Steve Santorelli was a crook. I said so to Steve.

"Madeline's a sharp woman," he said quietly, to avoid others overhearing, "but she gets most of her information about me from her assistant, who's a running buddy of my assistant. You've met Holly, so you know what she's like."

"Do you think the only reason Madeline's standing up for you is that her assistant tells her what Holly says about you?" I asked.

"I'm not that naive, Pink. Madeline wants to be president, and she's convinced she'll get the nomination, whether or not I'm in the running. I think she's doing this so she'll look like she's being fair and square."

"It's all a put-on?"

"Maybe not entirely. She and I are friends, and we've worked on a couple of bills together. But I have other friends on the Hill who don't believe I'm a crook—and notice how they're not saying anything? It's in Madeline's best interest to support me, because it makes her look magnanimous. And let's face it—even after we prove you're not guilty, my chances of nomination are zero. So what has she got to lose by supporting me? If I did turn out to be guilty of aiding and abetting your criminal activity, she would say how sad she was to know I'd strayed so far from truth and honor, yada, yada, yada."

I admit, I was surprised. "Steve, I had no idea you could be such a cynic."

He took a sip of his coffee and set the cup down easily, then turned it round and round. "Washington does that to you." He looked up from the cup and shrugged. "But it's like I've always told you—I don't care what the news reports or other people say, or how I'm perceived. So long as I can look in the mirror every day and know I did the right thing, that I didn't sell out, that I did the best job I could to represent the people of California, everything else is just a lot of noise."

"It's gonna kill you to lose your seat, isn't it."

"I'm not going to lose my seat. We're going to get the people who did this to you, and the whole world will know that you're not a scheming, evil woman, and that my interest in you isn't anything other than a man who wants a woman. When that happens, this will blow over and I'll go back to doing the job I was elected to do. Maybe I won't win reelection, but I'll cross that bridge when I get to it." He glanced at his watch. "Right now, we need to go to China."

He stood and offered his hand and we walked toward the boarding gate. I thought all over again that Steve would make an amazing president. And I hoped he was wrong, that once I was cleared, thereby clearing his name of the stink from collusion, the American people would be big enough to let it go, to see him for who he was—a deeply patriotic man who could lead the country with honor and integrity.

The flight to Beijing wasn't as bad as I had remembered. Maybe because we left from San Francisco, which cut several hours from the flying time. Then again, maybe the flight wasn't so bad because we sat in first class—a first for me. After being served champagne, eggs Benedict and fresh peaches, I was actually able to lie back and get some sleep. When I woke up, Angelina Jolie was kicking somebody's ass on the little drop-down screen above the seat. That reminded me to put more of the stinging crap on my lips. When I was done, I noticed Steve staring at me.

"What?"

"You already have great lips," he said in his psuedo-Russian accent. "Why do you do that for?"

"Because Sasha has—*had*—really big lips. Like Angelina."

He leaned close and I knew he was going to kiss me. I drew back quickly. "You will so regret it," I whispered in my normal voice. "Trust me. This stuff hurts like hell."

His frown spoke volumes. He sat back in his seat and closed his eyes.

I'd hurt his feelings. He didn't believe me. Well, fine. I grabbed his shirt, hauled him close and laid one on him. Within seconds, he jerked away from me, his eyes wide and his fingers reaching for his lips. I held them still. "Don't touch it, or your fingers will burn, too," I whispered.

"Sweet Mary! What is that stuff?"

"I think it's bee venom."

"Killer bees from hell?" He pulled a tissue from the little box between our seats and wiped his lips.

"I warned you."

"Then gave me the kiss of death, anyway?"

"Your feelings were hurt. I had to prove a point."

"Better my feelings than my face."

"Oh, stop whining. I've gotta use this stuff for as long as we're in China."

He glared at the little tube in my hand. "You can't do that. It's cruel and unusual pain."

"I don't mind."

"You misunderstand. If I can't kiss you the whole time we're in China, that's cruel and unusual pain for me."

"Gosh, Steve, you're so thoughtful and romantic."

"I try." He gave me a hard look. "You've got to remember not to call me Steve. And don't slip back into Texan. Stick with the accent, and remember who you're supposed to be, all the time."

Sitting up a little straighter, I tugged down the tight jacket of my spankin' new hot-pink suit until my cleavage was prominent. Then I gave him a let's-get-naked look. "Gromyko, where is my camera? I will take your photograph." I added a Russian phrase I'd learned on the Internet before we left the farm. Loosely translated, it meant something very nasty.

Steve's eyes widened and he leaned toward me. "Do you have any idea what you just said?"

I whispered, "Didn't I say you have a gi-normous Johnson?"

"Not hardly," he replied, also in a whisper. "You just suggested we have sex while standing up." He reached over and touched my cheek. "Backward."

"Oh." I cleared my throat and glanced around the first-class cabin, thankful that everyone appeared to be asleep.

When I looked at Steve again, he was smiling and shaking his head. "Maybe you better stick to English, with an accent." He raised one dark eyebrow. "Unless, of course, you meant what you said, in which case, please speak Russian to me some more."

Swear to God, I blushed. "Can't say that I've ever done that before."

"Said something dirty in Russian?"

"Asked someone to have standing-up, backward sex."

His incredible dark eyes looked right into mine and he whispered something in Russian.

Intrigued, I leaned an elbow on my armrest so that our faces were close enough that I could see every whisker of his beard and every lash fringing his eyes. "Did you just say something dirty?"

"Yes, but I'm a little fuzzy on which kind of dirt. I either asked you to give me a blow job with whipped cream, or I asked you to vacuum the dairy."

"I hate vacuuming."

"But you like whipped cream."

"Who doesn't?"

He sat back and closed his eyes. "Behave, Sasha. I am very hungry, and it's unkind to talk of food to a starving man."

I also sat back, feeling bad for teasing him. Cruel and unusual pain indeed.

* * *

We made it through Chinese customs with no problem at all. With stylish luggage and expensive jewelry, we looked like nothing more than a wealthy tourist couple with funny accents. Steve had arranged for a car and driver, and Mr. Jong was waiting for us in a crowd of drivers on the lower level of the Beijing airport, holding a cardboard sign that read Gromyko. It was almost eight o'clock in the morning, and the airport was jam-packed. We jostled through the crowd on the heels of Mr. Jong, until we made it outside.

The sky was gray, the color of dirt. The rising sun valiantly tried to shine through the murk, but it was a losing proposition in Beijing, despite the absence of any clouds. Even though I'd been there before, I was shocked all over again by the pollution. During my first visit to China, Aunt Fred took Mom and me to the Great Wall and I was disappointed that my eyes couldn't follow the path of the wall across the mountains. The distant snake of cream-colored brick faded into the fog of pollution.

I'd read that China was working on the problem, especially in anticipation of the Olympics, but from what I saw that morning, they weren't making much progress.

After a porter brought the luggage to the car, a black Audi, Mr. Jong helped him load it in the trunk. When we were all in the car, Steve immediately began telling Mr. Jong where to go—in perfect Chinese.

I stared at him, astonished all over again. I leaned close and said, "Is there any language you *don't* speak?"

His dark eyes met mine. "I'm a little slow when it comes to Pig Latin."

"Very funny. But really, how'd you learn Chinese?"

"Someday, when it doesn't make a difference, I'll tell you a few things. For now, you'll just have to be curious."

I sat back, looked out the window and let my curiosity and imagination run rampant. Steve was a mystery. Had been from the get-go. And I wondered if that was part of the attraction. I listened to him carry on an animated conversation with Mr. Jong, catching a few words here and there but really having no clue what they were talking about, and having even less of a clue what sort of man I was with.

"Have you been to China?" I asked.

"Yes." That was it. Just, *yes*. No story about when, or why. Just a bald *yes*.

Our first stop was the hotel, the Holiday Inn Lido, on the airport road. A lot of expats stay there, and many actually live there, in the section of the hotel that contains apartments. Unlike American Holiday Inns that are nice but pretty basic, the Lido in Beijing is more of a luxury hotel. It's large, and has a knowledgeable, English-speaking concierge and a pretty good restaurant that serves American food.

Our room was large and airy, if a little dated, and furnished in early-eighties light wood, with pale rose and forest green bedding and upholstery. I noted there was only one bed. King-size. While I unpacked, I considered asking Steve if he'd done that on purpose, but decided I'd ask later. If it was going to be awkward, I'd rather it be at the moment of truth—instead of while I was gearing up for my first performance as Sasha.

Still, the bed sort of loomed there, in the forefront of my consciousness. How could it not? We passed each other, coming and going from the closet to the bed, where our bags were lying open. When the last article of clothing had been ung up, I checked myself in the mirror while Steve sat on he bed and watched.

"More poison?"

I grimaced when the stinging sensation traveled to my brain, alerting it to severe pain. "You in for a blow job now?"

In the mirror I saw him flinch. "God help me, and I can't believe I'm gonna say this, but I'll have to pass. Someday I'd ike to have children, and I'm pretty sure that stuff would kill my chances of procreation."

"It's not permanent. And it does cause swelling."

He watched while I ran a comb through the short black hair of the wig. "That might explain Gromyko's curiously arge anatomy."

We left the hotel courtesy of Mr. Jong, who had a winning smile and gracious, almost formal manner. In the car, I called Aunt Fred from Steve's cell phone. She answered on the first ring.

"Are you in Beijing, Pink?"

"We're here."

"Can I tell you that it's a little bit of a rush, seeing the name of a U.S. senator on my cell phone?"

I smiled, glad to know she hadn't lost her love of the small things in life. My aunt Fred is maybe the happiest woman on earth. I used to think I would be just like her when I grew up. After checking out of life two days ago, I'd decided to grow up right away. "Thanks for helping us."

"Are you kidding? The minute you called and told me what that skunk Wang is up to, you couldn't keep me from it. Your uncle Alvin will have plenty to say about it, that's for sure. If not for Alvin, Robert would be back in the States, flipping burgers."

"You didn't tell Uncle Alvin, did you?"

"Of course not, but this is all gonna come out soon, and once it does, Robert won't have a friend left on two continents. Now, let's get started. You wanted me to get something to verify he's the same Robert Wang who owns that account, and I did. Last night, I rifled through his office and found verifications from the bank for deposits to the same account number you gave me. No doubt about it, Pink. He's your guy."

"Is he in his office right now?"

"No, he's out with your old boss, Parker Davis, looking over the food supply shipment we got in this morning."

I glanced at Steve, who gave me a questioning look. "Parker is in Beijing?"

"Got in late yesterday. He'd been meeting with the Chinese liaison all morning, probably explaining why CERF isn't going to be able to provide the same level of assistance as before."

I noticed Steve was looking at me expectantly. I realized we'd arrived at the earthquake-damaged area of the city and Mr. Jong had parked half a block from the small cluster of mobile offices provided by CERF. Time to hurry things up. "Do you think Robert will be out for a while?"

"I expect so. After their little tour, he was supposed to take Parker to lunch."

"Okay, we're going in. If you see anyone coming, call Steve's cell."

She agreed and we hung up.

"Let's go," I said to Steve, opening my door. "He's gone to lunch, so we should have time."

As we walked toward the offices, Steve made a low

whistle. "It's always unbelievably humbling to see some-hing like this."

I saw his gaze fixed on the landscape stretching away from he portable office complex. I was impressed by the amount of work they'd done since I was last there. "I know what you nean, but the mountains of debris are now small hills, so it's coming along." I squinted against the sun. "And it looks like hey're well on their way to finishing three apartment buildings. One thing you gotta give the Chinese—they don't waste any ime."

I was pleased that I remembered exactly which office was Robert's. Because of his position, he had a portable building all to himself.

Getting inside wasn't a problem because the door wasn't locked. One of the few upsides to a police state is the low crime rate. I could walk down the busiest Beijing street, naked, pulling a wagonload of cash, and no one would touch me. If they did, they'd be taken out in an alley and shot, along with a few other suspects, just to be sure they got the right guy.

Robert's office was just as I remembered—an anal-reten-tive's dream on the surface, their worst nightmare on further inspection. Nothing was filed in the right place, and I was as likely to find a used yellow Lipton teabag in a drawer as I was to find an invoice.

We failed to find what we wanted. The search was excru-ciatingly slow because neither of us could read Chinese characters. We knew the ones to look for because we'd mem-orized them after Fred faxed them to us at the farm, but it took forever to skim the papers we sorted through.

We'd been there at least forty-five minutes when Steve said, "He must keep everything at his house."

"I can't imagine where. Aside from his wife and son, his wife's mother lives with him, all in a tiny one-bedroom apartment. There's no room for storing anything, much less the kinds of records we're looking for."

We continued looking, and after another twenty minutes, finally found a manila envelope with some of the bride records. The envelope was stuffed inside one of at least a hundred supply-and-equipment type catalogs, which were thrown in a cardboard box.

"Do you think this is enough?" I asked, looking over the characters.

"If it isn't, we'll have to think up another way to go at this. We can't risk coming here again, and I'm not so sure we'd ever find what we're looking for." His eyes widened and he withdrew his vibrating cell from his jacket pocket. "It's your aunt. We gotta get out of here."

He didn't have to say it twice. I followed him through the door, and we got out and around to the side of the building just in time. We heard Robert talking to Parker as they approached the building. "I'm not sure about dinner, Mr. Davis. I was scheduled for another engagement tonight, but I've yet to hear from my friend."

"No problem," Parker said in his usual affable-sounding voice. "I've got some paperwork to catch up on anyway."

They said goodbye and Parker walked toward the street, where he got in a small red car and took off.

Steve and I walked away at a normal pace and got back to the Audi without incident. Mr. Jong pulled from the curb and we were on our way to meet Aunt Fred, who's better than the average bear at reading Chinese characters. We hoped she'd be able to give me enough information that I wouldn't

rip myself up when I called Robert. I needed to know where
.e and Sasha met, and what time. Any details that would
nake me appear legitimate.

We were to meet her at a location far away from the CERF
ffice, to avoid anyone seeing us together. I didn't want Aunt
red involved any more than necessary.

In the Chaoyang district, in a northeastern section of the
ity, we stopped at the Shard Box Store, off Silk Street. The
mall shop is filled with trinkets and jewelry and an assort-
nent of treasures, some cheap and cheesy and some stunning
.nd beautiful. Their primary inventory, however, is shard
oxes. Crafted of a silver metal similar to tin, they are small
rinket boxes with a shard of inlaid porcelain for the lids. The
hop says the shards are from antique porcelains destroyed
luring the Cultural Revolution, when it was illegal to own
hem. Some of the box lids are rounded, the shard originat-
ng from a bowl or jar, and some are flat, the shard from a
late or tray.

Being a cynic, I've always wondered if the shard-box
eople go over to Bei Ren Fa, the Chinese equivalent of Wal-
Mart, and stock up on cheap porcelain they can break and use
n some of their boxes. Many are lovely, obviously the
roduct of beautiful porcelain, but others are suspiciously
ike the rice bowls for sale at Bei Ren Fa.

At any rate, browsing the selection is fun, and I wasn't able
o resist buying a couple of boxes. Steve bought an antique
nuff bottle, but otherwise, he was restless and prowled
round the store while we waited for Aunt Fred to show up.

She's a great friend of the owner of the store, Mr. Songlin,
nd when she did finally arrive, he graciously showed the
hree of us to a back room so we could have some privacy

while we visited. As soon as we were alone, she stared from one to the other of us.

"Damnation, darlin', those are some disguises. If I didn' know for sure who you are, I'd never recognize you." Her gaze fell to my legs. "Your granny is rotating in her grave over that short skirt." Then she looked at Steve. "You look like Robin Hood."

"Aunt Fred, this is Senator Steve Santorelli."

She reached out to shake his hand. "I voted for you in your first election. California was our state of residence during the time my husband and I lived here."

"Does that mean you didn't vote for me in the second election?"

"Couldn't. We were in Texas by then." She grinned at him. "But you can sure count on me voting for you for president."

We took our seats around the small table and, as is the custom for business guests, we were served hot water by Mr. Songlin's assistant. Aunt Fred says this goes back to the fundamental frugality of the Chinese. If food is served, there is tea. But most business guests aren't offered food, so no tea. Just the water, served hot to assure it's sanitary.

"You've lost weight," I said to Fred, slightly astounded. She bears no resemblance to Mom, even though they're sisters. Fred's five feet tall and solidly plump, with lively blue eyes and a mass of curly blond hair. In a nation of thin people with coal black hair, she stands out. But her arms appeared thinner, and there was no doubt her face had lost much of its roundness.

"The food up there is sketchy at best," she explained, "and frankly, there isn't much time to eat. Even now, six weeks after the disaster, there are people turning up, needing housing and medical care."

"How's the cleanup going?"

"About how you'd expect. The Chinese government wants it done yesterday, so they've relocated an army of men from outlying areas to build more of those hideous concrete, cracker-box, high-rise apartments. We're charged with feeding them and supplying shelter, and that's on top of housing the people whose homes were destroyed. Winters's on the way, and the people need more shelter than a tent." She took a drink of her water, and her gaze went to the envelope on the table. "Lemme have a look-see."

While she paged through the papers, I met Steve's gaze and decided I would never not recognize him, because of the eyes. They were so dark, so expressive. I'd know him anywhere.

After about five minutes, Aunt Fred slid her reading glasses up on her nose and said, "He's lousy at writing Chinese characters, so it's hard to say for certain, but I think he collects the women at the Hongqiao Market, which is the pearl market, on Hongqiao Lu."

"Wonder why he'd do it in such a public place?"

"If the exchanges were done in a private place," Steve said, "and they were caught, it would be a lot harder to escape. Running through somewhere like the pearl market would offer opportunities to blend in and hide in plain sight."

Aunt Fred was still looking over the papers. "It appears our Mr. Wang has made quite a tidy profit on the bride trade. From just the sales in these records, which cover August, he earned close to twenty thousand U.S. His buddy Sasha earned thirty grand. And Mister Greedy Gromyko pulled down a cool hundred thousand." She looked up at me. "I have no idea how Chinese men can afford this. Twenty-five thousand dollars is the average price for a wife, and the average Chinese man would take ten years to earn that much."

"Maybe they're selling them to above-average Chinese men," Steve suggested.

Aunt Fred stared at him, her blue eyes wide. "The majority of above-average Chinese men are those affiliated with the Party, officials in the government who earn nice salaries and get kickbacks from foreign investors."

"There are hundreds of them," he pointed out, "from provincial government on up."

"But why," I asked, "would they need to buy a Siberian wife? It seems to me, on the marriage market those guys would be in high demand and any Chinese girl would be pretty fired up to land one."

Steve gave me a funny look. "I sure as hell hope that's not how you look at marriage."

"If I did, I'd have married you a month ago."

He had the good grace to apologize. "I'm sorry. It just sounded so…"

"Cold and crass?" Aunt Fred said. "Maybe so, Senator, but this is China, where marriage is still the best way to move up in the world."

"It doesn't answer the question of why these men would buy a wife from Siberia."

A vague memory crystallized in my head and I looked at Aunt Fred. "Do you remember how upset Mrs. Han was when she stumbled into the medical tent?"

"I'll never forget. Poor thing. I still wonder what became of her."

"That woman who came to translate, she had a hard time understanding Mrs. Han's dialect. At first, she interpreted that Mrs. Han said she lost her husband because he was unable to pay. It didn't make sense, and the woman said Mrs. Han must have meant she lost him because he was unable to leave work when the quake hit." I looked from her curious gaze to Steve's. "Suppose her first interpretation was correct. Suppose the men who can afford the women buy them, then sell them to working-class Chinese men, who have to pay out the fee with high interest rates."

"Capitalism in its purest form," Steve said. He looked at the records in front of Aunt Fred. "Can you find out if any of the names on those records are government officials?"

"I'm all over it." She stood and gathered up the papers.

Steve and I also stood, and I said, "We need two decoy brides."

"Not a problem. I've got friends who'll volunteer."

"They can't look wholly Chinese."

"No worries. The two I'm thinking of are of Mongolian descent. They can pass for Siberian. When do you plan to hand them off to Robert?"

"Tonight, if all goes according to plan. Tomorrow, I'll meet with him and explain we're going to hand over the list of brides to the Chinese government. We'll also hand over a copy of our video, unless he agrees to sign an affidavit and return to the U.S. to testify against Gromyko and exonerate me."

"What if we find out he's selling the women to government officials?" she asked. "That threat's gonna lose a lot of its weight."

Steve smiled, but it didn't quite reach his beautiful eyes. "If there's only one honest Party official, I can find him."

Fred looked at him for a long, quiet moment. Then she said, "Suppose Wang refuses to cooperate?"

"We'll make good on the threat, hand over the video, and he'll get what's coming to him." He looked at me. "Then Pink and I will flee the U.S. and live in anonymity off the coast of somewhere."

"That's not at all funny," Aunt Fred said with a frown.

Steve shifted his gaze to her. "Who's kidding? She is *not* going to prison, and if the system in our country could allow her to be convicted, I'd rather live somewhere else."

Aunt Fred looked well pleased with Steve. She shot me a look that said, *Way to go, Pink. This guy's a keeper.* Aloud, she asked, "What about the brides? Do you have some way of getting them back without alerting Robert? I can't think they'll volunteer unless their safety is assured."

"I've got some men who'll take care of it," Steve said.

We finalized the plans with Aunt Fred, and I told her I'd call as soon as I had the exchange time and place set up with Robert. She hugged me and made me promise to be careful, joking about it because that's her way.

"If something happens to you, I'll have to take care of your mother in her old age, and my life will suck for eternity."

"I love you," I said over her shoulder.

"I know, baby. I love you, too. Really—be careful."

Chapter 13

In a crowded, noisy restaurant patronized solely by Chinese, Steve and I ate a quick meal of chicken and roasted peppers and my favorite of all Chinese food—dumplings filled with vegetables and meat and served with hot chili sauce that can put hair on your chest.

During our final round of tea, I made the first of my calls, using Sasha's cell phone and her conveniently stored numbers. Before I could call Robert Wang, I had to call Gromyko, or risk Robert's suspicion if he discovered I hadn't.

While I looked at the make-believe Gromyko, sipping *cha* from a small, handleless cup, I spoke to the real Gromyko. Maybe because I was so determined to take down the scumbag, I concentrated as hard as I ever had about anything, and my accent, I believed, was flawless, without a trace of Texas.

Nonetheless, to cover the discrepancy in my voice and

Sasha's when he answered, I said, "It is Sasha. I have been ill and unable to talk. Even now, I'm not feeling well."

No sympathy from Gromyko. He was furious, because I'd failed to return his calls, but primarily because I had yet to transfer the money into the Wang Imports account. He let me know it in no uncertain terms. I couldn't help squirming a little at his threats of violence. The truly freaky part of it was that most of his threats were sexual. Gromyko used his gigantic pecker for much more than sexual gratification. He used it as a weapon. My God, the man was twisted.

I wondered if, rather than titillation, his reason for having Sasha take those pictures was to remind her of just how hurtful her punishment could be if she didn't follow orders.

When he was a little more rational, I said calmly, as I knew Sasha would do, "I cannot move the money, Gromyko, because it is no longer in the account. Ms. Pearl had a check drawn to the Global Fund for Women and there is no possibility of retrieving it."

Naturally, this set him off again, and I wondered at his extensive pornographic vocabulary. I drank my tea while he explained just how badly he would tear my vagina, and how loud I would scream for mercy. I twiddled my chopsticks while he described how badly my breasts would ache after he bit them. And I powdered my nose all during his description of the pain I would feel while he choked me to death with his penis. Swear to God, I had the insane desire to break in and ask, "Ya done yet? 'Cause you're putting me to sleep." Instead I held out the phone and let Steve get an earful.

He whispered, "Ouch."

I shrugged and listened until Gromyko calmed down and

asked about Olga. "You told me she was called back to Moscow."

"Yes, but I asked her to take care of Pearl before she left. You know I dislike hits, and I was in a hurry to leave for Vladivostok."

"Do you know she's dead? The Pearl woman killed her," he said.

"Interesting. She doesn't seem capable."

"She's far more capable than we thought in the beginning."

"And you, Gromyko? Did you meet success with the attorney?"

He didn't like that I brought that up, and I had to listen to a few more minutes of trash talk before I was able to say, "If Pearl and Ravenaldt are still alive, they will uncover further information."

He was quiet for a moment—mulling it over, I supposed. "I took care of the records at your apartment," he said at last, "and we've stopped shipping to Pearl. There is nothing left to discover."

"There is always something forgotten, Gromyko. After tonight's handoff to Robert, I am done. I've found other prospects that are not quite so risky, with principals who are more capable."

I expected him to blow up and hurl more threats at me, but his reaction was a complete shock. "Sasha, you are leaving me?"

My mind processed what it could mean. Were the threats some kind of sexual game? In my limited experience, sex is all about love and affection and giving and receiving pleasure. Disgusting threats of sexually charged pain infliction isn't what I'd consider fun. But then, I do tend to be naive.

"I'm not willing to face jail for you," I said. "If the charges against Ms. Pearl don't stick, if they start to look at you, I will disappear."

"I was a fool to believe your lies."

What lies? Had Sasha promised to remain the good and faithful sex partner to the end of time? "I didn't lie, but I have to look out for myself, Gromyko." I snapped the phone closed.

"I'm sorry, Pink," Steve said. "That couldn't have been easy."

While I dialed Robert, I said, "No big deal. While I listened to him go off I just imagined what'll happen to him in prison when they see the size of his equipment."

Steve flinched.

Robert answered and I said, "You are ready with the buyers?"

"Sasha! Where the hell have you been? I've called, and so has Gromyko. He is really angry."

"I have just spoken to him. Tell me if you're ready for the women and let's get on with it."

"Yes, I'm ready. How many?"

"Two."

"Is that all? I'd hoped for four."

"I have been ill and unable to solicit more. I will see you at the usual place, but I'd prefer to meet earlier."

"Not possible. I can't deliver the women until the usual time. I don't want to have them any longer than necessary."

I wanted to ask if that was because he was squeamish about herding humans for money, but I didn't. "When's the earliest you can meet me? I have a flight this evening."

"I just told you, I can't meet earlier."

He wasn't cooperating at all. I had no idea what the usual

time was. "If your only concern is having the women longer than ordinary, I don't care. Make it earlier, or forget it. I know someone in another place who would be happy to have these women, though not for wives."

"You would sell them to be prostituted?"

He sounded disgusted, which I found ironic. Amazing how people can justify things to themselves.

"As I said, I can take them elsewhere if you are unable to meet my request."

"All right, Sasha. I can be there at six, but that's the earliest."

"Upstairs, at Sharon's. I need to collect a set of pearls I charged her to make last time."

"It's so open there. I'd prefer to stick with our usual spot."

"At Sharon's. Otherwise, I'll—"

He huffed out an angry breath. "All right! Just know, I am tired of working this hard for less money, and after tonight, things are going to change."

"Perhaps you are right, Robert. After tonight, things should change. We'll discuss it later." I snapped the phone closed and nodded at Steve. "We're on for six o'clock at Sharon's."

Fifteen minutes later, we passed the Forbidden City. "I love going there."

Steve looked across the seat at me and smiled. "We've got several hours to kill before six. You want to go?"

I returned his smile. "Definitely."

We gave Mr. Jong instructions about when to pick us up, and took off to wander. I'd been there twice before, but it still fascinated me. My imagination always takes flight and I can visualize the pomp and ceremony of all those years of

emperors and the people who lived within the Imperial
Palace walls.

On the north side, where the golden-tiled roofs of the residence buildings stretch across the east and west, Steve
pointed to the section where the concubines lived. "Wonder
how the emperor decided who to sleep with every night."

"I suppose he went shopping and gave his list to the
eunuchs. It was good to be the emperor."

"But bad to be a eunuch." He shot me a look. "It must have
driven them insane, being around all those women but not
allowed to touch them."

If there wasn't hidden meaning in that, I was a rocket
scientist. "Isn't that why they were castrated, so they
wouldn't want to?"

"They were castrated so they couldn't, but I'm not sure it
killed all desire for female contact. After all, intimacy isn't
just about sex."

He was holding my hand, which was, I suppose, somewhat
intimate. I couldn't deny the undercurrent of our conversation,
and it seemed like a good time to throw things out on the table.
That damn bed was still just there, in my mind, bugging me,
because I didn't know what he expected. I looked into his dark
eyes and part of me wished I'd never met Ed, that I could go
goofy over Steve Santorelli and never look back.

"I kinda figured men out a long time ago, but I don't understand you at all."

"What's to understand? I want you to marry me."

"It just doesn't add up. We've never even slept together.
Suppose I said yes, and we got married, and the sex sucked?"

"The sex would not suck." He looked vaguely offended.

"How do you know? Sex isn't up to only one or the other.

It's a mutual activity, and whether or not two people are good together seems to be a matter of chemistry, or something more esoteric." Like love, which he'd failed to mention.

If I was waiting for a declaration of undying love and devotion, I needed to take a number and have a seat, because one was not forthcoming.

Instead, he said, "If it's worrying you so much, I know a really great way to put your mind at ease."

I dropped his hand. "Is that why we have one bed in our room?"

He walked away, toward another building. "Me and the boys are gonna check out the Palace of Abstinence, if you care to join us." Halfway across the pathway, he stopped and turned. "Are you coming?"

I followed and we walked around the building, looking up at the flying dragon eaves and the mosaic inlays in the red walls, next to a set of massive red doors. While he was bent low, checking out the small tiles, he said matter-of-factly, "The Lido was out of rooms with two beds, and there's no way I would let you stay in a room by yourself. Not after what you went through the other night. Dad told me it's likely you'll have some difficulty sleeping." He straightened and met my gaze. "If I said the thought of making love to you never crossed my mind, I'd be a liar, but I certainly don't expect it."

"See, that's the part I don't get about you. I keep waiting for an ultimatum, for you to tell me it's now or never."

He slid his hands into the pockets of his black trousers and leaned against the wall of the palace. "What good would that do me? At this point, I'm fairly sure you'd say never, and you'd be gone out of my life for good." Pushing away from the wall, he came close and rubbed his knuckles against my throat. The way he touched me was powerfully erotic, and I felt it all the way through my bones.

"Ed's a good guy, and you'd most likely be fairly happy with him over the long haul. But I'm convinced you'd be better off with me."

"Why?"

"Because we're so much alike. You're a wild child, and at the same time, you're straight and narrow. I suspect you spend a lot of time arguing with yourself about coloring outside the lines."

To say I was speechless would be like saying the Forbidden City is just a bunch of old buildings. I'd never known anyone, much less a man, to be that intuitive.

He grasped my hand and we walked back toward the Gate of Heavenly Peace, the entrance to the Forbidden City. "I know just how you feel. Rules and order and the formality of things like state dinners really appeal to me, but accomplishing things while circumventing the law has a certain draw that's not very presidential."

I thought of Carmine's. Then I thought of the shadowy man who aided CIA operatives, the one they called Santa. More than once I'd wondered if Steve was Santa, but always discounted the idea. He was a senator, for God's sake. Senators don't go around anonymously helping CIA operatives who get in over their heads.

But maybe there was one exception.

In the middle of the vast square before the Hall of Supreme Harmony, from which China's emperors once ruled the empire, I stopped walking and he drew up short. Still holding my hand, he came very close, until my breasts were touching him and our breaths mingled in the cool October air.

I looked at his lips, framed by the crisp black hair of his beard and mustache, not quite full but well on its way. Unlike Ed's sensual mouth, Steve's was thinner and firmer, more a straight line. My gaze traveled back to his eyes. "Is that why you want me to marry you? Do you see me as Mrs. Claus?"

He looked conflicted. Finally he said, "I'm not Santa."

Hmm. "But you do work for the organization. The same one Big Mama does, that is."

"Sometimes. When I'm available. If by some miracle I come through all of this with a glimmer of a chance to run for president, and if I stretch the miracle and win, I'd have to curtail my involvement almost completely."

"And you want me to take up the slack?"

"You'd have amazing opportunities as First Lady, Pink."

"Do you have a clue what you're asking me to do? To give up? Have you been running down dark alleys so long, you've forgotten what it's like to be just an average person?"

"You've never been an average person. And I don't run down dark alleys. Dad does that. Almost all of my job is done in private, and on the phone. It's more about strategy and thinking outside the box. You're a natural." He came closer and kissed me, softly.

I kissed him back, and because we were being brutally honest about things, I asked, "Was Lauren involved with Carmine's?"

"Lauren was totally straight and narrow." His lips moved across my lips to my chin. "Unlike you, who didn't hesitate to forge a check for a cool one hundred grand.... Do you have even the slightest idea what that did to me, knowing you could do something like that?"

His hand slid to the nape of my neck and his lips returned to my mouth. The kisses were getting less platonic and more sexual. I was feeling less platonic and more sexual, so I suppose things were working out.

"I was blown away that you had the guts to do it."

He parted my lips with his tongue and there we stood, in the middle of the Forbidden City, Frenching like we were alone. It's a wonder we weren't arrested. The Chinese frown heavily on public displays of affection. But at that moment, I just didn't care. Maybe he was on to something with his wild-child theory. Once again, I went into antigravity mode, kissing Steve like there was no tomorrow, like I was going to be executed in a matter of moments and had to get in one last thrill of living.

Eventually he broke the kiss, turned and started toward the entrance. I followed along, still holding his hand. "So Lauren wasn't involved, but did she know?"

"When she was alive, there was nothing to know. Three weeks after her funeral, a stranger called and told me about a plot to wipe out part of the New York subway system. I turned over the information to the FBI, and watched them try like hell but fail to get anywhere because their hands were tied. I decided to go in through the back door and see if I'd have better luck. Halfway through the operation, Dad stepped in, mostly so I could maintain my anonymity. Until about four minutes ago, he was the only person alive who knew."

"So Carmine's, and all the people who work from there…"

"It's me, Pink. Dad as Big Mama is always the face of

things. There are a handful of people who know about him, mostly his old buddies who are still in the military. Through them, and some who are in the State Department, we get the information we need to do things the United States can't."

We'd passed through the long, arched passageway, crossed the middle of the five bridges spanning the Imperial River, and were standing close to the street, facing Tiananmen Square and the Great Hall of the People. While we waited for Mr. Jong to pick us up, I watched the constant stream of bicycles, at least ten deep, as they passed. "Why me? And why get married? Just because I'd have more access to certain people and places as First Lady?"

He, too, was watching the bicycles, and he answered without looking at me. "You're so smart it's scary. You and Dad would work together beautifully. Only drawback is your accent and your difficulty picking up a different one. But I think you can overcome the problem."

Turning his head, he looked at me with a sad expression. "As for the second question, I've just told you something that could send me to prison. How much do you think I trust you? And do you really think I'd ask you to marry me for any reason other than that I want you to be my wife?"

"Until a few minutes ago I didn't, but you kind of put it that way, Steve. Like marriage to me would be so handy for your organization. And there is the sex thing. Other than über-religious men, I can't think of one who'd ask a woman to marry him before he's slept with her."

"This is really bugging you, isn't it? Maybe I should take you back to the hotel and fuck you until tomorrow. Would that prove that I'm serious, that there's no hidden agenda or ulterior motive? Because I'm game, Pink. More than game.

I've been living in the Palace of Abstinence for three years, and trust me, I'm way past ready to move out. Say the word and Mr. Jong's driving us on a condom run."

For the second time in an hour, I was speechless. I mean, how could I respond to that?

"See, that's why we're not going for condoms. You want to. I can see it in your eyes. But once we sleep together, you know it's all over with Ed and you're not ready to let go. Straight and narrow tells you it's wrong, that you can't have two lovers. Wild child says hell, yes, go for it. I'm a real bastard for tempting you, but I want you, Pink. If it takes a while for you to realize Ed's not the one, I'm okay with that. I waited three years to find you. I can wait a few months to sleep with you."

I stayed focused on those friggin' bicycles. Jesus, I had never seen so many bicycles. Hundreds upon hundreds of them. I formed no less that thirty sentences in my head and not a damn one of them ever made it to my lips.

"Are you speechless because you're shocked that Mister Do-Right Senator offered to fuck you for twenty-four hours? Maybe you're shocked because I said *fuck*. Or are you speechless because you're pissed off that you've got to make a difficult decision? Or are you just choked up because I'm a helluva sensitive guy?"

I looked at him and tried to smile, but gave up. "You're a Stepford man. You and your father. I should run away screaming."

"Trust me, we're far from perfect."

"Prove it."

At the car, he opened the curbside door, waited for me to get in, then followed. After he told Mr. Jong where to go, he urned to me and asked, "Remember the man who brought ou a Bolshevik sandwich?"

That was totally unexpected. "Yes."

"It was me."

"What?" If he'd said he was Mr. Rogers and owned a loset full of cardigan sweaters, I couldn't have been more hocked.

His next words were in the exact accent as Mr. Swarthy. If I were going to disappear with something of yours, it vouldn't be your soap."

"Oh, my God." I remembered what the dark man looked ike. There was no resemblance to Steve. Meeting his gaze, realized I would have known if I'd really looked into the nan's eyes. "You knew all along about the bank. You knew was going to forge the check." The significance of that hit ne broadside. "You didn't try to stop me. Instead, you elped me."

He didn't respond. Just watched me, as though he was vaiting for me to work through all the implications.

I replayed that day in my head, from the moment I walked nto Carmine's until the last time I walked out, after asking f I could keep the clothes and the wig and continue to be asha for a while longer. Sasha. "You knew what she looked ike. How did you know?"

"She came in the deli on occasion. Sasha was sexy and eautiful and there wasn't a man among us who didn't make point to talk to her, if we were anywhere on the premises. he day you walked in and wrote her name on the napkin, I vas stunned. We'd never heard her last name, or I might ave wondered about the coincidence of Sasha Valikov and Valikov Interiors. When I saw the name Sasha, I suspected it was the same woman. Then you described her and I knew for sure. But I didn't make the connection between her an Olga, for which I'm still kicking myself."

"But the check, Steve. Why did you let me do it, knowin the deep shit it could get me into?"

"If I'd told you it was unwise, that you shouldn't do i would you have listened?"

"No. But you didn't even try. I don't understand."

"I let you write the check for the reason you intended. I was the only way to shake up Sasha, to set her on the defen sive and give you some leverage."

"Why hide yourself from me? Was it just that you didn trust me yet?"

"I was already disguised, because I had some work to d there and, as I said, no one knows about me. When Da called and said he was sending you to Carmine's for help, volunteered. Had I told you who I was, you'd have acted dif ferently." He shrugged. "And a part of me wanted to see ho you operate on your own, with no one around that you know who you're comfortable with."

"You wanted to spy on me?"

"Pretty much, yeah." He looked suddenly inspired. "Ca that count as a flaw?"

"Definitely. Big one."

"Deal-breaker flaw?"

"If you made it a habit. That's unnerving."

"You're too smart to fake out a second time." He leane over and kissed me.

I kissed him back, more confused than ever.

Aunt Fred called on the way back to the hotel. Ever name in the records we'd found at Robert's office belonge o a Chinese official, some of them higher up, but most of hem intermediary positions.

"What do you think?" I asked Steve after I ended the call nd told him what she'd said.

He stared out the window for a while before he said quietly, "I think we're going to have to go as high as possible with the list. We have no way of knowing which officials have bought brides, and we can't take a chance on handing the list over to the wrong man."

"How high is as high as possible?"

Turning to me, he said solemnly, "We'll start at the top and work our way down."

Two hours later, after we freshened up and I made a few repairs to my face, with Steve's help because that plastic stuff is a bitch to get right, we left the Lido and Mr. Jong drove us o a small bookshop close to the Shard Box Store. There we picked up our fake brides. On the way to the pearl market, Steve went over the plan with the women and they nodded their understanding. I couldn't nod because I didn't understand.

Inside the market are four levels of everything from brand-name knockoffs, to clothing and linens, to leather goods and housewares. The pearls are all on the fourth level. There are rows upon rows of little booths, all staffed with industrious women stringing loose pearls with such speed and dexterity that their small hands are a blur. Each booth has a Chinese woman calling out to come and see the pearls, to find "best quality, best price."

We ignored them and went to a shop at the back of the fourth floor, the only pearl vendor who actually had walls,

and carpet and lighted display cases. Her name was Sharon
and she had photographs in the shop of Bill and Hillary
Clinton, George and Barbara Bush and a few other notable
Americans, all of whom had been to Sharon's. She's something of a celebrity in Beijing. I don't know that her pearls
are better than those of the little ladies in the booths, but I
suspect Sharon knows how to politick—and that's why she
has walls.

While the women and I waited close to the open doors,
Steve wandered around the shop, asking to look at various
items in the cases. My palms were sweating profusely, I was
so nervous. In my head, I went over and over what I would say
and reminded myself who I was, as I'd done that day at the bank.

It paid off, because when Robert showed up, I was certain
he had no clue I was anyone other than Sasha. I supposed
they'd only ever met to exchange money and women, so his
memory would be sketchy at best.

Steve continued looking at the case displays with his back
to us. We had no idea how well Robert knew Gromyko, or
how accurate Steve's disguise was. So to be on the safe side,
unless the situation warranted Gromyko's presence, Steve
was lying low. Of course, he was recording everything
through the end of the short umbrella he held under his arm.

"You have brought the money?" I demanded of Robert.

His ordinarily smiley face was nothing close to jolly as he
handed me a thick envelope. I opened it and thumbed through
the bills, estimating it to be ten thousand bucks—Sasha's
twenty percent of the fifty-thousand-dollar price tag on two
wives. My stomach lurched and it took everything in me to
keep from hauling off and smashing Robert's face in.

He appeared not to notice my disgust. "Gromyko says you're considering leaving the operation."

"Things have become too risky. I suspect this is the last that we will see of one another, as I intend to pursue other opportunities."

Shocking me completely, he reached out and grabbed my arm. "Will you be using the hundred thousand dollars you failed to transfer into my account?"

"Get your hand off me, swine, and do not accuse me of thievery. I can no longer transfer the money because it is no longer in the Valikov account. The Pearl woman took it."

"So Gromyko said, but he's more gullible where you're concerned. I think you took the money for yourself, knowing you were about to bail on us."

His fingers bit into my arm and I gritted my teeth to keep from crying out. "I tell you the Pearl woman stole it. She forged a check and had a cashier's check drawn to the Global Fund for Women. I have a receipt from the bank to prove it."

He shook me. Hard. The fake brides stood by, silent and acting afraid, their eyes wide and growing wider. Robert looked downright scary, he was so angry.

"Liar! You swiped the cash and expect us to believe Pink took it, but you forget, I know her. The woman wouldn't take ten cents from anyone, much less a hundred grand."

I wished I could be flattered that he believed in my integrity, but his opinion meant squat. "You are wrong."

"I don't think so. I suggest you cough up the receipt, or I'll tell Gromyko my suspicions."

"Tell him, and see how far you get. He will never take your side over mine."

"Never say never," came a voice from behind and to my left.

I twisted my neck to look and damn near passed out. The real Gromyko stood there, watching me intently from pale-blue eyes. Not Steve's beautiful dark eyes.

"Come, Sasha. We will discuss Robert's suspicions and an appropriate plan of action."

Oh, shit. I didn't dare look over my shoulder toward Steve, but I wished I knew what he was doing. Glancing down at the hand Gromyko extended toward me, I blinked.

And blinked again.

His watch was gold, with a raised gold Chinese character on a jade face and inset emeralds on the hours. It was unique—specially made for the man who wore it. I'd seen that watch hundreds of times before, usually as it was twisted round and round in a mindless habit by its owner.

I had one of those startling moments of clarity—so clear, I could almost hear the puzzle pieces locking into place.

Gromyko was Parker Davis. The executive director of CERF was the man responsible for ripping off over half a million bucks from the fund, for selling abducted young Siberian women to desperate Chinese men, for strangling Taylor Bunch, for setting me up.

And he was screwing Sasha Valikov. If his telephone conversation was any indication, they did it a lot, in very unique and unusual ways. I thought of Madeline Davis and instantly felt sorry for her.

Good God. Parker Davis. His disguise was excellent. Other than his eyes—and his watch—he looked nothing like the Parker Davis I knew. I was astonished. And my heart broke a little bit. I'd looked up to Parker, respected him, and admired his seeming selfless devotion to the alleviation of human suffering. As if. The man was a slave trader.

Twisting my arm from Robert's grasp, I smoothed the sleeve of my jacket, keeping my head down to avoid Parker's gaze. I couldn't let on that I knew, and equally important, I couldn't allow Parker to realize I wasn't Sasha.

Robert needed to leave the building with the women. He needed to take them outside and put them in a vehicle and take them away. We had to get it recorded, proof that they went with Robert, who'd given money for them. Still with my head down, I unzipped my purse and began digging through it. "The receipt is here, if you'll only wait a moment."

"You can look after we're in the car," he said, moving closer.

I continued digging and whispered to him, "Do not humiliate me. Send Robert on."

He muttered a command to Robert, and like an obedient dog, Robert grasped the women's arms and led them toward the stairs. I mumbled that I couldn't find the receipt, faking distress that turned too real when he grabbed my arm and jerked it so hard I winced in pain.

Where the hell was Steve? It was imperative that he follow Robert, and I couldn't make a run for it until he was gone.

Trying to buy time to allow him to get past us, as well as time before I had to come face to face with Parker, I allowed the purse to slide from my fingers and spill its contents all over the linoleum floor. I tugged my arm loose from his grasp and knelt down to collect the contents, expecting him to help. Wrong. He stood above me and demanded I hurry up.

"It would be faster if you assisted me."

He squatted beside me, and while we gathered up loose change and lipstick and Sasha's cell phone, I saw Steve's shoes pass by. Finally, I could leave.

Standing, I said to Parker, "I believe we are done."

Rising, he faced me, his expression something I can't describe, except to say I wanted to run away and hide from it. I saw the promise of freakish sex in his eyes and I swear my hootus drew up in terror. Especially when I remembered how huge he was and all the threats he'd made on the phone.

Then his expression changed and it was *worse* than the promise of violent sex. This one was more like the promise of murder.

"Who the hell are you?" he demanded, his hand circling my arm again, jerking me toward the stairs.

"I am Sasha!" I exclaimed. "What is wrong with you?"

"You are not Sasha, and I intend to find out who you are, and what you've done with her."

He hauled me down the stairs, and I considered how to get away from him. He would kill me, I was sure, and that would be after he made good on that look. God, it was frightening. Thoughts of twisted sheets with Ed, or Steve, were pleasant, stimulating, anticipatory. The thought of Parker Davis touching me made me nauseated with fear.

At the ground floor we headed for the exit. Outside, I saw the car, still parked across the street, and I noticed Steve standing to my right, his face hidden behind a map of Beijing. When he allowed the top half to fold down, Mr. Jong made a U-turn. Before Parker could move me any farther away from the market entrance, Steve came close and plowed a fist into his face. Whether from surprise, or pain, or self-defense, Parker let go of my arm, and I rushed to jump in the car. Steve was right behind me. The car took off before the door was fully closed.

I looked back to see Parker rubbing his face, staring after us in complete dismay.

After I caught my breath, I told Steve, "Gromyko is Parker

Davis. I'm sure of it. He was wearing Parker's watch, and after I noticed it, I could see the resemblance around his eyes. It all makes perfect sense. Who had more access to my office? Who knew all of my information, like my social security number? Aunt Fred said Parker was in Beijing."

Before Steve could react or say a word, Sasha's cell phone rang. It was Parker. "Who are you?"

"I'm the one whose life you screwed every which way from Sunday," I said in my own voice.

"Pink?"

"Damn straight, you sorry, scum-sucking piece of shit. You are so going down. Big mistake, wearing that watch."

"I don't think so. There's absolutely no way you can pin any of this on me."

"We just recorded Robert buying two women, and you're in the picture, along with your watch."

He was infuriatingly smug. "Robert will be arrested if you turn over the video, but Parker Davis won't be. Neither will Nikolai Gromyko, because he doesn't exist. As for the watch, I'll report it stolen."

"Robert will turn state's witness against Gromyko, and there's got to be a way they can tie you to him."

"No, there's not. I covered all my bases." He paused. "Where is Sasha?"

"With Olga."

"You killed her?"

"No, but she died with Olga. They were one and the same." I glanced out at the lights along the road to the Lido. "Get ready, Parker. You're going down."

"That's what I always liked about you, Pink. You never give up, even on lost causes." He ended the call.

I met Steve's gaze. "No need to repeat," he said quietly. "I heard everything."

"What am I going to do?"

"We'll stick with our plan. If we can't get Davis, we can still exonerate you. Robert will sign the affidavit acknowledging his role in the embezzlement, and name Gromyko as an accomplice. When we take it back to the States and present it to the Washington DA, you can tell them your suspicion that Gromyko is Parker Davis, then leave it up to them to find a way to prove it."

"How can you be so calm, Steve? Isn't it freaking you out that Parker is behind all of this?"

"In one way, yes, but in another, no. I always thought he was a social climber. People like that can get so caught up in it, they forget who they were to start with."

Steve's cell phone chirped. After a very brief, monosyllabic conversation, he ended the call. "That was one of the men who followed Robert to collect the women. Robert pulled over, and a few minutes later, Gromyko pulled up behind him."

His eyes met mine and I knew I wasn't gonna like what he was about to say.

"Robert's dead, Pink. Parker stabbed him."

Chapter 14

We had to go to plan B. Problem was, we didn't have a plan B. Back at the hotel, I took off all traces of Sasha and stayed in the shower an overlong time, my mind racing with ideas. Wrapped up in one of the hotel robes, I sat on the bed while Steve showered, and continued to think.

My mind methodically went through the process Parker had used to rip off CERF, and I came to the end of it wondering how he benefited. If the CERF money went to the Kansas account, then to Sasha's account, then to Robert Wang's account, where did Parker fit in? Where was his cut? Owl had told me there were no withdrawals from the Wang Imports account.

Over and over I ran through it, even got out a memo pad and diagrammed the flow of the money. Then I considered the length of time involved. They'd begun stealing the funds

just over a month ago. There'd been only one bank statemen
for Valikov Interiors.

On a hunch, I called Owl, forgetting until he answered ir
a sleepy voice that it's thirteen hours earlier in Texas than ir
China. It was 7:30 p.m. in Beijing, 6:30 a.m. in Midland. I
apologized for waking him up and he insisted I tell him why
I'd called, so I asked if he'd take another look at the Wang
Imports account and find out if there had been any recent dis-
bursements. He said he'd get back to me, and I gave him
Sasha's cell number.

Steve came out of the bathroom and headed for his laptop,
his robe swinging around his hairy calves. He plugged in a
USB cable, uploaded the video from the umbrella camera and
watched it, his concentration completely focused. "There's
the watch, in full view. And there's enough of his voice on
this, the FBI could match it to Parker's."

"Even with the fake accent?"

"Maybe not, but it's worth a try. Voice matching is more
about pitch and tone, and even with the accent, he's got the
same pitch." He turned and looked at me. "What have you got?"

"Not much." I told him about my call to Owl.

"Maybe it'll lead to something. In the meantime, let's
order something to eat. I'm starving."

We did, and while we worked our way through a smorgasbord of food, we continued to consider our options. The truth
of it was, we'd lost our ace in the hole when Parker offed
Robert. It bummed me out so badly, to find that someone I'd
liked and respected was a man with no conscience whatsoever.

"Before we leave, I've got to hand over the copy of the bride
list."

"Where is it?"

I pulled the papers out of my new purse and unfolded hem. Other than an icky smell and wavy wrinkles, the list was in perfect shape.

Steve held out his hand and I gave it to him. While he drank the rest of a Chinese beer and studied it, I studied him. I remembered the first time I ever saw him, sitting in a row of stern-looking senators, grilling me about Marvel Energy and Big Important CPAs. I'd thought he was an uptight politician with perfect hair. Looking at his hair now, I almost laughed. It was anything but perfect, constantly mussed because he had a habit of running a hand through it when he was deep in concentration. In the middle of my stare-fest, he glanced up.

"What? Have I got crumbs in my beard?"

"No. I was just remembering my first impression of you, and how totally wrong I was."

"Not sure where you're going with this, but I hope the impression changed for the better."

"Only a lot."

He laid the list on the desk, shoved the small rolling room-service table away and came toward me. Without even the semblance of asking, he pushed me backward on the bed and kissed me. I'm not sure he'd ever kissed me like that—all-consuming, with the weight of his body pressing mine into the mattress. Thoughts of anything other than the taste of his lips and the feel of his hands against my bare skin beneath the robe were shoved aside. There's something enormously erotic about kissing a man who's goofy for you, and knowing how he felt, what he wanted of me, I got carried away in the moment. And in a lot of moments that followed. I didn't lose my head completely. I didn't ruin it with Ed, but

I sure as hell pushed the envelope. What still haunts me is wondering if it was me who showed restraint, or Steve.

I have to think it was me. I was partially naked with a man who hadn't had sex in three years. No way could he be the one to resist going all the way. Could he? He said something deep and low, right in my ear, that I've yet to figure out. That's because he said it in Russian.

"Did you just ask me to vacuum the dairy?"

He moved his lips across my face, all the way to the other ear, and whispered, "No, but if you feel like tidying up, I'm not gonna stop you."

Oh, man. After that, everything is something of a blur, but certain things stand out. Like the taste of his skin, and the scent of it, and the way the hair grows across his chest, down to his groin, and the feel of his strong fingers against the most sensitive parts of me.

And when I remember, I wonder all over again if each of us climaxing nullified the restraint. Did the fact that we didn't actually have intercourse really make a difference? We were naked; the desire was there. All that stopped me was knowing I could never lie to Ed. And he would ask. I knew he would.

After he reached up and switched off the lamp, Steve took me in his arms and whispered, "I should apologize."

"If you did apologize, I wouldn't believe it anyway."

He held me closer, and after a while, his breathing became even and I knew he was asleep. Unfortunately, I was wide awake.

I was watching the thin line of parking-lot light from the center of the drapes when Sasha's phone rang. I extricated myself from Steve's arms and went to answer it.

Owl said, "Ancient Antiquities. Seventy-five percent of all

he money deposited into the Wang Imports account has been
ransferred out to Ancient Antiquities."

"Do you have the account number?"

"Pink, don't insult me this way. I have all the information
you need. Get a pen."

He wasn't lying about having all the information. He'd even
checked to see where the money in Ancient Antiquities went,
and the answer was nowhere. Evidently, the buck stopped there.

"The account signatory is William Mulholland. I did some
checking and he's a rich dude in New York. Sits on corporate boards. Has houses all over the world. On his third wife."

From his tone, I assumed Owl didn't approve of William
Mulholland. All I could think about was whether he was the
same Mulholland who'd pledged his support of Madeline
Davis for president.

In the middle of my musing, Owl said, "There's a political rally for Madeline Davis set for January in Manhattan,
and Mulholland is sponsoring it."

Bingo! I was expansively happy. "You're the man!"

"Uh, thanks, Pink. You know, I've noticed you sound different. Happier, maybe?"

"Well, Owl," I said, adopting his metaphysical vocabulary
so he'd understand, "you could say the past few days have
brought me closer to my spiritual center."

"Marvelous! I'll look forward to hearing all about it during
our tepee sit."

"I'll look forward to telling you." We hung up and it
occurred to me that I hadn't been lying. I really did see the
world in an entirely different way.

After a glance at Steve, who was out like a light, I focused
on the laptop and Googled Mulholland. I came up with hun-

dreds of links, and I clicked on several of them and read al
about the man, about his checkered background that includee
a sexual harassment suit. He had a finger in a lot of pies, anc
sat on the board of directors for three different corpora-
tions—one of them a Fortune 500 company. Braxton Technologies. The company was formed by the merger of two
smaller companies, and I remembered Mom bemoaning the
fact that she'd failed to buy stock in either of them before the
merger. The newly formed Braxton Technologies had broke
records on the American Stock Exchange.

I kept digging for any kind of connection between Parker
and Mulholland, but came up with nothing, other than they'd
both attended Boston University. I saw that Mulholland sup-
ported his old fraternity by donating money for renovations.
and on a hunch, went to the fraternity's Web site. Sure
enough, there was Parker's name as a contributing member.

I just couldn't figure out why a guy like Mulholland, a rich
man who ran with the social elite in New York, would be
involved with a small-potato company like Ancient Antiquities. A company that received dirty money. And why did
Parker go to all this trouble and commit heinous crimes for
money he didn't get? I considered the possibility that Mulholland was blackmailing Parker, but that really seemed a stretch.

Maybe Parker lied about Ancient Antiquities. Maybe he
did own a part of it. I went to the Web page that listed every
senator, along with a link to their latest asset rendition, and
looked for Madeline Davis. I was disappointed when I didn't
see Ancient Antiquities stock in her lengthy list of securities
and business interests.

But I nearly vibrated off my chair when I saw a huge
amount of Cardwell Systems. As of the date of the rendition,

which was three months earlier, Parker and Madeline owned thousands of shares. Cardwell was one of the companies merged to form Braxton, and anyone who owned their stock before the merger would have cleaned up afterward. If Parker and Madeline bought the stock anywhere close to the merger, I could make a case for insider trading. It was just too coincidental that Mulholland and Parker were fraternity brothers, that the money Parker stole from CERF all eventually ended up in an account owned by Mulholland, and that Mulholland sat on the board of directors for Cardwell before it was merged into Braxton. He would have known about the merger long before it happened.

I had no idea about certain elements, but instinct told me I was on to something huge. I wondered if Madeline was aware of her husband's illegal activities. Was she involved? Glancing at Steve, sleeping like the dead, I thought of the fallout for him if Madeline Davis turned out to be as big a crook as her husband. Steve would win the nomination for presidential candidate without half trying.

Looking back at the computer screen, I knew I couldn't tell him what I'd found. He couldn't be the one to bring this to light, if in fact there was something to it. He would look like a snitch, pointing the finger at the competition in an effort to appear righteous.

I closed the Senator Rendition page and went to check my e-mail address we'd set up under Ed's account, so that my Internet use couldn't be traced by the D.C. cops. I was breaking bail in a big way by being out of the country. He'd forwarded all my personal e-mails from my account, and I scrolled through until I saw one from him, sent less than an hour ago, when it was eight in the morning in California. He

said Mom had left to go home, and he would have gone with
her except that Lou had some crisis in San Francisco and
asked him to stay and look after things at the farm. Koi was
still off, and Rolly could use help.

I smiled when I read Ed's commentary. His leg was much
better, he said, but it hurt like hell after he was done feeding
five horses and thirty chickens. Not to mention two tiny dogs.
He wrapped up the e-mail by saying,

Be careful. Tell Santorelli I said hey. It would be nice to
know he never touched you, but I'm a guy. I know how
we think. I also know how you think when it comes to him.
Not that I want you to feel guilty. Just know that this is
driving me out of my fucking mind. And I lied—I want you
to be wretched with guilt. Come home soon.

He signed it simply, *Ed.* Not *Love, Ed.* Not *Love you, Ed.*
Not even a *Sincerely,* or *All the best, Ed.* Just, *Ed.*

I turned off the computer and went back to bed. Steve
stirred and gathered me up next to him, then mumbled against
my hair, "I love you," just before his breathing became steady
and even again.

When I woke up, Steve and the list were gone, and in their
place was a note instructing me to sit tight and wait for him.
He'd gone without me? Why? Had he gone as Gromyko? Or
as himself?

I got dressed, as me instead of Sasha, and it felt good to
look in the mirror and recognize myself.

Close to noon, my cell phone rang and I answered, expecting Steve. Instead, it was Parker. Or rather, Gromyko.

"I've got something of yours," he said, sounding smarmy. "If you want it back, you need to give me the money you stole."

"What have you got?"

"Your mother."

"Yeah, right. My mother's in Texas."

I heard a shuffle, then Mom's voice. "Pink, he's not lying. He grabbed me when I went out to see Fred."

My heart dropped into my brand-new pointy-toed black mules. "Oh, my God! Mom! What are you doing in Beijing?"

"Following you."

"Is Lou with you?"

"No, I came alone. I was worried about you getting in over your head, and now look what I've done. I'm so sorry."

Parker came back on the line. "Meet me at the Moko Internet Coffee Bar, in Dongcheng, in two hours."

"I will, but there's no way I can give back the money right now. I don't have the cashier's check."

"I don't care where you get the money. Just show up with one hundred thousand dollars, or your mother will get a taste of Gromyko."

Mad as hell and scared to death, I sucked it up and made my very first political phone call. Less than thirty minutes later, I'd set into motion something that would blow up ten times bigger than the Marvel Energy scandal. But this time, I wouldn't be the one in the middle of things. It wouldn't be me burning at the stake for standing up and pointing out the crook in the crowd. More importantly, none of it would touch Steve. He really did need to be president.

I called him, but he didn't answer. I redialed three times, and he never picked up. So I called Ed. When he didn't answer his cell phone, I dialed international information and got the number for the farm. As he answered, I heard a dog barking in the background. And a cat meowing.

"Ed, it's Pink. I need you to get me a hundred grand."

"Yeah, baby. Who's your daddy?"

"I'm serious."

"Okay, so I'll give you a hundred Gs. But first you gotta tell me why."

I did and he was quiet for a while, processing it.

"Okay, here's what we'll do. Give me the account information for Ancient Antiquities and I'll call my bank and have them do a wire transfer. Then I'll e-mail to let you know when it's done, and Parker can check the Antiquities account on the Internet at the café."

"That's a lot of cash to come up with on the spur of the moment. Isn't all your money in investments?"

"Isn't it kinda nosy of you to ask?"

"Yes," I said simply.

"The last settlement I won is still in the bank. Haven't had time to divvy it up into investments. Satisfied?"

"Enormously. But, Ed, should you use your own money?"

"You got a better idea? This is your mother we're talking about. Don't worry about it. I'm a lawyer and I know how to get it back, one way or the other. In the meantime, you can pay interest in the form of sexual favors."

"You're feeling better, aren't you."

"Much. Go get your mother and get your ass home." The dogs barked again and the cat shrieked.

"Is everything all right?"

"Hell, no. Damn dogs are pissing off the cat, who won't get out of the house. Keeps following me around. Gonna go for my nuts any minute now, I know it." On cue, the cat meowed. "For God's sake, Pink, please be careful."

I promised I would, then hung up and hurried out the door.

Explaining to the cabdriver where I wanted to go was a challenge, but with a map and a tiny grasp of fundamental Mandarin, I managed. Moko wasn't too far from the Forbidden City and I got there thirty minutes ahead of time. Most of the clientele were not Chinese, but a mish-mash of foreigners, all checking e-mails or otherwise taking care of business. I took a seat toward the rear, close to the back door, and pulled up my e-mail account to watch for Ed's message. While I waited I tried calling Steve again, but he still didn't answer. I had a vague sense of unease. Where was he?

In a corner of the small coffee shop was a TV, tuned to CNN Asia, which is in English, and I listened to the news while I watched the computer screen. When I heard Steve's name, I glanced up and nearly fell out of my chair. He stood in front of some official-looking government building, holding the list, telling the reporter about the China brides. Next to him was the Chinese secretary-general, the equivalent of our Secretary of State. Steve really had started at the top.

"Secretary-General Li has assured me he will do everything in his power to find these women and return them to their homes."

The reporter asked, "Have the people responsible for the wife sales been apprehended?"

"Not yet. The police have only just begun investigating."

"Senator, how did you come to be in China, with this list?"

"I've recently been the subject of conjecture, primarily because of my friendship with Whitney Pearl. In an effort to clear her name, I came to China to find the person responsible for embezzling the CERF funds."

"Have you been successful?"

"I'm making headway."

"If you came to find an embezzler, what's the bride list got to do with it?"

"The people behind the embezzlement are also behind the bride sales. At Ms. Pearl's request, I turned over this list of women to the authorities." He went on for a bit about my work with the earthquake relief, and how I found Mrs. Han and kept digging until I located the list. He wouldn't say how I got it, and when the reporter insinuated perhaps I was behind the bride sales, he got well and truly mad. Glaring at the man, he said, "Why would she sell these women, then turn over the list? Ask me an intelligent question and I'll answer it. Otherwise, this interview is over."

"All right, Senator. Was your trip to China sanctioned by the U.S. government?"

"No. I'm not here in an official capacity."

"Doesn't it strike you as out of the ordinary for a U.S. Senator to perform his own investigation into the alleged crimes of his girlfriend? To do so in a foreign country without the knowledge of the president or secretary of state?"

"It strikes me odd that the consensus is to string Whitney Pearl up without due process. Her efforts to help the people of China have been discounted and criticized. She obtained this list at great risk to herself because she felt it was important to bring it to light."

"Why wasn't the list given to the State Department, to be handled with China through diplomatic avenues?"

"Because I didn't want to wait ten more minutes to alert the

Chinese government about what's going on. These women need to be found and returned to their families as soon as possible."

"Again, Senator, don't you think it's unusual for you to be here, looking for another suspect in the CERF embezzlement? Aren't you concerned about how your constituents will view this?"

"Of course it's unusual, but I'm determined to find the people who framed her, and if that means losing my seat, or losing the next election, or losing anything at all aside from her, I can live with that. Some things are infinitely more important than politics."

The reporter appeared to be at a loss for words. He turned toward the camera, signed off, and then the screen cut to the news desk and a pretty brunette woman who began a new report.

Sasha's cell rang and I answered, hoping it was Steve. I needed to tell him I couldn't marry him because I wasn't worthy. He needed to marry Mother Teresa. After all, he did have a thing for nuns.

But it wasn't Steve. It was Lou. "He just sealed the deal to lose the nomination, but hell if I've ever been more proud. Wish his mother was alive to see it."

"You saw the report?" CNN must have broadcast it worldwide.

"I saw it, but then, I was expecting it. He called me on his way to hand over the list."

"Did he tell you about Parker, and Robert?"

"Yeah, Pink. I'm sorry the guy turned out to be a piece of shit." He changed the subject abruptly. "I'm looking for your mother. Have you heard from her?"

"She's here, in Beijing." I told him what was going on, that I was waiting for her and Parker to show up.

He sighed heavily, his breath whooshing across the line. "She tricked me. Kept insisting she wanted to go to China and I told her to stay out of it, that she'd only complicat things. Yesterday, she told me things aren't going to work ou then she packed and left. As angry as I am that she wen against my advice, at least I know she was lying."

"It's convoluted, but I know what you mean."

"She's likely to get killed. Pink, are you up for this?"

"The bastard has my mother. I am so up for this." I saw Mom at the entrance to the café. "Gotta go, Lou." I hung up on him and stood and waited for Mom and Parker, who wa dressed as Gromyko, to walk to me.

"Are you okay?" I asked Mom.

"Never better." To her credit, she didn't look frightened. She looked seriously angry.

"Let's have a seat," I suggested, taking my own. When Mom sat down, I saw the handcuffs Parker had around he wrist and his. He sat with his back to the room, effectively hiding the handcuffs from the other patrons.

"Come close," he commanded.

I'd expected as much, so I knelt before him and allowed him to feel every inch of me, to search for a wire. I concen trated on not going all squicky. The man disgusted me.

When he was done, I sat down and met his cool gaze. "My attorney wire-transferred the money into the Ancient An tiquities account about five minutes ago."

His eyes narrowed. "How did you know about that?"

"Does it matter?" Waving my hand toward the computer I said calmly, even conversationally, "Verify the deposit so I can take my mother home."

He reached for the keyboard and jerked Mom's arm in the

process. I started to say something, but she gave me a look and I kept quiet. Parker said, "Look the other way." Mom and turned our heads while he pecked at the keys. When he said he was done, I turned back around, and he was staring at me thoughtfully.

"Taylor discouraged me from hiring you because she said you aren't that smart, but I knew, because of the whistle-blower scandal with Marvel Energy, that you're extremely bright and intuitive."

I noticed Mom's shocked face. She'd just figured out that Gromyko was actually Parker Davis. "Is that why you hired me?" I asked him. "Because I'm so smart?"

"The embezzlement was bound to come to light, and with your past history, I knew you'd never sleep until you found the dirty rotten bastard who did it."

Maybe I wasn't as smart as he thought. "You wanted me to find you?"

"Not me. Mulholland." He smiled. "You've performed beyond my wildest expectations."

I glanced at Mom, who shrugged.

Parker crossed one leg over the other and picked at lint on his trousers. "Mulholland wants to be president, but because of the scandals in his past, he hasn't a prayer. He went for the next best thing and began an affair with my wife, almost a year ago. He's the reason she decided to run."

"How will it benefit him if Madeline is president?"

"The spouse of the first female president is sure to wield a certain amount of power, and Mulholland is all about power. He promised to marry her during her first term. She'll just be over her grieving period."

"They plan to kill you?" Mom asked.

"I have to die, because a divorce from a nice guy like me will hurt her chances. They've already tried. Twice. It was the near misses that gave me the idea of Gromyko, who allowed me to have some semblance of a life without having to look over my shoulder." He gave us a humorless smile. "On the pretense of a mutual interest in sailing, Gromyko cultivated a friendship with Mulholland. They say to keep your friends close, and your enemies closer."

"Mulholland has more money than God. Why would he open the Ancient Antiquities account, then allow a piddly few hundred grand, all of it dirty, to be funneled into it?"

"He wouldn't, unless he had some ulterior motive. Don't forget, his goal is to live in the White House. Aside from Madeline, who has the best chance of winning the next election?"

"Steve." Suddenly, everything became clear. I was blown away. "You set all of this up, with Mulholland at the end of the line, so it would appear he framed me to discredit Steve."

He looked at Mom. "See? Smart cookie."

Mom jerked the handcuff and glared at him. "Mulholland is a dupe just like Pink."

"True, but no one will see it that way when this blows wide open. Witnesses will testify they saw Gromyko and Mulholland together, many times. Other witnesses will testify they saw Gromyko at the scene of several different crimes, including the explosion of a San Francisco apartment building. And within the next few hours, bank records will show a large transfer from the Ancient Antiquities account to the account of Nikolai Gromyko." He threw me a look. "I know how you like everything nice and tidy."

"So it was a setup within a setup, from the beginning."

"I had two choices—allow them to kill me, or fight back."

"Why are you telling us all of this?"

"So you'll have accurate facts to give to the police. It's simple, really. You'll tell the cops everything, they'll investigate and find evidence against Mulholland, but nothing against me. Bill Mulholland will go to prison for a very long time, Madeline's chances of a presidency will be history and can get a divorce and go back to my life."

"You don't think they'll believe me when I tell them Parker Davis confessed all of this to me?"

He gave me a patient look. "Parker Davis is a saint, without a scratch on his reputation. There is nothing at all that can tie him to any of this. Nothing. I've planned everything down to the smallest detail, so all roads will lead to Mulholland." He glanced at his watch. "Now, where was I?"

"You were going to tell me why you hired me."

'Yes, well, because of Madeline's assistant, I've known for some time about your relationship with Santorelli. After the earthquake, I saw a piece in the *Wall Street Journal* about you volunteering in China. Did you know about it?"

I shook my head.

"I guess people still find you interesting because of the whistle-blowing fiasco. When I saw the article, it got me thinking about opportunities. Landing the CERF director position wasn't easy, but after that, everything fell into place. You discovered the Kansas account a bit too soon, but overall, I can't complain."

"Since you're in a tell-all mood, explain how my fingerprints came to be on the Valikov Interiors invoices."

"Every so often, I dropped a sheet of paper in the copy room. You'd come by, dutifully pick it up and return it to the

stack. I'd take it out and leave it in a stack in a cabinet, where
Gromyko, disguised as a package deliveryman, would collec
the paper every few days."

So my frugality and closet environmentalism had bit m
in the ass. "You came to the office disguised as Gromyko?"

"I told you, I thought of everything. The staff all saw
Gromyko on numerous occasions, and they'll tell the police."

"What about Taylor? Did you kill her just to set me up?"

"I needed you to be arrested, to make you desperate
enough to keep digging. And Taylor was too unpredictable.
I was afraid she'd get in the way as time passed."

"If you wanted me to get to the bottom of things and
expose Mulholland as a crook, why did you try to kill me?
And Ed?"

His expression indicated his aggravation. "Olga jumped
the gun, with Wu as well as Ravenaldt. She had no orders to
kill either of them. When she told me about your dinner conversation with Wu, I was surprised to find out you knew
about the brides."

"Yeah, I'll bet you were. How'd you get into the slave
trade, anyway?"

"Last year, during a trip to China with Madeline and a contingent of senators, I saw a need for brides and decided to fill
it. Until recently, it's been very lucrative." He frowned at me.
"When you found the list, you became a nuisance. I assumed
you confided what you learned to your attorney, so he needed
to be eliminated, as well. By then you'd uncovered enough
that after your death the police would have uncovered the
rest, including Mulholland at the end of the line."

"And Mulholland hired Gromyko to do all the dirty work."

"Right. Not long after this story breaks, Gromyko and the

money Mulholland paid him will disappear. People will assume Mulholland killed him to ensure his silence."

"Now it's about the money. Is that why you abducted my mother in broad daylight?"

"You took one hundred thousand dollars that wasn't yours. I wanted it back, and when I saw Jane out at the CERF offices, I saw an opportunity."

I had to give it to him. "All this, because your wife's having an affair. Did you ever consider marriage counseling?"

He missed my sarcasm. "Madeline and I haven't had a real marriage in years."

"Might be your sexual technique. You're a sick bastard."

Unexpectedly, he grinned at me. "Don't knock it 'til you try it."

I stared him down, then said, "I have the facts, and you have your money. Now give me my mother."

He retrieved a small key from the breast pocket of his dress shirt. When the handcuffs were off, they disappeared into the pocket of his trench coat, along with his hand. Thinking it was all over, at least until we were back in the States, I started to get up. But Parker had other plans. His hand reappeared from the pocket holding a switchblade that was just like Olga's.

"Sorry, Pink, but I only need one person to talk to the police. Otherwise, you've got corroboration if you're foolish enough to tell them about me."

Mom was rubbing her wrist and didn't see him coming at her until it was too late. She made a sad little gasping sound when the blade sliced through her linen duster and into her arm. Thank God she was rubbing her wrist, otherwise the blade would have plunged into her heart.

Trust me, there's nothing more horrifying than seeing your mother attacked. He drew back to cut her again and I lunged at him, grabbed for his hair and missed. Trying to get up from her chair but stumbling clumsily, Mom scrambled backward, holding her arm, blood trickling between her fingers. Parker advanced on her, and with fear and fury pumping through me, I gathered myself up to jump on his back. But before I could, something very large blocked my way.

Big Mama. *Lou.* He lifted Parker off his feet and threw him toward the back door. Parker hit it so hard, the door flew open and he went into the alley behind the café, the switchblade flying off into a pile of garbage. Lou went after him, moving fast, in spite of his bulk. Grabbing Parker by the shirt, he hauled him to his feet, then knocked him down. "I'm going to kill you. Stand up like a man, by God, and try to cut *this* woman!"

The fear in Parker was palpable. He got to his feet, turned tail and ran. Lou ran after him. Mom and I went to the doorway, along with a crowd of coffee drinkers, and saw him catch Parker by grabbing his coat. He spun him around and slammed his fist into his face, knocking off part of his fake beard, pushing him to the ground. Lou was in a rage, and I could see that he really did intend to kill Parker. I ran outside and caught up to him, just as he hauled Parker up for another round.

"Let him go!"

He turned his dark eyes to look at me and I realized Lou wasn't in there anywhere. This was a man possessed by something way beyond my understanding. Scared the shit out of me and that's no lie. But I couldn't let him kill Parker.

"He's got to live long enough to clear me. And he doesn't deserve to die quickly. Let him go."

Whoever was inside Lou wasn't having any part of that. His prey was right there, in his hands, and he could smell his fear. Hell, *I* could smell his fear. Not sure, but I think Parker peed his pants. Lou drew back his fist and nailed Parker so hard I heard the crush of bones in his face. He collapsed in a moaning heap. When Lou started to reach for him again, I stepped in front of him.

"Enough, dammit! Get a hold of yourself and leave it be!"

His hands were on my shoulders, about to shove me out of the way, and I knew if he did, I'd never get another chance to stop him from ruining his life. I don't know how, but I instinctively knew that yelling wasn't going to work. He was all about confrontation and violence and retribution, and any voice that matched those things wouldn't be heard. Before he could push me aside, I softly said, in a calm, even tone, "He's not the enemy. He's not worthy of the fight. He's just a pathetic excuse for a man."

Dark eyes met mine and I knew he had heard me.

"Mom needs you. So does Steve. And me. We can't have you if you're rotting in a Chinese prison."

The hands that held my shoulders loosened and he slipped his arms around me to draw me close to his ample, polysynthetic stuffed breasts. His breath ruffled my hair and he said on a sigh, "Ah, Pink."

"You were there the whole time, weren't you?"

"I followed you from the Lido. You don't know shit for avoiding tails, baby."

"Why are you in China?"

"After your mama left, she wouldn't answer my phone

calls, which isn't like her. If she didn't want to talk, she'd answer and tell me to screw off. I suspected she went to China, so I had Carmine's check flight manifests until I knew for sure. Being a guy who worries, I followed, but couldn't find her once I got here. Steve said you were at the Lido. I got there just about the time you took off."

"Did you come over in disguise?"

He tightened his arms around me. "I didn't have a current visa, and Big Mama did."

"What's the name on Big Mama's visa?"

He chuckled against my hair. "Tonya Weisberg."

From behind Lou, I heard Mom say, "You've got some serious whoop-ass, for a girl."

Lou dropped one arm and turned to face her with his other arm still around my shoulders. "You need to see a doctor," he said in a soft, feminine voice. It was a one-eighty from the deep, harsh shout of a few minutes earlier.

Mom was holding a small towel around her arm, one I suppose a coffee shop employee had given her. She cocked her head to one side and looked him up and down. Mom's a lot of things, but stupid isn't one of them. She settled on his eyes and they stared at each other for a long, drawn-out moment. I could see the instant she accepted who Big Mama really was. But she didn't give it away, maybe because she knew there was still an audience at the back door of Moko. Instead, she said in her usual, blunt manner, "I could show you how to do your eye shadow better. The way you've got it now, it makes your eyes look small. And you do have such nice eyes."

He walked toward her, his arm still around me, and looped his other arm around Mom. "I'd appreciate that, especially because I think you have the prettiest eyes in the world."

"Y'all are real cute," I said, "but shouldn't we do something about Parker?"

"No sweat, Pink," Lou said. "I called the American embassy a while ago and they're sending someone over to collect him. Turns out, the feds just subpoenaed Parker and Madeline Davis about possible insider trading."

I looked at Parker, flat on his face in a Beijing alley. "If they make a movie," I said to him, "they gotta get Gene Hackman to play you."

Chapter 15

B y the time the four of us arrived in Washington, the shit had already hit the fan. We were met at the airport by Steve and Lou's old family friend Richard Harcourt, the retired speaker of the house, aka Very Handsome and Wonderful Old Man, along with a small contingent of head honchos from the FBI, the CIA and the State Department. Oh, and the SEC. I doubt there'd been a collection of that many agency heads and lesser minions in one place since Kennedy was shot. They were there to follow us to an undisclosed location where we'd each be debriefed.

Richard took my hand and placed it on his arm to walk with him to the limousine, which was waiting for us on the tarmac. We'd deplaned away from the terminal to avoid the crowd of reporters and onlookers that had congregated there when our arrival time was leaked. The FBI director took the laptop Steve handed him and gave it to an agent, who got in a small sedan and drove away with it. In addition to watching the video of the bride swap at the pearl market, they would check the fingerprints on the keys, as well as the recent cache of Web sites, which would include the bank where Ancient Antiquities had an account. They'd also be able to find the password to access the account, which Parker had typed in, never realizing that the computer he was using wasn't like the others in the Internet café. It belonged to Steve. At the end, when Parker was so sure he'd won, he tripped himself up.

Ed was in the limo and I wound up wedged between him and Steve. I looked up at him and asked, "Are you on the clock?"

His gaze went over my head, to Steve, then refocused on me. "If you mean, am I here to act as your legal counsel, yes. If you mean, will I charge you for it, no. But don't forget that interest we discussed."

In the seat across from us, Richard said, "Pink, after you called me things happened very quickly. The SEC looked into the stock trades and you were right—the Cardwell Systems stock was bought by Parker only two weeks before the announcement of the merger, and they sold the merged Braxton Technologies stock two weeks after that, when it was trading for an obscene amount."

"If Mulholland wanted Madeline to win the election, why would he tell her something that could get her in trouble?"

"He claims he didn't tell Madeline, and she concurs. The stock was actually bought and sold by Parker, and they're claiming he learned about the merger via bugs he planted in Mulholland's office and car when he grew suspicious of them having an affair."

"Did he do it for the money, or to ruin Madeline's chances in the election?" Mom asked. "He's convinced Madeline and Mulholland were trying to kill him, to get him out of the way so she could win as a widow, then marry Mulholland."

Richard said soberly, "He's under a lot of pressure because of the enormous amount of debt he and Madeline had racked up trying to keep up appearances, so he needs money. But he's clearly paranoid, so he may have done it for both reasons."

"What about everything he told Mom and me at the café?"

"It's being checked out," Ed said, "but no matter what they find, nothing can refute the fingerprints on the laptop or the cache and the account password. The only way Parker could have known the password was if he set up the account himself."

"That's true," Richard added. "If Mulholland set it up, he'd never share the information with Parker. They've despised one another since college, ironically, because they were in competition for Madeline."

From my left, Steve asked quietly, "Did Madeline know any of this?"

"I'm inclined to think not," Richard said, "but I do think she's involved with Mulholland. Maybe not an affair, but he does spend a lot of time with her. The man's grabs for power are transparent. He gives huge amounts to political campaigns, then demands positions."

"Which he never gets," Lou said, "because he's a loose cannon."

"Madeline's political career will be over, one way or the other. Voters don't like it when politicians are involved with criminals."

I glanced at Ed. "Am I off the hook?"

"Your hearing is tomorrow, and I think we have enough to present to the DA that he'll drop the charges. Just after you called to tell me what happened in Beijing, I hired an expert to compare the J. Smith handwriting on the sign-in sheet at Taylor's to Parker's handwriting. The unobservant, worthless security guy still can't say for sure if J. Smith was male or female, but there's DNA evidence that Parker was in Taylor's apartment. They also found some trace evidence that's most likely hair from a wig or a fake beard." He gazed down at me. "The Chinese history guy says the supposed antiques Sasha sent are all fakes. Total of everything is worth maybe two grand."

"Looks like their case is losing walls," Steve said, just as we arrived at the building where we would be debriefed.

The next several hours were spent retelling the sequence of events and answering a thousand questions. When I explained about forging the check, it got pretty intense, and I asked to speak to Mr. Brookes, the head of the CIA, with only Ed present.

As we left the room, I felt Steve's gaze and I glanced at him. He smiled crookedly.

In a small adjacent room, I asked Mr. Brookes, "You have the check, don't you?"

"It's addressed to Santa. Why do you believe Santa is at the CIA?"

"Look, we could play around with this all day, but I'm tired and want to go home. I know you have the check. You know I'm aware of a guy named Santa. When I got the check, I wanted to mail it somewhere safe, to someone who would hold it until the right time. I figured if I addressed it to Santa, it wouldn't be lost in the paper chase because it would drive you guys crazy trying to figure out why I did it. And I know you know it was me, because the first thing you did was run prints."

Mr. Brookes looked at Ed, who said in his best lawyer voice, "She has no clue who he is, so no matter how many times you ask, she still can't tell you. As for how she knows anything at all, well, let's just assume she's delusional, because she'll never say."

When Mr. Brookes still looked stubborn about it, I said, "Why is it so important to know? Whoever he is, he's gotten some of your guys out of some serious trouble. Look at it as a gift and move on. Now, will you call and have somebody bring over the check, so they'll believe I didn't rip off the money for myself?"

He gazed at me for a long time before he said, "When did you first hear of him?"

I looked at Ed.

He stood up a little straighter and said, "My client isn't answering questions any longer. If you and the others need more information, you'll have to subpoena her." He grasped my arm. "Let's go, Pink."

We were to the door when he relented. "Okay, I'll have the check sent over."

After that, it went pretty fast. In light of my reasons for forging the check, and the fact that the cashier's check was made out to a legitimate charitable organization, the FBI director said I wouldn't be charged with any crime. He also said he'd see to it that Ed got his money back once they were through investigating Ancient Antiquities. As for the cashier's check, he couldn't be sure, but he expected it would be voided and the funds redirected to the Red Cross for further aid to the Chinese earthquake victims.

Mom and Lou had left hours before, so it was just me and Ed and Steve who left the building in the early afternoon. When we got to Steve's house in Georgetown, we had to fight our way through the army of people on the sidewalk. I will say, the mood was positive. They appeared to think Steve was the second coming. Funny the difference a few days and random acts of heroism can make.

We found Mom and Lou in the living room, listening to the Beatles and drinking whiskey. Mom, I noticed, had on those ratty jeans and the white linen blouse, and she was barefoot. She'd lost her luggage when Parker abducted her, so I suspected the clothes belonged to Jenny. I kind of thought she would have been okay with that. She would like that Lou was starting over.

The following day, as Ed predicted, the DA dropped all the charges. Steve got his bail money back. Parker, who was cooling his heels in jail, was arraigned and charged with murder, embezzlement, fraud, identity theft and a laundry list of lesser crimes. The judge set no bail.

I spent the day gathering up my stuff that was still in the loft. Some of it I boxed up and shipped back to Midland, some I gave away to a homeless shelter and the rest I packed in two big suitcases. Ed was anxious to get back to Midland. But I didn't go with him when he left. Oh, I was dying to go home, to get back to the wide-open flatlands of Midland, but I wasn't ready. So I said goodbye to Mom and Lou and Ed, then went home with Steve.

That night, we stayed up late talking. Steve asked me to come to work for him, to manage the money for his campaign. That blew me away, not just because he had that much faith in me, but because it would be maybe the coolest job ever. But I had Mom to consider. I worked for her, and if I left for a while it would leave her in a bind.

There also was Ed.

Steve repeated his marriage proposal and I was closer than ever to saying yes. The picture he painted was so damn tempting, and when he told me he loved me, wide awake and with all his clothes on, I jumped without a chute and told him I loved him, too. It wasn't a lie, and I wasn't caught up in a moment. I absolutely did love him. But did I love him the right way? And Ed... I just had to work things out in my head before I could make a decision.

Steve took me to the airport the next morning and kissed me goodbye at the entrance to the gate area. Some people recognized us and we quickly gained an audience that applauded when we broke the kiss.

He hugged me close and whispered, "I'll be right here, waiting for you."

Walking away from him, I had to wonder how long he would wait. I also had to wonder what was going to happen that would push me to decide. Just before I had to turn a corner, I looked back and saw him there, in his faded Levi's, staring after me. No kidding, it was the hardest thing I've ever done to turn and keep walking.

I had quite the surprise waiting for me in Midland. First, I had a notice in the mail that my mortgage had been denied. I wasn't surprised. They'd been reviewing my application while I was charged with embezzlement and murder. But I was still hugely disappointed.

What did surprise me was being unable to get into my

apartment. I went to see the manager and he said I'd failed
to renew my lease. He was right, and I'd done it on purpose,
in anticipation of moving to a house, but I'd meant to talk
to him, to get a short extension of my lease until I could
move. I just forgot. Getting arrested for heinous crimes will
do that to you. So I was evicted, and my stuff, what there
was of it after I'd made the temporary move to D.C., was
stacked in his little storage building. I asked to sign a lease
for another apartment and he said there were none available.

I figured I'd have to stay at Mom's until I found another
apartment, but then I remembered that Lou was staying for
a while. I love Lou to death, but there are just certain things
you don't do in life. Hanging out at Mom's while she and Lou
were falling in love is one of them.

I considered calling Sam, my manager at Mom's firm and
a good friend who'd saved my butt a few times during my
whistle-blower experience and another recent harrowing ad-
venture in Midland. He'd put me up until I found a place to
live. And he had a cat. That would be a nice bonus. All in all,
calling Sam was a great idea—or would have been if he
hadn't been on vacation surfing in California.

Instead, I wound up on Ed's doorstep at nine o'clock at
night. He swung the door open and took a look at the suitcase.

"Did you run away from home again?"

"Ed, I've got nowhere to go. Can I stay with you?"

He reached for the suitcase, stepped back and waited for
me to come inside. I heard the door close, followed by what
sounded like a *meow*. A wee kitty meow. While I stared in
total confusion, a gray and white kitten came rolling across

the floor of the entry hall. It pounced on the leg of Ed's sweatpants and stuck there like a burr.

I shot him a quizzical look.

He sighed as he bent and picked the ball of fur off his leg, then straightened and handed it to me. "It's yours. I was going to surprise you with it tomorrow."

Holding the soft, warm kitty in my hands, I looked up into his face and said, "You're amazing."

His smile was slow and seductive. "Yeah, I'll show you amazing. Take your clothes off."

* * * * *

*Silhouette Bombshell is proud to bring you
cutting-edge stories featuring the savviest heroines
around!*
*Turn the page for a sneak preview of
one of next month's sexy, suspenseful releases,*

THE SPY WITH THE SILVER LINING
by Wendy Rosnau

*Available May 2006 wherever
Silhouette Books are sold.*

Globe-named "The Access," Casmir had recovered precious gems, exposed the most cunning terrorists and carried

The world is a stage, Cassie. Play to your audience and get them to love you. Life is an investment. It's like buying a satin suit and fabulous shoes. You get what you pay for.

Head up, shoulders straight and remember, never buy cheap.

For twenty-eight years Casmir Balasi had lived by her mother's words, as well as her motto: quality, not quantity. She'd been a trendsetter in her youth, a runway model by age nineteen, and for the past five years, Ruza's teachings had turned the blonde with attitude into one of the most valued femmes fatales at EURO-Quest.

Her model figure and fashion sense, along with her catlike ability to land on her feet, had allowed her to infiltrate some of the most dangerous criminal circles in the world.

Code-named "The Actress," Casmir had recovered precious gems, exposed the most cunning terrorists and carried top-secret documents across enemy lines while entertaining evil in the process. And each time, she had managed to keep her identity a secret in order to play the game another day.

She'd been as elusive as a grain of sand in a sandstorm.

Until tonight.

Tonight, the black wide-brimmed Tularo shielding her green eyes and the silver Devicca suit outlining her curves had fallen short. Nasty Nicky was seated at the bar, and he was looking straight at her.

Normally that wouldn't have raised a red flag, but the smug look on his face told Casmir that he wasn't just enjoying the sight of an attractive woman in a crowd.

There was something else in that look.

It was a look of recognition…and something more. As if he knew her secret life behind her secret life.

Casmir scanned the club and the throngs of beautiful people who had ventured out tonight to play at the Kelt. If Nicky was here, Yurii Petrov must be somewhere close by. Which meant the Russian mobster had escaped the maximum-security prison in Prague where he'd been eating and sleeping and dreaming of freedom for the past seven months.

And if that was true, it meant Yurii knew everything— who, what and why.

Even more damning, it meant he knew that she was responsible for his recent address change.

Had she underestimated Yurii? If he was here, then, yes, she had.

A year ago her assignment had been specific. Trip up Yurii Petrov. Find his weakness and exploit it. Get close to him.

During her research she'd learned why she'd been picked

or the job. Yurii had only two weaknesses—apricots from is homeland in Armenia, and long-legged blondes.

She'd turned his head within a week, and had literally rought him to his knees two months later.

The vision of Yurii on bended knee, pulling a velvet box rom his pocket, flashed in Casmir's mind, and she glanced own at her left hand. She should never have kept the ring, ut it really was beautiful—a ten-carat marquise diamond set n a circle of flawless rubies.

"Never take your eyes off the target. That's what I romised myself that day on the Riviera. Remember, Kisa?"

His Russian accent was thick, his breath spiked with the amiliar brandy-soaked cigars he favored. His lips brushed he side of her neck, reminding her that they were a little too hin for her taste. Still, he knew how to use them. After all, e was the detail man and appreciated perfection in all things.

It was a rare woman who could resist the forty-nine-year-old Caucasian when he'd marked her as his.

Yurii captured her hand and spun her quickly, and suddenly Casmir was looking into a pair of deep-set earthy rown eyes. He raised her hand and kissed it, his penetrating eyes locked on the ring he'd given her months ago.

There was an awkward moment of silence, as if he'd forgotten what he was going to say. Then he recovered. "I should e furious with you. But how can I be angry, my love?" His humb slowly passed over the diamond engagement ring on er finger. "You're still wearing my gift. So just maybe I'll ave to rethink killing you."

"Kill your fiancée? Why would you want to? I thought you oved me, Yurii."

"And I thought the feeling was mutual. But I heard a disturbing rumor while I was living in my home away from home."

"Rumors are so unreliable."

"Tell me you didn't set out to betray me, Kisa. Tell me it wasn't all a lie. Tell me I didn't let an enemy into my heart."

If prison had been a hardship, Casmir couldn't tell. Yurii looked fit and healthy, his wavy black hair cut short with just a touch more gray at his temples than she remembered.

To go along with his dangerous good looks, in public he favored black shirts beneath expensive black suits—and always a bloodred silk tie. The picture he presented tonight was a carbon copy of the old Yurii, right down to the scent of his mordant cologne and an imported cigar pinched between his fingers.

Although his five-foot-nine height made his build more round than lean, his charisma was as powerful as his high-ranked position in the criminal world.

A real sweet deal is how Ruza would have described him at a glance.

"Deny the betrayal. Let me hear the words from your hot red lips. Lips that have haunted my dreams nightly since we've been apart. Tell me it's all a terrible mistake, my love. Speak the truth."

"I'm wearing your ring. I haven't taken it off since you gave it to me. That is the only truth I know, Yurii."

He searched her eyes. Suddenly his hand closed around hers and squeezed. "Not exactly a confession of innocence, my love. Come. We will discuss it in private. My car is waiting."

She felt something dig into her side. Without needing to look, she knew Yurii had drawn his Gyurza. The Russian pistol was famous for its cored bullets and penetration ability. A deadly weapon that could go through two sheets of titanium at a hundred meters.

Casmir didn't flinch. Instead she glanced left, then right. The nightclub was packed wall to wall, but Pasha had to be here somewhere. A little help from her contact would be appreciated about now.

"If you're looking for your dark-haired friend, I'm afraid he won't be coming. She's met with a tragic accident. A lovely creature, but she's certainly not you."

If Pasha was dead, that meant Yurii knew for certain that she was a spy for EURO-Quest.

Casmir didn't react to the bad news. She was a professional, after all. She hadn't earned her stripes by wilting under pressure, or spilling tears in the face of the enemy.

She would cry for Pasha later—after she escaped.

* * * * *

The Marian priestesses were destroyed long ago,
but their daughters live on. The time has come
for the heiresses to learn of their legacy, to unite
the pieces of a powerful mosaic and bring light to
a secret their ancestors died to protect.

The Madonna Key

Follow their quests each month.

Lost Calling by Evelyn Vaughn,
July 2006

Haunted Echoes by Cindy Dees,
August 2006

Dark Revelations by Lorna Tedder,
September 2006

Shadow Lines by Carol Stephenson,
October 2006

Hidden Sanctuary by Sharron McClellan,
November 2006

Veiled Legacy by Jenna Mills,
December 2006

Seventh Key by Evelyn Vaughn,
January 2007

It's a dating jungle out there!

Four thirtysomething women with a fear of dating form a network of support to empower each other as they face the trials and travails of modern matchmaking in Los Angeles.

The I Hate To Date Club

by
Elda Minger

COMING NEXT MONTH

#89 THE SPY WITH THE SILVER LINING—Wendy Rosnau
Spy Games

Chic superspy Casmir Balasi had played the game too well this time—getting love-struck master criminal Yuri Petrov to propose on bended knee…and fall into her trap. But when he escaped prison and vowed to enforce the "'til death do us part" clause of their sham marriage, all Casmir had for protection was her arrogant if irresistible bodyguard. Would her protector's secret agenda lead her into the hands of the enemy? Or into his arms?

#90 LOOK-ALIKE—Meredith Fletcher
Athena Force

Agent Elle St. John's loyalty to Russia clashed with her twin sister Sam's to America, but they were on the same team when it came to finding the truth behind their spy parents' deaths. Scouring Europe for clues—and fighting her attraction to the shadowy German helping her—Elle soon discovered a web of deceit entwining her parents, an Athena Academy blackmailer and security secrets from both twins' homelands.

#91 NO SAFE PLACE—Judy Fitzwater

When her estranged husband's dead body turned up—not once, but twice!—Elizabeth Larocca knew his dangerous secret life had caught up with him…and was about to catch up with her. So she took her grown daughter and ran. But her husband's associates were after her, men whose offers of help came across more as threats. Trusting no one, Elizabeth's only hope was to solve her husband's murder—and maybe prevent her own….

#92 INVISIBLE RECRUIT—Mary Buckham
IR-5

Jet-setter Vaughn Monroe needed a change. Why not try spying on for size? After all, her daddy was the CIA director. But it was tough joining the IR Agency, a group of covert women operatives, because her instructor mistook the debutante for dilettante. She proved him wrong—using connections to access a sinister private auction in India that other agencies couldn't infiltrate. Now, the fate of millions rested on Vaughn's next move….

SBCNM0406